Farewell to Matyora

Farewell to Matyora

A NOVEL BY *Valentin Rasputin*

TRANSLATED BY *Antonina W. Bouis*

WITH A FOREWORD BY *Kathleen Parthé*

NORTHWESTERN UNIVERSITY PRESS

EVANSTON, ILLINOIS

Northwestern University Press
Evanston, Illinois 60201

Farewell to Matyora copyright © 1979 by Macmillan Publishing Co., Inc.
Foreword copyright © 1991 by Northwestern University Press. This
edition is published 1991 by arrangement with Macmillan Publishing Company,
a division of Macmillan, Inc. All rights reserved.

Printed in the United States of America

96 95 94 93 92 91   6 5 4 3 2 1

Library of Congress Cataloging-in-Publication Data

Rasputin, Valentin Grigor 'evich.
    [Proshchanie s Materoĭ. English]
    Farewell to Matyora / Valentin Rasputin ; translated by Antonina
W. Bouis with a foreword by Kathleen Parthé.
        p.   cm.
    Translation of: Proshchanie s Materoĭ.
    ISBN 0-8101-0997-2 (pbk. : alk. paper)
    I. Title.
    PG3485.5.A85P7613   1991
    891.73'44—dc20   91-8165
                                                                      CIP

The paper used in this publication meets the minimum requirements
of American National Standard for Information Sciences—Permanence
of Paper for Printed Library Materials, ANSI Z39.48-1984

Contents

Foreword: Master of the Island

Kathleen Parthé

> The dam will flood my little home,
> It will disappear—well, let it go . . .
> —Yevgeny Yevtushenko, "Bratsk Station"

One of the most striking features of the future-oriented Soviet literature that appeared after 1930 was the way it defined progress as Man's victory over Nature: writers told of how rivers were being dammed and their energy used to run generators, how forests were being cut down, how valuable ores were being extracted from the earth, and how age-old farming methods were making way for agricultural assembly lines. The path to the "radiant future" was plotted out in such works as Katacv's *Time, Forward!* Pilnyak's *The Volga Falls to the Caspian Sea,* Ilyenkov's *Driving Axle,* Zhuravlev's *Combines,* and Sholokhov's *Virgin Soil Upturned.* Even in the years after Stalin's death in 1953, writers like Yevgeny Yevtushenko, who rejected many of the constraints of Socialist Realism and who regularly challenged the censors, still enthusiastically accepted the Soviet premise that the future well-being of the country lay in harnessing the natural riches of the USSR to fuel rapid urbanization and industrialization. The Thaw literature of the 1950s expressed frustration, not with the Promethean goal itself, but with the inefficiencies of farm and factory management and with the lack of trust in local and individual expertise, all factors that hindered growth. Youth Prose and Urban Prose reflected a sense of alienation that—while tied to specific problems of Soviet life—was a reaction to urban life everywhere in the mid-twentieth century. Even the literature of the Soviet underground (*samizdat*) was generally oriented toward progress and growth, although often on a Western rather than a Soviet model. The only genuine literary challenge to the overly positive portrayal of rapid development came from Russian Village Prose (*derevenskaia proza*), the largest and most coherent body of aesthetically interesting and ideologically significant literature to be published in the Soviet Union during the three decades following Stalin's death.

Russian Village Prose began in the 1950s with articles critical of the way collective farms were being run, and developed into an insider's view of rural life that revolved around nostalgic visits to the village of one's childhood. Rejecting palpably false and badly written collective-farm novels, these writers bypassed Socialist Realism for pre-Revolutionary literature. They saw themselves as the peasant heirs of nineteenth- and early twentieth-century gentry writers like Turgenev, Tolstoy, and Bunin, and their picture of the Russian countryside picked up where the literary "grandfathers" left off, with an elegy for the waning of the traditional rural way of life. There was in Village Prose a search for—and a celebration of—the values and rituals of the disappearing Russian village; there was also a strong sense of the need to protect the environment from those who would destroy it in the name of urban-style progress. In Village Prose there is a turning away from the "radiant future" and a move backward to the "radiant past." Among the Soviet Russian writers who took part in the development of the new rural literature are Valentin Ovechkin, Efim Dorosh, Vladimir Soloukhin, Yury Kazakov, Fedor Abramov, Alexander Solzhenitsyn, Vasily Shukshin, Vladimir Tendriakov, Alexander Yashin, Vasily Belov, Viktor Astafiev, and Valentin Rasputin.[1]

Village Prose can be contrasted at almost every point to Socialist Realist Collective-Farm Literature. Contrast—between old/new, endings/beginnings, old age/youth, submitting to nature/ruling nature, preservation/destruction, local/national, spiritual/material, continuity/revolution, past/present, and hand/machine—is used in both of these types of rural literature as a structural principle, but to opposite effect. What is celebrated in a work that focuses on a collective farm is mourned in a story set in a village threatened with extinction.

The main characteristics of Russian Village Prose are the centrality of the village, nature, the peasant home and its simple inventory, all that is implied by the Russian word *rodnoe* (which refers to things that are both "native" and "dear"); an orientation in time that focuses on the past, cyclical (rather than linear) time, memory, nostalgia, and childhood; and an interest in and reverence for authentic language.

Canonical Village Prose flourished for more than two decades, until the latter part of the 1970s. Valentin Rasputin's *Farewell to Matyora* (1976) is by common consent the single most important work in this movement, and the one that seemed to both its author and the critics to "logically complete the village theme."[2] The apocalyptic finale of the work was the strongest possible image for expressing the sense that the traditional village had reached the end of its history. The elegiacal period of Village Prose, centered on the memories of a rural childhood, drew to a close, experiencing the natural fate of all literary movements. Also, as a memory-driven "witness" literature, it could not survive the aging of the last generation of writers who had grown up in Russian villages that still had kept many of the old customs. In the years following the publication of *Farewell to Matyora,* the rural writers finished up lengthy historical novels, began archives on collectivization (a rural counterpart to Alexander Solzhenitsyn's "Gulag" cycle), wrote philosophical and political essays on the decline of peasant Russia, and moved their primary fictional settings to urban areas. When new movements in Soviet Russian literature began to take shape in the mid-1980s, once again it was Valentin Rasputin whose writing proved to be seminal. His 1985 story "The Fire" was the first major work of what has been called "cruel realism" (*zhestokii realizm*), and it is seen as an "emblem" of the Gorbachev years.[3]

"The Fire" is actually the third part of a Rasputin trilogy on the destruction of centuries-old Siberian communities by the floodwaters of progress, specifically the Angara River hydroelectric project, about which the poet Yevtushenko expressed such epic enthusiasm. In "Downstream" (1972)—the first and most autobiographical of the three works—Viktor, a young writer, travels down the river by steamship to see his family.[4] His previous trip had been on the eve of the flooding of his coastal village to form a reservoir for the hydroelectric project. His village and several others were moved inland and consolidated; five years later the old village is an indistinguishable part of a large new settlement. Viktor has trouble adjusting to the new setting, which to him seems not *rodnoi* (native) but *chuzhoi* (foreign, alien), and he abruptly terminates his visit. At the end of "Downstream" he is on his way back to the city, where he will try to accept the realities of his displaced home and waning youth, and then return as a "different" person to see the place as if for the first time. The story is really a model for Village Prose: the rural-born writer tries to accept change but comes into painful conflict with the main source of his creativity, his radiant childhood memories.

As Viktor travels downstream, the sides of the steamship scrape against trees from islands flooded by the same project. He suddenly realizes that colorfully named islands like Khlebnik and Beryozovik no longer exist.[5] These islands were an important part of a boyhood spent on the river. Here he had picked berries and mushrooms, wild onions and garlic; here he had fished with his grandfather, grazed horses, plowed fields, and cut hay. Here he had watched the terrifying—but exciting—first thunderstorm of spring that freed the river ice and sent it rushing noisily downstream. Childhood had preserved these river memories in a distinct place. "They lived like a warm, heartfelt sorrow beside which he would often rest and warm himself before moving on" ("Downstream," 387). "Downstream," like *Farewell to Matyora* and much of Russian Village Prose, is the story of first and last things. The first things are the primordial settings, the ties to pre-Revolutionary life and literature, and the memories of childhood. The last things are the ways in which traditional peasant life and the very existence of the small villages were coming to an end.

"Downstream" is structured on a series of lyrical digressions; the main character floats down the river, recalling as he goes various points along the current of his past and comparing these recollections with the present-day reality of life in his transplanted community. In *Farewell to Matyora* Rasputin took on the much more difficult task of depicting the disorienting moment of change itself. Rasputin's inclusion of an island spirit—called simply the

Master—and communication between the living and the dead does nothing to weaken the impact of his observations about the pain involved in transforming rural Russia. Mixing serious social and political commentary with the fantastic is a Russian literary tradition that goes back at least as far as Alexander Pushkin and includes works by such writers as Gogol, Dostoevsky, Bely, Zamyatin, Bulgakov, and Sinyavsky. And although the nonrealistic side of *Matyora* may bear the idiosyncratic stamp of its author, it strongly reflects Russian "dual faith" (*dvoeverie*), that amalgam of folk belief and Russian Orthodoxy that is so characteristic of rural Russia.

The third-person narrative of *Matyora* is dominated by the voice and thoughts of one old villager, Darya Pinigina, much as Solzhenitsyn's narrative in *One Day in the Life of Ivan Denisovich* is circumscribed by the experiences and limitations of the main character. We hear Darya's voice in her interactions with her son and grandson and during lengthy conversations with the remaining villagers; what appear to be leisurely interchanges are not mere "gossip" but the village's time-honored way of keeping its history and defining itself. "The making of this continuous communal portrait is not a vanity or a pastime: it is an organic part of the life of the village. Should it cease, the village would disintegrate."[6] The village is in fact disintegrating, but Darya helps to preserve the memory of the village by keeping everyone talking, literally until the end of Matyora's existence, when she and her friends sit in Bogodul's darkened hut, the only structure left on the island on the eve of the flooding. Along with conversations, many of Darya's important observations come in the form of interior monologues that merge seamlessly with the narrator's inner voice. Rasputin—and this is typical of Village Prose writers—uses the voice and the point of view of older peasant women to enrich and even shape his narrative. Rural writers were brought up in homes and villages that had lost most of their men to wars, to the rural purges that accompanied collectivization, and to the lure of the city. Young village boys listened to their mothers, grandmothers, and aunts talk about the daily routine, about the tragedies that had taken the men away, and about the village past. Like the poet Pushkin, these writers had heard countless fairy tales and other folk stories from simple peasant women (though in the case of the aristocratic Pushkin the storyteller was a nanny and not a relative). The writers' own experiences, and the reality of life in the Russian countryside after the Revolution, meant that in rural prose female characters would be foregrounded.[7]

Darya and a few other villagers wait out the final summer of the island's long existence; everyone else has left for the new settlement, returning only to help bring in the hay. The luminous treatment of the haymaking scene is intended to give an indication of the harmonious way of life being carelessly abandoned. Like the heroine of Solzhenitsyn's "Matryona's Home," Darya is the moral center of her village, its memory and its conscience. But whereas Solzhenitsyn ends his tale with the warning that without the Matryonas, the nation could not stand, Rasputin's narrator says confidently that every village has one or even two old people with Darya's qualities, and that inevitably "if one such old woman lives out her days and dies, her place will immediately be taken by another woman who has grown old, strengthening her position among the others with her firm and just temperament" (70). There is an implicit warning in this book, but it concerns the dangerous deterioration of man's relationship both with nature and with his past.

Rasputin emphasizes the importance of cyclical time to the farming community of Matyora. What counts in this context is not a date on a calendar but the annual cycle of the seasons and the various tasks appropriate to a given season. The book begins with the statement "Once more spring had come, one more in the never-ending cycle, but for Matyora this spring would be the last." The forces of progress, of Russia's historical destiny, will break up the island's cyclical life and bring it to an end. Patterns of everyday life (*byt*) in the countryside and the ways that these patterns are interrupted and destroyed by historical forces—war, collectivization, urbanization, an epic story of loss—structure the narrative of Village Prose more than any conventional plot.

The concept of *rod* (kinship community, relatedness in time and place) is even more important to *Matyora* than cyclical time. Not only is Darya the moral and social center of the village; she is also, while she is alive, the caretaker of her whole *rod*.[8] The village cemetery is full of people who are her near or distant relatives, and her chief anxiety about the flooding of Matyora is that the graves of her relatives—already despoiled by outsiders sent to clear the island—will be lost beneath the waves. While her grandson Andrei—a conventional Socialist Realist hero—feels a responsibility to build for the Soviet future, Darya's responsibility lies entirely with the past and the family dead. In Russian folk belief, a person has to remember and honor the dead in order to be assured of a place among them; the Russian Orthodox calendar includes many days on which special attention is paid to deceased family members. Darya's actions in the second half of the book cannot be fully appreciated without understanding how important this duty is to her. She fears breaking the chain of remembrance and leaving past generations of her *rod* stranded in the oblivion of the unremembered dead. When in doubt about the proper way to say farewell to Matyora, she consults with the people she trusts the most—her dead. She receives from them the message that she must bid a proper, ritual farewell to her home, the center of her family's simple life for generations. She prepares her house for its "funeral" with great dignity and affection in what is one of the most powerful scenes in postwar Russian literature.[9]

The Master of the island, that small, catlike creature, invisible to human eyes, who knows everyone and everything past, present, and to come, is an extension of the folk idea of the place spirit. There was hardly a peasant home, barn, bathhouse, or threshing floor that did not have a resident spirit. The woods had its wood goblin, and the water its water sprite, but chief among these was the *domovoi,* the guardian spirit of the peasant dwelling, its second "master" whose origins lay in an ancestor cult. He took an active interest in the life of the household and was especially upset by loss or change. To move and not to respectfully invite him to accompany the family to the new home was to court almost certain disaster. The Master is the *domovoi* of the whole island of Matyora. A creature of the night, he roams his kingdom, listening to the voices of houses doomed to extinction and to the whispering of trees and animals. He knows that the dead come to the living at night in what seem to be dreams but which are really recollections. And the Master also knows that he is the last in his line; as a place spirit he cannot survive the disappearance of his kingdom beneath the waves.

Of the other characters in *Farewell to Matyora,* the most colorful is Bogodul (from the Russian word *bogokhul,* "blasphemer"), whose earthy comments are mostly limited to the all-purpose word *kurva* (which literally means "slut" or "tart" but which Bogodul uses in a variety of contexts). He is a shaggy and seemingly ageless link to the primordial past, "as though God had decided to keep at least one man alive through several generations" (25). The women's affectionate tolerance of his blaspheming ways is a reflection of the Russian attitude toward the *yurodivy,* the wandering "fool-for-Christ," whose humble appearance and seemingly crazy behavior were interpreted as signs of holiness.

Darya's son Pavel is a man caught between past and future, tradition and innovation; Darya speaks of him as being pulled through life by impersonal forces beyond his control. He is at home neither in the past, as his mother is, nor in the future, as his son Andrei is. It is fitting that at the very end of the story he is literally adrift between the island and the shore, hopelessly lost.

The tsar larch, standing in majesty on a hill, is much more than a mere tree. As Darya took care of the dead, and the Master kept watch over the living, the larch anchored the island itself to the river bottom. "As long as it stood so would Matyora" (183). It had long served as a focal point for the island's indigenous folklore, and it proves in the story to be strangely impervious to modern man's tools of destruction. At the end the larch is the only natural survivor of an island once lushly covered with forest and field.

Rasputin chose to focus in this book on the imminent flooding from the point of view of one of the islands, rather than from a shoreline village (as he had done in "Downstream"), because of the greater symbolic value of an island. The very name "Matyora" has multiple etymological associations in Russian, all of them related to the word for "mother."[10] The most important resonance is that of Damp Mother Earth (*mat'-syra-zemlia*), the female earth spirit in Russian folk belief which brings forth and nurtures all living things and which receives the dead.[11] Matyora is both itself and all of traditional rural Russia, where villages were like little "islands" in the forest, cut off for much of the year from other settlements, and where everyone outside your village was to some extent alien. Matyora is also emblematic of the isolation of rural Russia from urban Russia, of the country as a whole from other nations, and of the earth vis-à-vis the universe. The disorderly but relentless march toward a radiant future that was observed with misgivings in Rasputin's earlier work here takes on a significance that goes far beyond Angara's shores. Andrei Sinyavsky's words from another island—the Gulag Archipelago—come to mind: "I have always thought of our existence as an island, but now realize that it has the dimensions of a whole continent, and that all the people who have ever been here, whether living or dead, forever remain part of it."[12]

Rasputin's story "The Fire" fulfills the promise he made after *Matyora* to "follow" his characters to the new settlements to see what their lives would be like there. In "The Fire," the apprehensions expressed in 1976 about the new life have become a reality. The former villagers can only look to a place in the river where their Egorovka used to be. After years in the new lumber town of Sosnovka, it is painfully clear that the old villages "died" twice; first they disappeared physically, and then the transplanted inhabitants forgot the old ways that had helped them cope with trials much worse than the fire now sweeping through the town's warehouses. When fields were submerged along with the villages, the former villagers lost the whole way of life that accompanied agricultural work. Their new occupation—lumbering—encourages an indifference toward nature and, eventually, toward the common good. The luminous ancestral memory of *Matyora* has given way in "The Fire" to a dark, angry pain. It is an important but bleak work.

Valentin Rasputin is a native son of the Siberia he portrays so passionately in his stories. He was born in 1937 in Ust-Uda on the shores of the Angara River and spent his childhood in another shoreline village, Atalanka. Although he was too young and too far away from the battlefields to remember much of World War II, he does have a vivid recollection of how the conflict brought local people together in the struggle to survive and to support the war effort. For the Siberians, European Russia was the *prarodina*, "ancient homeland," distant from them in time, place, and way of life. Rasputin had to leave his community to attend secondary school; from there he went to the university in the Siberian city of Irkutsk. During his years in college, the transformation of Siberia by the construction of the Angara hydroelectric system had begun. In order to provide energy for the projected growth of this region, the Angara River was to be dammed; the resulting inland seas would flood both the islands in the middle of the river and low-lying villages along the shore, and Rasputin's own village of Atalanka was moved inland to a new shoreline. Rasputin wrote about this massive undertaking for newspapers and television. In 1966 he published a book of essays in which his enthusiasm for the growth of his native region was not unlike that of his fellow Siberian, Yevgeny Yevtushenko. Another Rasputin book, published in the same year, contained lyrical essays and stories on the vanishing traditions of a Siberian tribe; it is here that the author—breaking free from the considerable linguistic and ideological shackles of Soviet journalism—began to reveal his literary interests and his potential. The path he had chosen as a writer would not lead him forward to a rapidly developing Siberia but would take him back into the past. Rasputin would write of progress from "the point of view of those who have to make way for it, both in the human world and in nature."[13] His theme would not be rapid gain but rapid loss.

In the decade between Rasputin's abandonment of journalism for literature and the publication of *Matyora,* he wrote an impressive series of essays and stories that made him one of the most respected young writers in the post-Stalinist period. His three longer works (*povesti*)—*Money for Maria* (1968), *Borrowed Time* (1970), and *Live and Remember* (1974)—told stories that are, like *Farewell to Matyora,* descriptive of life in Siberia, but that achieve a universal significance. The first two novellas describe, respectively, a villager caught up in the loss of collective-farm funds, and the passing away of an old woman and its effect on her children. In *Live and Remember,* Rasputin's sympathetic portrait of a woman who shelters her deserter husband from the authorities stretched the limits of official tolerance for nonheroic depictions of the war years. A less persuasive writer might have stumbled badly with characters like Andrey and Nastena.

Rasputin's greatest impact on the reading public and critics alike came two years later with *Farewell to Matyora.* Even those who were by now tired of the village theme or were worried about the use that was being made of Village Prose by reactionary critics were impressed by Rasputin's artistic confidence, and by the way even this tragic tale is told with a luminous touch.

Valentin Rasputin's career in the years since the publication of *Matyora* has taken several turns that even a novelist would have had trouble imagining. In March 1980 he was viciously beaten in his Irkutsk apartment building by thieves who were after his jeans. It was several years and a number of operations later before he was able to write full-time again, and it was only in 1985, with the publication of "The Fire," that he resumed his role as one of the most prominent literary figures in the USSR.

Many of those who read "The Fire" saw a marked change in the writer's style to a more publicistic, more rhetorical tone, one that was reminiscent of Aleksandr Solzhenitsyn. This observation has been borne out by the writer's turn to the essay form in the second half of the 1980s. His essays cover a number of areas, from the history and ethnography of his native Siberia to the preservation of the environment—on which he has been one of the most fearless and effective voices in the country—to the state of the Russian people and their culture. He is distressed by what he and a number of other literary and nonliterary figures view as a pervasive hatred of Russia, and they fear the gradual destruction of the Russian people as a distinct entity, going so far as to speak of "Russo-phobia" and national "genocide." In searching for someone to blame for the perceived threat to their national identity, Rasputin and his fellow conservatives have pointed to things like the Revolution, collectivization, mass culture, the avant-garde, and peres-troika, and to a host of harmful "outsiders" (*chuzhie*), including Westerners in general, non-Russian Soviet citizens, and, most prominently, Soviet Jews.

It is because of his negative comments on Soviet Jews that Rasputin has gained a prominence in the West that eluded him as a writer of lyrical fiction. Like a number of writers before him—Dostoevsky for example—his artistic sense is not matched by polit-ical wisdom or by a generosity of spirit toward those whom he identifies as *chuzhoi*. He has had the misfortune—mostly of his own making—to become best known abroad as a Russian chauvinist, rather than as one of the finest writers of the post-Stalinist period. His appointment to Gorbachev's inner council in the spring of 1990 was even seen—incorrectly—as an endorsement of Russian chauvinism by Gorbachev.[14]

Nationalist feeling in Russia is not one kind of emotion or polit-ical stance; it ranges from the "cultural ecology" of the academician Dmitry Likhachev at one end of the spectrum to something close to neo-Nazism at the other end. Rasputin is somewhere in the middle, refusing to condemn the idea of a group like Pamyat (Memory) while also avoiding any direct identification with them and their bullying tactics. There are many factors in the rise of an extreme form of Russian nationalism in the 1980s, only one of which is the legacy of Village Prose and the political activity of rural writers like Rasputin. Xenophobia and anti-Semitism have, unfortunately, a centuries-long history in Russia, and periodic outbreaks are independent of a particular writer or group of writers or type of literature.

Rasputin has said that whenever he thinks back to his child-hood, he always remembers being on the shores of the Angara (before it was flooded), next to his native village of Atalanka "with the islands across the water from me and the sun setting on the opposite shore. I've seen many objects of beauty both natural and man-made, but I will die with that picture before me which is dearer to me than anything else in the world. . . . It is how I see my homeland."[15] The wistful backward looks to a rural boyhood structure much of Russian Village Prose and give it its luminous tone in what would otherwise be a tragic story of the upheavals of collectivization, the war, and the destruction of rural life. Rural writers like Rasputin have preserved not only the social history of rural Russia but also its atmosphere, giving an insider's view of village life which is all too rare in Russian literature. To understand *Farewell to Matyora,* we need to recall the child on the shore, looking out at sunset, dreaming of becoming Master of the island. Like the Master, Rasputin is devoted to his homeland, to the exclusion of all else, and he is abnormally sensitive to its pain. He watches over it zealously and sees his fate as irrevocably linked to its continued existence and its spiritual well-being. If Rasputin's political vision in recent years has seemed clouded and deeply flawed, his artistic vision in *Farewell to Matyora* astonishes the reader with its confident lyricism. This is a story of loss, but a very beautiful one.

A Selected Bibliography of Rasputin's Work in Translation

"Downstream." Translated by Valentina Brougher and Helen Poot. In *Contemporary Russian Prose,* edited by Carl Proffer and Ellendea Proffer, pp. 379–430. Ann Arbor, Mich.: Ardis, 1982.

Live and Remember. Translated by Antonina Bouis. New York: Macmillan, 1978.

Money for Maria; Borrowed Time: Two Village Tales. Translated by Kevin Windle and Margaret Wettlin. New York: Quartet Books, 1981.

Siberia on Fire: Stories and Essays. Translated by Gerald Mikkelson and Margaret Winchell. DeKalb: Northern Illinois University Press, 1989.

You Live and Love and Other Stories. Translated by Alan Myers. New York: Vanguard, 1986.

Notes

1 For a more complete discussion of Russian Village Prose see Kathleen Parthé, *The Radiant Past: Russian Village Prose from Ovechkin to Rasputin* (Princeton, N.J.: Princeton University Press, forthcoming).

2 Liliia Vil'chek, "Vniz po techeniiu derevenskoi prozy," *Voprosy literatury,* no. 6 (1985): 72.

3 Gerald Mikkelson and Margaret Winchell, "Valentin Rasputin and His Siberia," Introduction to *Siberia on Fire: Stories and Essays by Valentin Rasputin* (DeKalb: Northern Illinois University Press, 1989), p. xvii.

4 Valentin Rasputin, "Vniz i vverkh po techeniiu," in *Vniz i vverkh po techeniiu* (Moscow: Sov. Rossiia, 1972); Rasputin, "Downstream," trans. Valentina Brougher and Helen Poot, in *Contemporary Russian Prose,* ed. Carl Proffer and Ellendea Proffer (Ann Arbor, Mich.: Ardis, 1982).

5 Khlebnik is related to *khleb,* "bread, grain"; Beryozovik to *bereza,* "birch tree," and *berezovik,* "brown mushroom."

6 John Berger, *Pig Earth* (New York: Pantheon, 1979), pp. 8–11. Berger describes how each village (he is talking of France but what he says applies to rural life in general) had its own communal "living portrait," built out of the events of the day supplemented by narratives handed down from one generation to another. In the village, says Berger, "everybody is portrayed and everybody portrays."

7 While there is at least one well-known female rural poet—Olga Fokkina—there are virtually no female Village Prose writers. Women were deeply involved in oral folk culture; they were less likely than men to leave the village for urban areas, where one had to go to get the literary training and contacts necessary to launch a career as a writer. Often future writers left the village when they were drafted into the army and never returned there to live.

8 Teresa Polowy, *The Novellas of Valentin Rasputin: Genre, Language and Style* (New York: Peter Lang, 1989), p. 11.

9 This has been captured very successfully in *Proshchanie* (Farewell/The Parting), the Soviet film based on this work. The film has its own poignant history. The director, Larisa Shepitko, and four members of her crew were killed on location at the beginning of their work on the film. Her husband, the director Elem Klimov, completed the project for her. He added a scene at the beginning in which five hooded figures in what seem to be translucent white monk's robes (which turn out on closer inspection to be raincoats) silently cross the mist-shrouded Angara River in a small boat. As they land, the four men—government workers—go off to clear the island; the fifth figure disappears from view. This tribute to Shepitko and her coworkers, though obviously not in the original text, fits beautifully and eerily the film's elegiacal sensibilities. Rasputin generally liked the film, although he thinks it would have been better had Shepitko lived to complete it.

10 A more precise transliteration of this word from the Cyrillic is "Matera." The word for "mother" in modern standard Russian is *mat'*; an archaic, bookish variant of this is *mater'* (cf. Eng. "maternal"). Other associations that come to mind are *materik* (in dialect *matera*), "continent, a steep bank," and *materoi,* "full-grown, experienced, old" (cf. Eng. "mature").

11 A number of critics have discussed the concept of Mother Earth in *Farewell to Matyora,* e.g., Irina Corten, "Solzenitsyn's Matrena and Rasputin's Dar'ja: Two Studies in Russian Peasant Spirituality," *Russian Language Journal* 33, no. 114 (1979): 95.

12 Abram Tertz [Andrei Sinyavsky], *A Voice from the Chorus,* trans. Kyril Fitzlyon and Max Hayward (New York: Bantam, 1978), p. 303. This book consists of letters Sinyavsky wrote to his wife from a Soviet prison camp, where he spent over five years for having published his stories abroad without official permission. The prison camp of Solzhenitsyn's story *One Day in the Life of Ivan Denisovich* likewise can be seen as emblematic of Russia or the Soviet Union as a whole.

13 David Gillespie, *Valentin Rasputin and Soviet Russian Village Prose* (London: Modern Humanities Research Association, 1986), p. 39.

14 Along with Rasputin, Gorbachev appointed another prominent figure from the literary world, the liberal Central Asian writer Chingiz Aitmatov. Aitmatov resigned from the council in October 1990 to become ambassador to Luxembourg. The council contained representatives of a number of different interest groups in the Soviet Union. The council itself was abolished in December 1990.

15 Valentin Rasputin, "Nuzhno vzvolnovannoe slovo," *Sovetskaia kul'tura,* 19 March 1985.

1

ONCE MORE SPRING HAD COME, one more in the never-ending cycle, but for Matyora this spring would be the last, the last for both the island and the village that bore the same name. Once more, rumbling passionately, the ice broke, piling up mounds on the banks, and the liberated Angara River opened up, stretching out into a mighty, sparkling flow. Once more the water gushed boisterously at the island's upper tip, before cascading down both channels of the riverbed; once more greenery flared on the ground and in the trees, the first rains soaked the earth, the swifts and swallows flew back, and at dusk in the bogs the awakened frogs croaked their love of life. It all had happened many times before, and many times Matyora had been caught up in nature's changes, neither falling behind nor running ahead of each day.

And so this year, too, the people planted their gardens—but not all of them: three families had moved out in the fall, going off to various cities, and three other families had left even earlier, as soon as it became clear that the rumors were true. As usual, they planted wheat, but not in all the fields: they didn't touch the fields beyond the river, planting only on the island, close by. And they sowed the potatoes and carrots in their gardens not at the proper time, but whenever they had a chance: many were living in two houses nowadays, with a good fifteen kilometers by hill and water between them, and it was tearing them apart. And Matyora wasn't the same: the buildings were in place, only one small house and a bathhouse had been torn down for firewood, everything was still alive and in motion. The roosters still sang out loudly, the cows bellowed, and the dogs barked noisily, but the village was fading, you could see that it had already faded: like a half-chopped tree, it had lost its roots, it was out of cycle. Everything was in place, but everything was wrong: the nettles crept forward thicker and more brazen, the windows in the empty houses were frozen, and the gates to the yards were open—people closed them to preserve appearances, but some evil spirit kept opening them again and again, to make a draft, to make the gates creak and slam; fences and gates sagged every-where; sheds, barns, and lean-tos blackened and sagged, poles and boards lay scattered uselessly—the owner's hand that had fixed things and kept them in repair for long service no longer touched them. Many houses weren't whitewashed and stood dirty and half empty; some things had been moved away to the new houses, revealing sullen, soiled corners, and some things left be-hind, for they still had to come here and they still had work to do here. But now the only full-time residents in Matyora were the old men and women, who took care of the gardens and houses, tended the animals, and played with the children, giving the vil-lage an inhabited air and keeping it from being too desolate. In the evenings they gathered, talking softly—and always about the same thing: what was to happen—sighing deeply and frequently, looking guardedly in the direction of the right bank, beyond the

Angara River, where a large new settlement was being built. Various rumors came back from there.

That first peasant who decided to settle on the island over three hundred years ago was a far-sighted and clever man, who had judged rightly that he would find no better land. The island stretched over five versts, and not in a skinny ribbon, but in the plump shape of an iron—there was room for pastures, and forests, and a swamp with frogs, and on the lower side, beyond a shallow crooked stream there was another island close to Matyora which they called Podmoga, and sometimes Podnoga. Podmoga, made from the word "to help," made sense: what they lacked on their own land they got there. But why they called it Podnoga—no one could have explained it back then and now it was hopeless. Some-one's tongue must have stumbled, and the new name caught on, for it's a fact that the stranger a word the more the tongue likes it. There is another name in this story that seemed to come from nowhere, and that's Bogodul, the name given to an old man who had moved to the island and who pronounced it with a Ukrainian accent, Bokhgodul. But you can at least guess at how the nick-name came into being. The old man, who passed himself off as a Pole, loved Russian swearwords and apparently a visiting edu-cated person must have heard him and said "bogokhul," which means blasphemer, and the villagers either misunderstood or twisted it around on purpose, changing it to Bogodul. Whether this is what happened or not no one can say for sure, but the explanation seems natural.

The village had seen everything in its day. In ancient times bearded Cossacks passed it on their way up the Angara to set up the Irkutsk prison; merchants, hurrying every which way, would show up for a night's lodging; convicts were transported on the river and when they saw populated land right in front of their noses, the convoys stopped, came ashore, and boiled up a stew with fresh-caught fish; for two full days a battle roared between Kolchak's White army, who had taken the island, and the parti-sans who attacked from both sides by boat. The Kolchak forces left behind a wooden shack that they had built on the upper end of the island, and for the last few years Bogodul had moved in every summer, as soon as it got warm, living like a roach. The village had known floodwaters that submerged half the island and left treacherous whirlpools swirling over Podmoga—which was lower and flatter—and it had known fire, hunger, and pillage.

The village had its own church, situated as it should be, on high, clean ground, visible from afar from either branch of the river; the church had been turned into a warehouse during collectivization. Of course, services had ceased much earlier for lack of a priest, but the cross had remained and old women had bowed to it in the morning. And then the cross was knocked down as well. There was a mill in the upper bow channel, which seemed to have been dug especially for it, and the milling, while not profitable, was at least self-sufficient, enough for their own bread. During the last few years a plane landed twice a week in the old pasture and the locals had learned to take to the air to get to the city or the district capital.

And so the village had lived on in its lean and simple way, clinging to its spot on the bluff by the left bank, greeting and seeing off the years, like the water that joined them to other settlements and had helped feed them since time immemorial. And just as the flowing water seemed to have no end or limit, the village seemed ageless: some went off to their Maker, others were born, old buildings collapsed, new ones were built. And the village lived on, through hard times and troubles, for three hundred and more years, during which time half a verst of land was washed away at the upper tip, until the rumor thundered down on them that the village would be no more. A dam was being built downriver on the Angara for a hydroelectric power station, and the water would rise in the rivers and streams, flooding much land, including, first and foremost, Matyora. Even if you were to pile five islands like Matyora one on top of the other, they would still be flooded and you wouldn't be able to show the spot where people once lived. They would have to move. It wasn't easy to believe that it really would come to pass, that the end of the

world, with which the superstitious used to threaten the unenlightened, was really nigh for the village. A year after the first
rumors an evaluating commission came by cutter and began as-
sessing the depreciation of the buildings and determining how
much money they were worth. There was no more doubt about
the fate of Matyora, it was living out its last years. Somewhere on
the right bank they were building a new settlement for the
sovkhoz, or state-owned farm, into which they were bringing all
the neighboring kolkhozes and some that were not so neighboring, and it was decided, so as not to have to deal with rubbish, to
set fire to the old villages.

And now only the very last summer was left: the water would
rise in the fall.

2

THREE OLD WOMEN SAT AROUND THE SAMOVAR, sometimes lapsing into silence, pouring tea and slurping it from their saucers, and then reluctantly and wearily taking up the weak, fragmented conversation. They were at Darya's, the oldest of the women; none of them knew their own age precisely, because that precision was left in the church baptismal records, which had been taken away somewhere—and could not be found. The old women used to talk this way about age:

"I was a girl and pulling my brother Vaska around in a sled when you were born." That was Darya talking to Nastasya. "I could remember things by then, I remember."

"You are three years older than me, I guess."

"Three, hah! I was getting married, and you—what were you

then—think back! You were still running around without a shirt. You must remember when I got married, don't you?"

"I remember."

"Well, there. How can you compare yourself to me! Next to me, you're a youngster."

The third woman, Sima, could not participate in these reminiscences; she was a newcomer, blown into Matyora by a random wind less than ten years ago. She came to Matyora from Podvolochna, a village on the Angara, and she came there from somewhere below Tula, and she said that she had seen Moscow twice, once before the war and once after, but the village had a way of not believing things that couldn't be proven, and they snickered at her claim. How could Sima, a homeless old woman, have seen Moscow if none of them had? So what if she had lived right near it—they don't let just anyone into Moscow like that. Sima did not grow angry or insist, saying nothing, but then she would tell them again, which earned her the nickname Moskvishna. It suited her, by the way, for Sima was clean and neat, she could read a bit and had a songbook, and when she was in the mood, she would pick out sad and drawn-out songs about bitter fate from it. It looked as though fate had truly given her a life of sorrow, since she had to wander about so much, leaving the home where she had been born during the war, giving birth to just one daughter, who was mute at that, and then in her declining years being stuck with a little boy and no time or means to raise him. But Sima still had hopes of finding an old man she could cuddle up to and look after—washing, cooking, serving. That's why she had come to Matyora in the first place: she had heard that Grandpa Maxim had been widowed, and she waited a proper time and then left Podvolochna, where she was living, and set off for the island to find happiness. But happiness didn't come: Grandpa Maxim put up a fight, and the other women, who didn't know her well enough, didn't help; nobody needed Grandpa, but he was their own, and they didn't want to see him go to a stranger. Most likely it was Valka, Sima's mute daughter, who scared Grandpa off, because she was grown by then and made loud and very unpleasant sounds, always wanting something and very high-strung. The unsuccessful matchmaking prompted the village wags to say: "She was Sima, but she missed"; but Sima wasn't insulted. She didn't go back to Podvolochna but stayed on Matyora, moving into a tiny abandoned house on the lower end. She planted a garden, set up a loom, and wove runners from rags—that's how she earned a living. And Valka, while she lived with her mother, worked in the kolkhoz.

Kolka, Sima's four-year-old grandson, Valka's surprise package, played near Sima. The boy didn't take after his mother; he wasn't mute, but he talked poorly and very little and was growing up to be a wild, scaredy-cat boy who never left his grandmother's skirts. The old women pitied him and petted him—he just pressed closer to Sima and watched them with a comprehension that was not childlike, but bitter and meek.

"Who are you to be looking at me like that?" Darya asked. "What do you see behind me—my death? I know about it without you. Look, the dummy's stare is fixed—like a nail."

"He's not a dummy," Sima said, hurt, pulling the boy closer.

"He may not be a dummy, but he doesn't talk."

The conversation flagged again, for they were made sleepy by the tea and the bright setting sun that poured in the window that opened on the sunset. Old Darya, tall and lean, a head taller than Sima who sat next to her, was nodding agreeably to something, her stern bloodless face with its sunken cheeks turned to the table. Despite her years, Darya stood on her own feet, controlled her hands, and managed the work involved in running the house. Her son and daughter-in-law were in the new settlement, coming here only once a week or less, so the yard and garden were on her shoulders, and the yard had a cow with a calf, a little bull from the winter calving, a piglet, chickens, and a dog. The old woman had been told, of course, to turn to her neighbor Vera if she couldn't do it or was sick, but it hadn't come to that yet, Darya was managing alone.

June had just begun, and there was day after clear sunny day, barely interrupted by short nights that were like a prolonged twilight. It was never too hot on the island surrounded by water; in the evening, when the breeze died down and the warm earth let off a light steam, it became so peaceful and beautiful, the greenery glowed so thick and fresh, raising the island even higher above the water, the Angara rolled over the rocks with such a clear, merry ring, and everything seemed so permanent and eternal that you couldn't believe any of it—not the move, not the flooding, not the parting. And there were the sprouts in the fields and gardens, and the rains that came on time and the warm weather that also came on time, a rare coordination that promised a good harvest; the unhurried, desired crescendo of summer . . .

"I wake up in the morning and remember first thing . . . oh, my heart stops, it won't go," Nastasya was saying. "Oh, Lord! . . . And Egor just weeps and weeps. I tell him: 'Don't cry, Egor, don't.' And he says: 'How can I not cry, Nastasya, how can I not cry?' And I go off with a stone heart to clean up. I go and I see Darya, I see Vera, Domnida—and I feel a little better, I get used to it. I think, maybe they just want to scare us and won't do anything."

"Why would they just want to scare us?" Darya asked.

"So that there won't be any who aren't scared."

After Nastaysa and Egor were left alone (two sons didn't return from the war, the third drowned when his tractor fell through the ice, and their daughter died of cancer in the city), Nastasya became a little strange, telling tales about her old man, all of them pathetic and morbid: either he had burned to death and she had barely escaped, or he had screamed all night because someone was choking him from inside, or he was weeping ("his second days have started, and he's crying, washing himself in tears"), even though everyone knew Grandpa Egor wouldn't shed a tear easily. At first he tried to shame her out of it, threatening, teaching her—nothing worked, and he gave up. She was a normal, healthy person in every other respect, but this was like threading that had twisted askew and couldn't be made to fit— she kept talking about things that couldn't possibly be. Kind people tried not to notice Nastasya's harmless quirk, and mean ones liked to ask: "How's Egor today—is he alive?"

"Oh!" Nastasya would exclaim joyfully. "Egor . . . poor Egor . . . he almost died last night. The old man is losing his mind, he pulled off a wart and bled and bled. A basin full of blood."

"And now—has he stopped bleeding?"

"It's all gone, so it stopped. He's hardly breathing. Oh, I feel so sorry for the old fool. I'll run home and see how he is."

And meanwhile Egor would be hobbling along on the other side of the street, angrily and helplessly squinting at Nastasya: the feeble-minded woman was at it again, may her tongue fall off, telling fairy tales about him.

They were facing the earliest farewell to Matyora. When it came to determining who would move where, Grandpa Egor signed up, either out of spite or in confusion, for the very city where they were building the hydroelectric power station. They were putting up two big buildings for people like them, alone and refugees from the flood zone. The terms were a trade: they wouldn't get a cent for their house, but they would get an apartment in the city. Later Grandpa Egor, not without prompting and nagging from Nastasya, tried to switch to the sovkhoz, where they gave you money as well as an apartment for your house, but it was too late.

"The sovkhoz is setting aside apartments for workers, and what kind of worker are you now?" Vorontsov, the chairman of the village soviet, tried to tell him.

"I gave my whole life to the kolkhoz."

"The kolkhoz is something else. There is no more kolkhoz."

The district capital sent people to hurry Egor to move, the apartment for him and Nastasya was ready, awaiting them, but the old people kept dragging things out, not moving, trying to breathe a few more gulps of native air before they died. Nastasya planted a garden, started one project after another, putting it off, trying to fool herself. The last time the man from the capital had really yelled at them, threatening them with the loss of the apartment which would leave them with nothing, and Egor decided: if they had to leave, they might as well leave. And he announced: "Be ready by Whitsunday."

And there were only two weeks to Whitsunday.

"At least you won't have any cares," Darya said to Nastasya, either in comfort or mockery. "I visited my daughter in the city—it's amazing: you have the Angara and the forest right there, and a toilet-bath. You don't have to come out on the street for a year if you don't want to. There's a faucet, like that one on the samovar, and you turn it and water comes out; one has cold, the other hot. And you don't have to throw logs in the stove, it also has a faucet you turn and the heat comes. Cook and fry. There's so much—it spoils a woman! And the bread doesn't come from your stove, no, it comes from the store. I had never seen the faucets and wasn't used to them and so I oohed and aahed over them—and they laughed that it was strange for me. What's even stranger is that the bath and toilet are in the same corner, just the way heathens have, by the kitchen. That's wrong. You sit, and worry, and tremble that they don't hear at the table. And the bath . . . that's no bath, it's a joke, you could rinse off an infant and have room for nothing else. But they splash in it and climb out wet. And so you'll live like a lady, Nastasya, lying around; everything is in the house, you won't have to lift a finger. And there's also that . . . tephelone. It says 'ring-ring,' you say 'lo-'lo,' talk, and then back you lie down."

"Oh, don't torture my heart!" Nastasya said, clutching her chest with her aged hands and shutting her eyes. "I'll die of sadness in one week there. Living among strangers! How can you transplant an old tree?"

"We're all being transplanted, girl, not just you. We're all going that way now. Hurry, Lord, and take us."

Nastasya shook her head in disagreement.

"Don't compare me, Darya, don't. You'll all be in one place, and I'll be alone. All you women from Matyora will visit each other, and you'll feel happy and almost like home. And me? Oh, how can you say that."

"How many of us are there?" Darya replied patiently. "There's no one left. Take a look: they took away Agafya, they took away Vasilisa, they're luring Liza to go to the capital. Katerina's boy still hasn't found himself a place, he's running around like a crazy man. And how can he find time to make up his mind when there's still wine to be drunk. Natalya says she may go live with her daughter on the Lena River . . ."

"Tatyana, Domnida, Manya, you, Tunguska . . . that's a goodly group. But not for me."

"That's all of Matyora?! Lord!"

"I'm keeping quiet about me. Quiet, quiet," Sima wailed and pulled Kolka closer. "Kolka and I will get in a rowboat, push off, and go where our eyes lead us, into the deep blue sea . . ."

Sima had no possessions, no relatives, and there was only one road for her—to an old folk's home, but now there was even an obstacle on that road: Kolka, whom she adored. They weren't too eager to take her into a home with a boy. Valka, Sima's mute daughter, had disappeared. When she grew up and came to know a man, and then another, and another, and another, Valka grew to like it and got into the swing of things so much that she used to ask for a night's games herself. And very soon she won Kolka in one of the games. Sima chased after Valka with a stick, mothers and wives called her every name under the sun, and crazed Valka ran off, and it was more than a year since they'd heard anything from her. They told Sima to go to missing persons, but with the constant movement and madness on the Angara now, and with Valka's muteness, and lack of records, it would not be easy to find her.

"Even if she is found, I won't give Kolka to her anyway," Sima said. "Kolka and I may have to crawl, but we'll be tied to the same rope."

"Why don't you teach the boy to talk right?" Darya reproached her. "When he grows up he won't thank you."

"I'm teaching him. He can talk. Kolka is a quiet one, that's all."

"The boy had it hard. He understands everything."

"He has had it hard."

Without asking Nastasya, Darya took her glass, splashed in some brewed tea, and then set it under the samovar—a large merchant one, old-fashioned, with a beautiful pure copper glow, an elaborate grillwork that revealed the sparkling coals, and prettily curved but sturdy legs. A strong and steady stream, without splatters, poured from the faucet—that meant there was still plenty of boiling water—and the disturbed samovar wheezed lightly. Then Darya poured Sima's glass and added some tea to her own—after a rest and some preparation, wiping away the sweat on their faces, they started another round, bowing, creaking, blowing on their saucers, sipping carefully with outstretched lips.

"This is the fourth glass, you know," Nastasya calculated.

"Drink, girl, while the tea is alive. You won't set up a samovar over there. You'll make it in a sauce pan on the stove."

"Why in a pan? I'll have a teapot."

"It's still not tea without a samovar. At least it's not dry. But there's no taste. Just water, that's all."

And Darya laughed, remembering that they were building city-style apartments at the sovkhoz, too, and that she would be forced to live in the same conditions as Nastasya. And she shouldn't be scaring Nastasya—who knew whether she would be able to set up her samovar, either. No, she wouldn't give it up, she'd set it up on the bed if she had to, and as for the rest, she'd see. And out of turn, having lost the train of their conversation, she announced with a bitterness that had caught her unawares: "As for me, I'd just as soon not go anywhere. Let them drown me, if that's what they want."

"And they will," Sima said.

"Let them. You die once. What's there to be afraid of?"

"Oh, but I don't want to drown," Nastasya said in fear. "It's a sin, don't you know. Let them bury me in the ground. All our people are in the ground, and that's where we should be too."

"Your family will soon be floating."

"Floating. Yes, that's so," Nastasya agreed drily and carefully.

And to change the subject, which she herself had brought up, Darya remembered: "Why isn't Bogodul here today?"

"I can't even think back to when Bogodul missed tea."

"It's sinful with him, and lonely without him."

"Ah, that Bogodul! He's just like one of the Lord's birdies, but a swearing one."

"For shame, Nastasya!"

"Forgive me, Lord!" Nastasya obediently crossed herself in the direction of the icon in the corner and sighed uncomfortably with a sob, took a sip from the saucer, and blessed herself again, adding a little whispered prayer.

The glowing coals in the samovar gave off a sweet charcoal smell, and the sunny motes hung obliquely and lazily over the table, thick and barely stirring; a rooster flapped his wings and crowed in the garden, stepped out under the window, self-importantly lifting his sturdy twisted legs, and peered into the window with his insolent red eyes. Through the other window they could see the Angara's left sleeve, the glistening current giving off sparks in the hot sun and the bank, its meadows ornate with birches and wild cherry trees blazing with blossoms. The dry and rotten odor of the heated wooden sidewalks wafted in through the open door. A chicken hopped up on the doorstep, extended her ugly, half-plucked neck, and looked at the old women: were they alive or not? Kolka stamped his foot at it, the chicken jumped and started clucking madly, without taking its irritation very far away, staying on the porch. And suddenly it grew excited, fluttering its wings, bumping into the walls, and knocking the ladle off the tub, flew into the room in final desperation, and landed on the floor, ready for the ax. Right behind it came a shaggy, barefoot old man muttering to himself, who prodded it with his staff and threw the chicken out on the porch. Then he straightened up and raised his tiny eyes, overgrown from all sides, at the old women, saying: "Kur-rva!"

"There he is, the holy spirit on crutches," Darya said without the least surprise and got up for a glass. "He's not shy. And we were just saying Bogodul isn't coming for some reason. Sit down while the samovar isn't completely cold."

"Kur-rva!" he shouted again, croaking like a raven. "Samovarr! They're rrobbing the dead! Samovarrr, bah!"

"Who are they robbing? What are you going on about?" Darya poured his tea, but stopped warily, leaving the glass under the faucet. These were times when you couldn't believe things, but had to: if someone said that the island took off and was being swept downstream like a twig, you had to run out and look to see if it really wasn't floating downstream. Everything that just recently had seemed eternal and solid as rock was so quickly turned into rack and ruin you just wanted to shut your eyes and forget.

"They're chopping down the crosses, sawing the tombstones!" Bogodul shouted and struck the floor with his staff.

"Where—at the cemetery? Make sense."

"There."

"Who? Don't drag it out, for God's sake," Darya stood up and edged out from the table. "Who's chopping?"

"Strangers, kur-rva!"

"Oh, who could it be?" Nastasya gasped.

Hurriedly tying her kerchief, which had come loose during tea, Darya ordered: "Come on, girls. Either he's crazy, or he's telling the truth."

3

THE CEMETERY LAY BEYOND THE VILLAGE on the road to the mill, on a dry sandy knoll among birches and pines, and you could see far along the Angara and its shores from there. First, leaning forward and stretching her arms as though picking berries, came Darya with firmly set lips, which betrayed her toothless mouth; Nastasya barely managed to keep up: she suffered from shortness of breath, and gasping, she bobbed her head frequently. Behind them, holding the boy by the hand, minced Sima. Bogodul fell behind to arouse the village, and the old women flew into the cemetery alone.

They were finishing up their work there, putting the downed headstones, beds, and crosses into a pile to make a bonfire. A huge bearlike man in a green waterproof jacket and matching pants, trampling the graves, was carrying the ancient wooden grave markers in his arms when Darya, using the last of her energy to surge ahead, hit his arm with a stick she had picked up. The blow was weak, but the shock made the man drop his burden on the ground and exclaim: "What's the matter, what is it, old woman?"

"Hup, now march out of here, you evil spirit!" Darya shouted, choking on fear and rage, and brandished the stick once more. The man jumped back.

"Come on, old lady. You—you watch your hands. Or I'll tie them up. You—you—" His big rusty eyes slid over the old women. "Where did you all come from? The graves?"

"March—who am I talking to?" Darya advanced on the man. He was backing away, stunned by her terrible, prepared-for-anything look. "Get out of here right now, damn your soul! Destroying graves . . ." Darya howled. "Did you bury them? Are your father and mother here? Your children? You never had a mother and father, you bastard. You're not human. What human could do this?!" She looked at the crosses and stones thrown every which way and howled even louder. "Ow-ow-ow! Strike him down on the spot, Lord! Don't have mercy on him! No-o!" She attacked the man again. "You won't get out of here that easy. You'll answer for this. You'll answer to the whole world."

"Get away from me, woman!" the man cried. "Answer for this. They ordered me to do it, and I'm doing it. I don't need your dead."

"Who ordered you? Who?" Sima hobbled over to him sideways, without letting go of Kolka's hand. The boy, sobbing, pulled her back, away from the huge, angered man, and Sima, giving it to him, still screamed as she retreated: "There's nothing holy left in the world for you. Herods!"

The racket drew a second man out of the bushes—he was smaller, younger, and cleaner, but not good-looking either, and he too was wearing a waterproof outfit—he came out with an ax in his hand and stopped and squinted.

"Take a look," the bear said, happy to see him. "They're attacking me, waving sticks around."

"What's the problem, citizens-about-to-be-flooded?" the second man asked seriously. "We're a sanitary brigade, clearing out the territory. On the orders of the sanepidstation."

The difficult word seemed a mocking one to Nastasya.

"What sam-asp-station stuff is that?" she yelled. "Mocking old women! You're an asp yourself! You're both insatiable asps! There isn't punishment enough for the likes of you. And don't try to scare me with that ax. I said, don't scare me with that, put it down."

"Well, well," the second man said and stuck the ax in a nearby pine.

"And don't squint. Look how he's closing his thieving eyes. You look us in the eye. What have you done, asps?"

"What have you done?!" Darya asked, picking up the question. The lonely, naked graves, reduced to anonymous silent hillocks, at which she was looking in her flaming sorrow, trying to grasp the enormity of the deed and getting more and more depressed by it, suddenly lashed at her with their mutilated image. Forgetting herself, Darya attacked the bear with her stick because he was closer, but he grabbed it away from her. Darya fell to her knees. She didn't have the strength to get up right away, but she heard Sima screaming wildly and the boy scream, and the men scream back at them, and the shouting of many voices, swelling, rising; someone helped her up, and Darya saw that the people had come from the village. Katerina was there, and Tatyana, and Liza, and children, Vera, Grandpa Egor, Tunguska, Bogodul, and some others. The uproar was unbelievable. They surrounded the men, who couldn't answer all of them. Bogodul got hold of the ax that had been stuck in the pine tree, and shoving his sharp staff in the bear's chest with one hand, he menacingly waved the upraised ax with the other. Grandpa Egor silently and dully stared at the crosses and stars that had fallen from the stones and then at the men who had done it. Vera Nosaryova, a sturdy, fearless woman, saw her mother's photograph on one of the headstones and at-

tacked the men with such ferocity that the men, jumping away
and protecting themselves, truly feared for their safety. The noise
increased even more.

"Why talk to them—just do away with them right here. It's the
most appropriate place."

"So that they learn better, the godless ones."

"And their hands didn't fall off! Where do they find men like
them?"

"Pulled them out like carrots . . . You have to think hard to
come up with that!"

"We should free the earth of them. It'll thank us."

"Kur-rva!"

The second, younger man, tossing his head back like a rooster
and twisting from side to side, tried to yell over the noise of the
crowd.

"It's not us! It's not us! You must understand. They gave us an
order, they brought us here. It wasn't our idea."

"He's lying," they interrupted. "They came here secretly."

"Let me tell you," the man insisted. "We didn't come secretly,
the representative came with us. And your Vorontsov is here,
too."

"That can't be!"

"Take us to the village, you'll see. They're there."

"Right, let's go to the village."

"That's a mistake! They should be tried where they committed
the crime."

"They won't get away from us. Let's go."

And they herded the men into the village. They hurried with
relief and joy: the old women, unable to keep up, demanded that
they slow down. Bogodul hopped along, like a fettered horse,
never letting go of the tall man and poking him in the back with
his stick. The man turned around and complained, whereupon
Bogodul gave a satisfied, gap-toothed grin and showed him the ax
in his hand. The entire noisy, angry, and heated procession—the
children in front and bringing up the rear, and in the middle,
crowding the two men in from all sides, were the raw old men

and women, unkept, aroused, bent over in two or three places, shuffling and shouting in common cause, raising all the dust on the road—collided at the entrance to the village with two men who were hurrying out to meet them: one was Vorontsov, the chairman of the village soviet and now of the settlement soviet in the new settlement, and the other, an unfamiliar man who looked like a clerk with a straw hat and gypsy face.

"What's this? What's going on?" Vorontsov demanded still at a distance from them, as he ran.

The old women began shouting all at once, waving their arms, interrupting each other, and pointing at the men who, feeling somewhat braver, had made their way out of the circle and pushed through to the gypsy.

"We were doing what we were supposed to, and they attacked us," the young one explained to him.

"Like dogs," the tall one added and searched the crowd for Bogodul. "I'll show you, you old scarecrow—"

He didn't finish. Vorontsov stopped him and the old women, who had responded to the "dogs" with indignant howls.

"Qui-et!" he commanded. "Are we going to listen or sell fish? Are we going to understand the situation or aren't we? They,"— Vorontsov nodded to the men—"were in the process of a sanitary cleanup of the cemetery. This is required everywhere. Do you understand. Everywhere. Required. And here is Comrade Zhuk, from the department on the flood zone. This is his job and he will explain things to you. Comrade Zhuk is an official personage."

"And if he's a personage, then let him answer to the people. We thought they were lying, but here he is, the personage. Who ordered leveling our cemetery to the ground? There are people there, not animals. Who dared do that to graves? Let him answer us. The dead will also ask."

"You don't get away with things like that."

"Merciful Virgin! What have we lived to see? You could just drown yourself in shame."

"Are we going to listen or not?" Vorontsov repeated, sharpening his tone.

Zhuk waited calmly and even with an accustomed air for them to quiet down. He looked tired, his gypsy face ashen. Obviously, his work wasn't easy, if you realized that he had to explain these things to the locals in more than one place. But he began speaking slowly and confidently, with a sort of condescension in his voice:

"Comrades! There is a misunderstanding here on your part. There is a special resolution"—Zhuk knew the power of such words as *decree, regulation, resolution,* even when spoken softly —"There is a special resolution on the sanitary cleanup of the entire floor of the reservoir. And that includes cemeteries. Before we release the water, we have to organize the territory, prepare it—"

Grandpa Egor couldn't stand it.

"Don't drag the cat by the tail. Just tell us why you had to knock down the crosses."

"I am telling you," Zhuk grumbled, and insulted, began speaking faster. "You know that the sea will flow into here; there will be big ships, people traveling . . . tourists and intourists. And your crosses will be floating along. They'll wash up and float away, they won't stay the way they're supposed to on the graves under water. You have to think about these things."

"Did you think about us?" Vera Nosaryova shouted. "We're live people, and we're still living here. You're thinking ahead about tourists but I just picked up Mama's photograph from the ground after these robbers got through. How can that be? Where will I look for her grave now, who'll show me where it is? The ships will come . . . that's way in the future, but what am I supposed to do now? You can take your tourists—" Vera choked. "As long as I live here, the land is under me, and don't you insult it. You could have done this cleanup at the end, so we wouldn't have to see it—"

"When at the end? We have seventy places to relocate, and each one has a cemetery. This is the end. You can't drag it out any more."

"Don't blabber away." The villagers know: it's hard to rile

Grandpa Egor, but once he's riled, watch out, there's no stopping
him. And this was it, Grandpa was getting angrier and angrier.
"Go back where you came from," he ordered. "Don't touch the
cemetery again. Or I'll take to my rifle. I don't care if you are a
personage. A personage must have respect for people and not just
a hat. Big deal, you're here! Some work you found for yourselves!
In the olden days, for work like that you'd get—"

"What's the matter with them?!" Zhuk, pale, turned to Vorontsov for aid. "They don't seem to understand . . . They refuse to
understand. What's the matter with them? Don't they know
what's happening here?"

"Kur-rva!" Bogodul stepped forward.

Vorontsov barreled out his chest and shouted:

"What's all this ruckus? What's all this noise? This isn't a mar-
ketplace!"

"Listen, Vorontsov, don't you raise your voice to us," Grandpa
Egor interrupted, moving in on him. "You're still wet behind the
ears. You're a tourist yourself . . . you only came because of the
sea. You don't give a damn where you live—here or somewhere
else. But I was born in Matyora. And my grandfather. I'm the
master here. And while I'm here, don't you talk to me like that."
Grandpa Egor waved his black, gnarled finger under Vorontsov's
nose. "And don't mock me. Let me live out my days without
shame."

"Look, Karpov, don't excite the people. We'll do what has to
be done. Without asking you."

"You go to——" Grandpa Egor said, sending Vorontsov pretty
far away.

"That's another thing," Vorontsov said. "We'll remember that."

"Go ahead. I'm not afraid of you."

"Some defender you are."

"There's plenty like you!"

"Get out of here, before you're sorry."

The old women boiled over again, shouting, and formed a tight
circle around Vorontsov, Zhuk, and the men. Vera was shoving
her mother's photograph under Zhuk's nose and he was moving

away, grimacing; Darya and Nastasya were pressing in on him from the other side. Zhuk's hat was askew, revealing his dark curly hair, making him look even more like a gypsy—it seemed that any minute he would jump up with a gypsy squeal and babble in his tongue right and left, fighting them all off. Old Katerina took on Vorontsov, attacking and shouting: "There are no such laws! There are no such laws!" When Vorontsov tried to move away, Tunguska, who had been quietly puffing on her pipe throughout all this, appeared before him and silently motioned for him to listen to Katerina. Grandpa Egor's deep bass thundered as the main voice. And with all the hullaballoo, which increased constantly, Vorontsov and Zhuk, who had barely managed a few words, fought their way from the crowd and headed for the village. The tall fat one tried to take the ax from Bogodul, but Bogodul roared and brandished it—and Grandpa Egor, who was nearby, offered this advice to the stranger:

"I wouldn't mess with him, fellow. He's here in exile. He's already patted one man with an ax handle."

"A criminal, eh?" the tall man inquired.

"Uh-huh."

"Maybe I'm one, too."

"Well, then, try it. We'll watch."

But the tall man fumbled around, took another look at Bogodul, who was winking at him with his horrible, glowing red eye, turned and ran to catch up with his pals. An hour later all four had left Matyora.

4

THERE WEREN'T MANY PEOPLE LEFT who remembered when
Bogodul first appeared in Matyora—now it seemed that he had
always been here, that he had been bequeathed to the villagers
for their sins or something by the others who had now departed.
They did remember that there was a time when Bogodul would
come by boat, dropping in on Matyora along his route to the
shore villages. They knew him then as a barterer: he traded awls
for oil. And he would fill up a sack with thread, needles, mugs,
spoons, buttons, soap, buckles, and papers and trade them for
eggs, butter, bread, but most of all for eggs. He knew that not
every village had a store and things that you need for the house
weren't always handy, but Bogodul would be there, knocking: Do
you need this, or that? Of course I do! and they'd invite him in

and give him tea, place orders, add an extra egg or two to his dozen, sometimes even six extra, for everyone had chickens, and he'd take the eggs to the village general stores and sell them. He certainly wouldn't get rich with his trade, but he ate, and as long as his legs carried him, he seemed to eat well.

Either they treated Bogodul better in Matyora than in other villages, or he liked the island for some other reason, but as soon as it came to finding a home port, Bogodul chose Matyora. He came as usual but didn't leave; he stuck. In the summer, sometimes, he'd take off for a while—apparently the call of the road was too strong, driving him somewhere, collecting its due, but he never stirred in the winter: he'd spend a week at one old woman's house, then a week at another's, and sometimes after the bathhouse had been used and warmed up, he'd spend the night there, and before you knew it, it was spring again, and with the warm weather Bogodul moved to his "apartments"—the Kolchak house.

For many years they knew Bogodul as an ancient old man, and for many years he hadn't changed, remaining just as he had appeared, as though God had decided to keep at least one man alive through several generations. He was still on his feet, stepping slowly and broadly, with a heavy, rolling gait, bending his back and lifting his large shaggy head, in which sparrows could easily have nested. The impenetrable thickets on his face revealed only the knob of his bumpy nose and his glowing, bloodshot eyes. From snow to snow Bogodul walked barefoot, indifferent to stones and nettles; his feet, blackened and broad, had lost all semblance of skin; they were so hard they seemed petrified, as if bone had grown over the old bones. There was a time when the kids caught snakes: they trapped them with forked sticks on the ground, picked them up near the head, and ran to scare the girls and women; once he saw an escaped snake slithering down the road surrounded by jumping children, and Bogodul, without a second's thought, offered it his naked foot—the snake tried to bite it but couldn't, bumping against it as though it were rock. From that moment, the boys had found a new game: they brought all the snakes they caught to Bogodul, who would sit on

Kurva – mean poor

a stone in front of his hut, lift his leg with his hands, and tease them, chortling as if tickled whenever the snake tried to strike and penetrate his foot, and blissfully mutter: "Kur-rva!"

That one word took the place of a good thousand words that no other person could manage without. Bogodul managed perfectly. Whether he was a Pole or not, he rarely spoke Russian; it wasn't even conversation, but a simpleminded explanation of what was necessary, liberally sprinkled with his old *kurva* and its relations. There were men who swore more colorfully, more saltily, but no one swore with greater relish: he didn't drop words carelessly, he lovingly baked the curse word, basting it with butter, adding tenderness or anger. And a word that another man might utter as an empty and habitual curse, which would fall by the roadside, not even reaching the listener's ears, was Bogodul's entire statement: like it or not, good or bad, it expressed his precise and genuine feeling for the topic under discussion. Once in a while it did happen that Bogodul spoke to the old women—of course, even then *kurva* followed upon *kurva*, but still it was a meaningful connected story that could have been understood by an outsider.

The old women liked Bogodul. It wasn't clear what charmed them about him, but as soon as he appeared on Darya's doorstep, she dropped whatever she was doing and rushed to greet him and make him welcome.

"Hello, Darya!" he roared in a hoarse voice that seemed full of holes.

"Hello yourself," she replied with suppressed joy. "You're here?"

"Like God—and curses."

Darya blessed herself in front of the icon, begging God for forgiveness for everything that Bogodul said and would say, and hurried to put on the samovar.

"Nastasya! Come have tea, Bogodul is here," she called over the fence. "Call Tatyana, invite her too."

And since the old women liked him, it went without saying that the old men didn't. He was a stranger and an eccentric, a sponger and hanger-on, you couldn't talk to him or find out anything about him—only the devil knew what kind of a man he was, that old women's pet. An old woman would forget to make tea for her own man, a hundred times over her own, but not for him, no, he really was like a god for her, come down to the suffering earth at last, testing the people with his sinful, Christ-like image. The old men grumbled: "He's a criminal." (There was a rumor that Bogodul had been sent to Siberia for murder.) They grumbled but put up with it; it was better not to tangle with the old women, and he was a human being after all, not a dog. Though he was as useless and evil a man as you would find in the world.

In the last few years, when the rumors began and were followed by all the worries with the move, Bogodul was the only person who seemed to be totally unaffected by them—either he figured he'd die before then or, like here, he'd just sponge off the old women there. Their whole life had narrowed to that one thing now, and no matter what they began talking about, no matter what time they harkened to, no matter whom they were discussing, it always ended the same way—with the imminent flooding of Matyora and the move. Bogodul would sit right there with them, scratching his overhardened feet with a scraping sound like stone on stone, or he would sigh heavily after his tea and wheeze and glower:

"They don't have the right."

"Of course they do, if they have it," the old women attacked him with despair and hope. "Is it us they're going to ask for permission?"

"They don't. Flooding . . . kur-rva . . . people . . . they don't. I know the law."

And raising his threatening finger over his head, he looked at it with stern hostility.

"And where will you go, poor thing?" the old women asked pityingly.

"Not a step from here!" Bogodul shouted. "Japanese gods! They don't have the right. I'm alive, kur-rva!"

"You won't be able to stop the water alone, if they let it go. They'll do something with you, send you somewhere."

"I'm alive . . . kur-rva!" he insisted.

The day after the incident at the cemetery he showed up at Darya's, not in the evening as usual, but in the morning; she didn't rise to greet him, didn't talk, she just sat glumly on the bed, head lowered and her hands, dry, large-knuckled, and weathered with hard work, folded between her knees. Bogodul creaked and groaned as he settled down on the bench by the door—Pavel, Darya's son, had taken the good, store-bought furniture to the new apartment across the ice, leaving the old stuff here—Bogodul creaked and groaned, muttered something grumpily, and sat quietly, waiting for Darya to say something. But she showed no interest in talking or in tea, and sat quietly, sighing heavily from time to time and just as heavily lifting her eyes, unseeing, staring off into space, as though she didn't recognize Bogodul or couldn't understand why he was there.

It was late morning, and quiet; the sun, already high in the sky, shone bright and hot but without great force or insistence, with controlled strength, and you could feel it even inside. The light beyond the windows seemed limp, and the various sounds didn't seem to collect together in one place to be heard, but seeped off in all directions. The unheated house was comfortably warm, with a medium temperature, when you're neither hot nor cold—it was completely impalpable, as if in a dream; flies droned wearily and monotonously in the windows, striking the panes; the slop pail, prepared for the animals and not brought outside, gave off a sour smell; the table hadn't been cleared from the night before and the glass of tea poured for Bogodul still stood untouched. Bogodul saw the glass, walked over and drank it. Darya stirred and asked: "Should I put on some fresh water, eh?"

He shook his head *don't*, but she got up anyway and put on the water. And having taken hold of work by the corner, she went on with it: she took out the slop, fed the chickens, who rushed toward the feed noisily and with great turbulence, cleared the table, and by the time the samovar was making noise out on the porch she had placed two pinches of black cake tea in the porcelain teapot and set it on the crown. And then, the samovar inside, the tea steeping, Darya waited for it to brew and finally spoke—without whining, simply, as though she had been interrupted only for a minute and was now continuing.

"Last night I didn't even milk the cow. All the milk is just going sour. I make sour cream, and that spoils too, all the jars are full. And Pavel, he comes here, has a mug of milk, and gets back in his boat, and he's gone again. And I drink a little. And not because I want to, but because I'm sorry to see it go to waste—so I have a mug. Well, soon all this free milk will be gone. And then when you want some in your tea, there won't be any, and then you'll remember this."

She poured the tea, pushed Bogodul's glass over to him, splashed some from her glass into the saucer, and took a sip. And just as if listening to something, trying to catch something, she raised her head and froze, and then once she heard it, she lowered her head again and took another sip, bringing the saucer to her dry, sharp lips that seemed to be covered with snakeskin. And she changed the subject sharply.

"I was thinking today: what if they ask me? They'll ask: How did you allow this disgrace, what were you thinking of? We depended on you, they'll say, and what did you do? I won't have an answer. I was here, after all, it was up to me to keep an eye out. And now that the water will come, it's sort of my fault too. And that I'll be buried alone. Better that I don't live that long—oh, God, how good that would be! No, I have to, it's my lot. Mine. For what sins?" Darya looked over at the icon, but didn't cross herself, stopping her hand in midair. "They're all together: father, mother, my brothers, my old man—only I will be taken away to strange earth. And I'll be flooded too, I suppose, and my bones will eventually float away too, but I'll never catch up with them.

"Father used to say . . . Father was good to me. He said: 'Live, Darya, as long as you're alive. Good or bad, you live, that's what your life has to be. If you swim in sorrow and anger and you get exhausted and want to join us—don't; you live, move, make the world remember that we once lived there. No one's ever been afraid to come join us, there's never been and never will be such a person in our family.' He thought that there wouldn't be, but I'm afraid. I should have gone much earlier, I don't belong here . . . I belong to them, to the other side. And it's been so long since I've lived my own life, my way, I don't understand anymore where I am going, or why. But I'm still alive. The world is going to crack in half: that's what's happening! And it'll break across us, the old people . . . we don't belong here or there. Lord have mercy! Maybe it's hard to tell from us what people were like in the old days, but no one looks behind himself anymore. Everyone's rushing headlong. They're out of breath, stumbling on every step, but they keep on running . . . No time to look back, there's no time to look underfoot . . . as though someone's chasing them."

"Japanese gods!" Bogodul agreed.

Darya kept pouring from the samovar into her glass, from her glass into the saucer, sipping gently and carefully, savoring the tea, not swallowing right away, neatly licking her lips and slowly, dreamily talking, as though not choosing her words but taking them out at random, talking and talking, not taking the conversation in any one direction, but bending it this way and that.

"It's hard without tea," she confessed to the pleasure of drinking it. "I feel a little better. But this morning it was like a bridle around my chest, I was so sick . . . I had no strength left. I forced myself to milk the cow, the poor thing had been crying, and I let her out—I couldn't see the windows, it was so black before my eyes. I thought: I must put on the samovar. And I felt even sicker and said to myself: what do you need a samovar for? You were sitting around the samovar, chattering away, while the godless ones knocked down the last memories of your father and mother. No samovar for you, don't ask for it. When I think of them, when I think . . . my heart stops and disappears. I push away the thoughts—and it beats once or twice, but . . . as soon as I think of it again . . . it stops. And I thought, where will they take me, where will they put me? When Raika Serkina's boy died, they looked for a plot for three days, they wanted to start a new cemetery, and then later they decided to put it somewhere else. And the poor child was put to rest in the wrong place, all alone . . . away off to the side. How can that little one be all alone in the woods with the animals? Will he say thank you to his parents for that later?

"Father and Mother died at almost the same time. They weren't old, compared with me. Mama went first, and death jumped on her. In the morning she was walking around, cleaning up, then lay down on her bed for rest, lay for a while and then screamed: 'Oh, death, death is pressing on me!' And she plucked at her throat and her chest. We ran over, but no one knew what to do, we just saved our arms around and kept saying: 'What, Mama, what, where?' She turned blue right before our eyes, in spots, and rattled . . . We lifted her up, sat her up, but it was already time to lay her out. There were marks on her neck where death was choking her . . . That's how it happened. Father later said: 'It was aiming for me, I called to it, but it missed, it attacked the wrong one.' And he was sick, seven years or so. They put a new millstone in the mill and he fell under it, he tripped and fell right under it. I don't know how he stayed alive. He coughed up blood, his insides were hurt. He probably would have lasted longer if he had taken care of himself, but he didn't know how to take care of himself, and he went on working like he was healthy and didn't watch after himself. We buried Mother in the winter, around Christmas, and him soon after, around Pentecost. We dug out Mother's coffin from the side, and it hadn't turned black at all, like we had put her in the ground yesterday. We put Father's coffin next to her. May they rest in peace! They lived together, and they're together there too, so no one is hurt.

"There is a grave on this island . . . now it's lost forever, somewhere below the village on our bank of the slope. I remember it from when I was little. They say a merchant lies in it; he used to carry merchandise on the Angara. And once he was traveling along with his merchandise and he saw Matyora, and he had them row toward it. And he liked it so much, our Matyora . . . he came to the men who lived here, then, he came to them and said: 'I'm so-and-so, and when death takes me, I want to be buried on a high hill on your island. And I'll build you a Christian church for that.' The men, being no fools, agreed. And he did leave them money, the merchant was a rich one . . . thousands he left, either ten, or a hundred. And he sent his chief clerk to build it. And so they built our church, blessed it, the merchant himself came for the blessing. And soon after that they brought him here, as he willed, for eternity. That's what the old folks used to say, but whether it happened or not, I don't know. But why would they make it up?

"When Father was dying, he was fully conscious, and he kept teaching me . . . He said: 'Darya, don't take on too much—you'll wear yourself out, you take on only the most important thing: to have a conscience and not to be bothered by it.' In the old days conscience was very important. If someone tried living without one, it was obvious right away, everyone lived an open life then. There were all kinds of people then, too. Some would have been happy to follow their conscience, but what do you do if you're born without one? You can't buy it with money. And some went off the deep end with it, that's no joy, either. They steal his last shirt from him and he takes it off to help, and thanks them too for undressing him. We had a relative, Ivan, like that. He was the best bricklayer for a stove in the whole world. People came to ask him to do their stoves from a hundred versts around. He never said no, he went to work for whoever asked, and he was too shy to ask for money, so he did it for free. His wife would scold sinfully: 'You'll be gone a week, who'll work in the field for you? Who'll work at home, you fool, you're no man.' And he really was a fool. 'People ask me . . .' And he let his house go to ruin . . . 'People ask.' You might as well just leave forever. The commune was formed then and he joined up . . ."

Darya drawled the last words, she was thinking about something else, her mind moving to the present: "I went crazy last night looking for Ivan's grave. But it was dark and I couldn't tell which was what. Could they have knocked it down too? There was a red star over it, his son had brought a metal tombstone from the city, and there was a star on top, sitting like a birdie. I have to check today. Oh, God, catch those monsters and punish them for us. If there is sin in the world, what could be worse than that?" To keep from getting overly upset again, Darya carefully shook her head and, breathing deeply, got up, went in the kitchen, and brought out five chocolate candies wrapped in brightly colored paper. She pushed three toward Bogodul and left two for herself.

"Have some sweets, I know you like them. I remember back during the war there was nothing, but you used to come up with lumps of sugar and give them to us. You'd get so mad if we saved it for the children, you made us crunch it up ourselves. I don't know anything sweeter than that sugar. It was so sweet because there wasn't any around."

"Wine—yck!" Bogodul pronounced and shook his head to indicate that he couldn't stand wine and never had.

"Let the devil drink it," Darya agreed, sitting down again. "What was I talking about Ivan for? My memory is worn out. Ah, about conscience. In the old days, you could see it: whether a person had it or not. Those who had it were conscientious, those without it were conscienceless. And now only the devil can tell, everything is mixed up in one pile. They bring it up needlessly with every word, mauling the poor thing so much it's barely alive. Almost like it's impossible to have it anymore. Oh-ho-ho! There's many more people, but conscience is the same—and so it's wearing thin, now it's not for yourself, not for asking questions of, it's just for show. Or they're doing such big things that they've forgotten about the small deeds, and the conscience is like iron for big deeds, it has no bite. And our conscience is getting old, it's an old woman, and no one looks at it anymore. Oh, God! How can I talk about conscience when such things are going on!

"After last night I couldn't sleep and I kept thinking and thinking; all sorts of nonsense kept getting into my head. I never feared anything in my life, and now this fear gripped me: I kept seeing that something was about to happen, something was going to happen. And I couldn't stand it, I got so wound up from waiting... I went outside, stood in the middle of the garden, and waited— for heavenly lightning to strike and destroy us because we're evil people, or for something else. The fear made me want to go back inside, but I stood without moving. I heard noises: a door slamming here, a door there—I wasn't the only one feeling this, then. I looked up to the sky, and the stars were burning up there, peppering the whole sky, there wasn't a clean spot up there. They were so large and hot—it was terrible! And they were coming closer, lower, closer to me . . . The stars made me dizzy . . . I seemed to pass out, I didn't remember who I was, where I was, what had happened. I was taken somewhere. When I came to, I looked around, it was getting light, the stars were back in the sky, and I was cold, shivering. And I felt so good, so comfortable, as though light had been shed in my soul. Why, I thought, what happened? I felt good, and it hurt that it was so good, it embarrassed me. I tried to remember if I had seen anything, and I think I did. It was like a voice. 'Go to sleep, Darya, and wait. Each will be asked,' the voice seemed to say. And I went. I didn't sleep, but I did feel better, I could stand it. But what kind of voice it was, where it came from, I don't remember, I couldn't say.

"Our menfolk, you know, were always our own, from Matyora. We didn't take to strangers. In my time only Orlik managed to get in, but Orlik is the devil's brother. If he wanted to, he could set down on water and not get his feet wet. He was a real talker, he could spin a hundred yarns and not get dry in the throat, his tongue was like a shuttle. That's why the men let him stay, of course, because he made them laugh. Men like that aren't born here. They'd gather and laugh and laugh so that you could hear them all over Matyora, and he'd be sitting in the middle: red headed, a robber's face, all covered with freckles, and spaces between his teeth. They're right when they say that gap-toothed people are liars—everything can get through them. And he'd rinse and rinse his few teeth—with whatever came to mind! He made the men fall down laughing. But he was a worker, too, what a worker! If he hammered in a stake, something would grow there. So, Dunka was married to him and had a daughter by him. Well, she was nothing like her father: never lied, always scared. And she had two boys, they were more daring, never at a loss for words. Well, one was taken as a German spy, so he wouldn't tease, and the other bit his tongue and left Matyora. Where he went, or if he's alive today, I don't know. I forgot that he ever existed, but it wouldn't take long to ask Dunka about him.

"Well, the menfolk are our own, but they liked to bring in the women. It's been that way for a long, long time. And for our girls that were left over, men came by boat to take them away, fighting each other: everyone was happy to marry into Matyora stock. People here have always lived well. And the girls fathered here were all pedigreed, strong—the merchandise didn't stay on the shelves long. Even today you can see Matyora in a woman's blood. Father brought in my mother, too, somewhere from the Buriat side of the river. He teased her about her talk: 'oy-yo-yok.' That's where mother was from, Oy-yo-yok, or however you call it. But they didn't have any water there at all, or just a tiny stream you could cross in one jump, and she was deathly afraid of water. At first, Father said, she would stand on the riverbank and shut her eyes to keep from seeing the water. But where could she go?—the Angara is all around. You have to cross water to get to Podmoga, and that's where we had our hay. She never did get used to it to her dying day. We teased her, the Angara was like home to us, we grew up on it, but Mother would say: 'Oh, it'll bring sorrow, it will, you don't have a fear like this for nothing.' But no, no one in our family ever drowned, and as for flooding, when the Angara went over its banks, well, that happened to everyone, not just our land. Only now Mother's fear has surfaced, now I see she was right . . . just think, now . . ." Darya stopped in confusion, lowering her voice until it was barely audible, completely lost now: "So that's how it is: the water will catch up with Mother after all. I never occurred to me. So that's it."

Stunned by this unexpected news, which she should have known a long time ago, but which had gotten lost and only now slipped out of the many forgotten things in her mind, Darya dropped her tea and stared ahead, her eyes running back and forth with fixed concentration, seeking something, something that was unnecessary and difficult. The sun, approaching midday, was even murkier, shedding pale weak light on the whitewashed walls with its hardened clumps of lime, on the floor with wide indentations scuffed into its surface, on the cracked windowsills—everywhere that the light fell, things seemed lonely and pathetic, oppressed by irreversible old age. In the middle of the room behind Bogodul's back, a spider, called a sitnik in these parts, slipped down through space, stopped briefly, swaying lightly in the air, resting or looking around, and then fell further. A motorboat buzzed across the expanse of the Angara visible through the window like a beetle, leaving a wake; in the other window, the white swollen sky lay on top of the fence. And the more Darya looked, drinking it all in with her eyes and seeing nothing, not noticing details, the more disturbed she became. And the more she felt that she was doing the wrong thing again, sitting around the samovar, like yesterday . . . something was prodding and pushing her, not letting her rest, stretching her soul every which way.

She got up and quickly, as though late for something, said to Bogodul: "Well, we've had our tea. We've had it—enough. Now you go, if you have to. Or stay, but I'm going. We sat too long again, sitting and talking, and there's nothing to talk about . . . Our talks are like milksop—no weight and no point. Just a memory that there had been wheat. There was a time . . ."

"Darya, where to?" Bogodul asked sternly, looking up.

She stopped in confusion for a moment and refused him.

"No, no, I'm going alone. I have to go there alone."

"Where, there" she didn't know, and stopping in thought by the gate, she started for the Angara, knowing that she would turn, and she turned, leaving the village beyond the gardens—her feet were taking her to the cemetery. But she didn't reach the cemetery: she realized that there was no point in going there with an unsettled soul, that she would disturb the peace of the dead, who were outraged by last night's incident as it was. She wouldn't be able to reach them with a knowing word—she didn't have it and it wouldn't come to her; they wouldn't reply. Completely lost, she sank helplessly to the ground on a dry, grassy knoll, and found herself facing the lower reaches of the river. Seeking something to calm her, she looked around. She looked once, and once more, and then a third time.

From here, the top of the island, she could see everything spread out below her—the Angara, the distant foreign shores, and her Matyora, looking like a single village with Podmoga beyond the pine barrens, so that the island's lands stretched almost to the horizon and it was only at the very edge that there was a shiny strip of water. The broad right sleeve of the river, sticking out at the bend, crowded the low opposite bank, digging into it, and then straightened out in the distance, falling smoothly and neatly; the left sleeve, calmer and closer, at that hour in the quiet sunlight seemed motionless. In Matyora they called it Our Angara. The village faced that way, and it was here that they set out their boats and went down for water, and it was from here that the children first looked out into the world; they knew everything here down to the last stone, and beyond the channel, when they still had the kolkhoz, they kept their fields, which were abandoned only now.

And the island lay quietly and peacefully, all the more familiar and fated to be her home because it had clear boundaries, beyond which there was no more solid ground, but water. But from edge to edge, from shore to shore, there was enough space, and wealth, and beauty, and wildlife, and animals in pairs—it had enough of everything, standing alone away from the mainland—was that why it had the proud name of Matyora? And it lay quiet, hushed —gathering the juices of early summer: the right field from the hill on which Darya sat had a thick cover of green winter wheat, and behind it rose the still-pale forest, its leaves not yet unfurled, with dark splotches of pine and fir; above and below, the road passed through it, leading to Podmoga. Closer than the forest and to the left of the road a pasture was fenced off from two sides; the two sides leading to Our Angara and to the village were left open—cows wandered around in there, and the cowbell one of them was wearing rang thinly, like a rattle. There, like the tsar of trees, towered a huge three-armsful around, centuries-old larch, with mighty branches that stuck straight out, and a crown that had been lopped off by a storm. Nearby stood a birch that looked as if it had been creeping up to it but stopped, either frightened by the larch's awesome appearance or dumbstruck by an execution; Darya remembered it well when it was young, a slim birch, and now its trunk had clumsily split in two, and the bark had hardened and started peeling, and the heavy branches drooped and bent down. And that was all, the rest of the pasture was empty—the cattle had plucked and trampled the rest.

But Darya saw, she saw what was beyond the forest—the fields with tall aspen groves, the rolling damp right bank covered with osier and gooseberries, and closer to Podmoga, the swamp, where ugly birches crowded together on knolls, drying up young from the bad water, sticking out nakedly and misleadingly: if you grab a tree like that for support, it will crack and break. The birches were quite different on the high left bank—they were tall, clean, and rich, leaving a thin white coating on your hand at the slightest touch, standing wide and merry, seemingly set up for some game, in twos and threes. And the young people had always chosen that meadow for their games. It was the site of more than one assignation, and more than one fine young woman earned her reputation on that grass, leaving the spot in the same clothes that she came in, but not in the same state of intactness. And sometimes the entire village would hitch up the horses and come out here in the blazing sun for a holiday, and the fellows would dive from the high promontory into the dark water, and as the old story has it, one long-ago summer a fellow named Pronya never climbed back up and has been wandering here at night all those years, a merman, calling to someone quietly and indecipherably.

Darya's memory let her see even further—more fields on either side of the road, solitary old trees here and there on the fields, primarily dried-out trees that back in the days of private ownership marked the boundaries of properties, and crows sat silently and lazily on the trees, confused by the pallid, fading sun and the unusual stillness. The road led to the old threshing floor, where sparrows fluttered in the chaff, through which seeds sprouted and blackened hay lay in the pans—there were so many old things around, having outlived their time and usefulness, remaining unnecessarily, but rotting away unwillingly and slowly. What could you do with them? What could you do? It was all right here, everything here would be burned and flooded, but what about other places? And it seemed to Darya there was nothing more unfair in the world than when something, be it tree or man, lived on to uselessness, to the point when it became a burden; that of the multitude of sins let loose upon the world to be prayed away and redeemed, this was the only one that was unbearable. The tree at least would fall, rot, and fertilize the earth. But a man? Is he at least good for that? Then why bear old age if it brings nothing but discomfort and suffering? Why seek some higher truth and service, when all the truth is in the fact that you're worth nothing and won't be worth anything anymore, that everything that you came into the world to do, you've done long ago, and that your only work now is to be a burden to others. "Is that so? Is it?" Darya probed fearfully, and not knowing the answer, rather knowing only her own answer, fell silent, depressed and confused.

And down there—the blunt end of Matyora, a silty shore in front of the channel that had to be forded in order to reach Podmoga, or Podnoga. When the water was clear they calmly herded the cattle over there—the kolkhoz herd summered there every year, but when the river rose and acted up, you had to be careful even in a boat. Podmoga's tip stuck out into the Angara and passed Matyora a bit, as though the lower island had once decided to pass the upper one and had started, picked up speed, turned off, and then suddenly got stuck. And Matyora had to take on Podmoga as a tug: they hung a cable across the ford so that there would be something to hold on to in bad waters. Swifts liked sitting on it, the ones that lived on the promontory on Our Angara, and they sat there now, like buoys twitching their tails and peering down.

And you couldn't tell if the island was in sunlight or if the sun had gone down: it was in the sky, there was some light in the air and on the ground, but it was weak, barely tinted, giving no shade. It was sleepy, patient, and silent—the old village lay silently to the left with the blind windows that seemed to be covered with cowhide; the beheaded tsar larch was frozen in the pasture, blindly spreading its huge branches; the green fields seemed pale and dull; the forests seemed diluted, without full greenery and full height, and of course, also in silence, humbly and powerfully, without revealing any secrets, another, richer village lay nearby, closed now to any new inhabitants: the cemetery, the resting place of their elders . . .

Soon, soon everything would end.

Darya tries but can't raise a heavy, too heavy thought: perhaps this is the way it must be? Backing off from it, she tries to find the answer to an easier thought: what "must be"? What was she thinking of? What was she trying to understand? But she didn't know that either. She had to live a long and wretched life to admit to herself at its end that she hadn't understood anything about it. While she had been moving toward old age, her human life had disappeared somewhere too. Let others chase after it now. But they wouldn't catch it either. They only imagine that they'll catch up—no, they too will have to watch it disappear sadly and impotently, the way she was watching it recede now.

Somewhere behind her back on the big Angara River a ship screamed out, and a crow tore away from one of the solitary trees on the fields, "On the deep blue sea, on the island of Buyan . . ." Darya suddenly remembered an old and horrible spell.

5

PAVEL CAME TOWARD EVENING. Darya lifted her head at the slam of the gate, watched Pavel come into the yard and toss off the sagging backpack, that city-style bag, and she guessed: he'll take some potatoes. And so she asked, when Pavel came in the house: "Finished off the potatoes, eh?"

"Yes."

"I told you to take more. You left by freight boat. And yet you didn't take even half a bag—how long could that last you big eaters?"

"More would have spoiled," Pavel replied, sitting down on the bench and preparing to take off the heavy tarpaulin boots.

"Spoil?" Darya said in surprise. "You said you had a root cellar there."

"We do," Pavel said, struggling with the boots that stuck to his legs. "There is a cellar. Except we're going to use it for a well. It's full of water. You could put a pump there."

"We-el-el. So why did they build it where there was water? Why didn't you check what they were giving you?"

"Check or not, everyone has water. Who needs the Angara?"

"What is going on!? How can they build like that? Didn't they stick a shovel in the ground first to see what was in it?"

"Because a stranger built it. That's how they can build like that."

"That's even worse!"

And Darya stopped talking: it all added up. Really, how could you explain what has no explanation, what is its own answer? Only children ask questions like that: why is bread called bread and a house a house? Because *bread* and *house* have their own, ancient names that gave rise to other words, and what would change if someone knew why and wherefore—as long as there was bread, and there were houses, and they didn't set people's homes down blindly!

She saw how tired Pavel was. He pulled off his boots with difficulty, took them outside so that they wouldn't smell up the house, then walked barefoot to the front corner and sat down on the bed, carefully placing his white, worn feet in front of him. This year in spring, just before Easter, he turned fifty—he was Darya's oldest now, though actually he was the second son; the first had been killed in the war. And she had lost another son during the war; he was too young and had stayed home, but found death felling trees thirty kilometers from Matyora. They brought him home in a closed coffin and buried him without showing him to his mother, saying that there was nothing to see. How simple and horrible, beyond comprehension: she bore him, fed him, brought him up, and he was racing to be a man, manhood was close, and a tree tore away and in one second left nothing for the coffin. Who had pointed at him and why him? She couldn't believe that these things just happened blindly: that whomever it fell on, blindly, would fall; no, there was a predetermined aim and meaning to the falling tree, it knew whom it was after. And there was an incomprehensible and terrible truth in it: of Darya's three buried children all had grown and entered life—one was ready for war, the other for work, and the third, her eldest daughter, who died in Podvolochna giving birth to her second child, had lived with her own family. She was buried in Podvolochna, which meant that she too would go under water. Only her son who was buried in foreign land in a mass grave with many others would perhaps stay in the ground—who knew how they treated land and water there, and which the living needed more?

And Darya had as many—three—left among the living: a daughter in Irkutsk, a son who had recently moved from the old, faraway lumber project to a just-opened one near Matyora, and Pavel. It would be a sin to complain about them; all of them, probably, honored their mother: the ones who were far away wrote and invited her to visit, and Pavel never spoke a harsh word to her and ordered his wife never to, either. Not everyone is as lucky in her old age—what more did she want? No one was starving or freezing nowadays, and so it was their relatives' behavior toward them that was important for old people.

Pavel sat in silence, staring in deep thought at the floor, and probably because he noticed that the floor wasn't swept, asked: "How are you managing here? Does Vera come by?"

"When Vera comes I tell her I don't need her. I do it myself. I just let things go now. Last night I didn't even go to the cow, I dropped everything."

"Were you sick?"

"Do you know what they're doing, Pavel?! What they're doing?! The mind can't imagine!" She had begun calmly but burst into tears, covering her face and bowing in dry, rasping sobs. Pavel, without asking or rushing her, waited. And when, slightly calmer, his mother told him about yesterday's scene, stressing that Vorontsov and Zhuk said that they had to do what they did to the cemetery, he still didn't reply with a single word, but looked even more weary and heavy, bending over with his hands between his knees like an old man, still lost in difficult, unceasing thought. Not getting an answer from him, Darya begged.

"Maybe, we could at least move your grandfather and grandmother, eh, Pavel? The Koltsovs took their people with them . . . two coffins. And Anfisa got her boy and moved him to the new place. It's a sin, of course, to move the dead . . . But it's a worse sin to leave them behind. Look what they're doing! And if they let the water loose . . ."

"I can't think about that now, Mother," Pavel replied. "I'm exhausted as it is—I don't have time to breathe. When I have more time, we'll move them. I've been thinking about it. I'll arrange it with someone else, so that I'm not alone, and we'll move them."

And, not knowing whether she would be happy that she brought it up and arranged it, but still happy, still suddenly given hope, she asked him about something else.

"Will you be mowing this time?"

"I don't know, Mother. I don't know anything yet."

She felt sorry for him and didn't bother him with more questions.

But she hadn't brought up the mowing without good reason: it was time to decide whether they should keep the cow. It was a decision that everyone who was moving to the sovkhoz faced. Reports, each stranger than the other, came from there, from the new sovkhoz settlement. They said, and not only said but actually knew, had personally seen, that people from twelve villages were moving into the settlement, some from nearby and some from distant villages, that they were building two-family houses with separate entrances and separate living quarters, and that the apartments for each family took two stories, connected by a steep staircase, almost like a ladder. And that's the way it was—no exceptions, everyone just the same. And that the staircase was steep, too steep, not only for an old person but even for a sick man, was obvious from the fact that there already had been accidents: drunken Samovar—that's what they called the hot and big-bellied kolkhoz accountant—was running up and down the stairs one night, and flew down counting them and ended up less two ribs and was now in the hospital; and a little girl from some other village also fell down and hurt her head. Well, that alone would have passed—they were used to walking on flat ground, now they needed time to learn something new. Darya had decided immediately that if she had to live in an apartment like that she wouldn't go up the stairs in search of her own death. And the apartments, they bragged, were beautiful, the walls were covered with flowers and leaves, the kitchen, like a city one, didn't have the Russian stove that used logs and coals, no, it had an electric one with switches; the toilet was on the other side of the wall, so you wouldn't have to run out into the street, and upstairs, if you could get upstairs, there were two large rooms with all sorts of closets and doors for eternally joyous living.

That was the housing. And next to it, right there in the yard, up against the wall, there was a tiny garden, for which you had to haul in soil to grow anything because it was set up in stones and clay—and that was very strange too: why was it so backwards—you didn't have a garden on the soil, you had to have soil on top of the garden. And what a garden it was! one-hundredth and a half of a hectare—a joke! There was a pen for chickens, a pen for pigs, but there was no stall for a cow, and there was no place to set one up, either. They said a gypsy managed somehow and set one up, but they came from the soviet and said no, take it away, this is no gypsy camp but an urban-type settlement, where everything must fit the plan. Darya didn't believe the part about the gypsy too much: where would a gypsy get a cow? They had never even bothered with cattle, they wouldn't ever steal a cow, they were only interested in horses. A gypsy would made a cattle breeder as a wolf would make a shepherd. But they told the story about a gypsy for some reason. When Darya asked Pavel whether it was true that they don't let you build a stall he frowned and waved off the question uncertainly and imcompletely.

"They'll let you ... that's not the problem."

Of course, the greatest problem was hay: there were no hay fields and no pastures in the new place, and no one really knew how they were going to feed the commonly held cattle, not to mention private stock. They were stubbing out fields; for a dozen miles around, the taiga hummed and buzzed with the sounds of machinery, but human hands hadn't tended it yet. To break the soil of one habit and teach it another takes years and years. For the first winter, of course, they could mow the old lands, and that short and undependable "could" upset and confused the people most of all: you could for one winter, and then? What then? Wouldn't it be better to break clean now? And on the other hand, how could you break if you were used to your cow which fed you in the leanest years, and if you still "could" this winter? You could, but that "could" was filled with potholes so easy to fall into: how do you find the time to mow?—this wasn't a kolkhoz where everyone had the same concerns and where it was understood; how would you get the hay over the Angara before high water, and then how do you get it up the hill? And if you did manage all that—mow, ford, haul, and get it home—where do you put it? And where do you keep the cow? There were so many problems that you just let your hands fall helplessly, let it all go to rack and ruin.

This last, crucial year seemed terrifying. And what seemed particularly terrible and unfair was that the year moved on in its usual way and the days with their usual speed got closer to that which would be, and there was no way to hold back what would be. Later, when it was all over and they were in the new life and they would see what they would be—whether they'd be peasants, but of a different kind, not like now, or landed gentry—once they harnessed themselves into this new life and pulled, it would probably become easier for them, but for now everything ahead frightened them, everything seemed strange and unsteady, steep and not for everyone, just like those stairs that some can use easily, and some not at all. It was easier for the young people, they could hop up on one foot—and it was easier for the young to part with Matyora. Klavka Strigunova used to say:

"It should have been flooded long ago. It doesn't even smell of habitation . . . not people, just fleas and cockroaches. What a place to live, in the middle of water, like frogs."

And she waited, she couldn't wait for the hour when she could set fire to her father's and grandfather's house and collect the remaining money for it. She would have burned it down a long time ago and left without looking back, but there were houses close by on either side, and the people in them weren't ready to leave, and their houses might catch too. And so they held Klavka back, and she cursed Matyora and the people who clung to the village, calling down thunder and lightning on their heads.

"I'll burn it," she would threaten, coming over from the sovkhoz. "It's easy for me. If you don't want to leave, if you want to burn—go ahead and burn. I don't intend to suffer because of you."

The same concern—how to get the second installment of the money for the house—worried Petrukha, the son of old Katerina. But Petrukha was held back by another disaster. Two years ago some people who walked around Matyora and rapped on and examined almost all the buildings attached a metal sign to Petrukha's house: "An example of wooden folk architecture. Property of the Acad. Sciences." They told Petrukha that they would cart off his house to a museum, and at first he was very proud: they picked out Petrukha's house and no one else's, people would pay money to take a look at the house, at the rare and delicate fretwork on the windows and shutters, the patterns on the fringe, the sleeping planks between the ceiling and stove, and the logs it was made of. And even though the mill and the storehouse also had plaques, they were a mill and a storehouse and his was an inhabited house—how could they be compared? That was a temporary plaque, and the one in the museum would read: "The house of a peasant from Matyora, Petrukha Zotov . . ."—or better: ". . . peasant from Matyora, Nikita Alekseyevich Zotov." Everyone would read it and envy Petrukha–Nikita Alekseyevich Zotov. At his birth he really had been named and registered as Nikita, but his dumbness, shiftlessness, and scoundrelhood turned his name into Petrukha. No one even remembered that he was Nikita, even his own mother called him Petrukha; he himself only pulled out and signed his legal name in his dreams, when he was being decorated and praised as a rare, acclaimed man, and in real life he used Petrukha too. But on the plaque, at least, he would have his full legal name.

But the months passed and the people who had fallen in love

with Petrukha's house never came back, and Petrukha began worrying. The advance, half of the compensation for the house had been used up, drunk up, long ago, and to get the second half, Petrukha had to make sure his house as such no longer existed. Petrukha had spent the entire year writing letters and demanding that the "Acad. Sciences" take away its property. No one answered his letters. He no longer cared about the museum—to hell with the glory, the eternal plaque—he wanted the money. After the kolkhoz was disbanded Petrukha didn't find anything, had no job, only picked up a little money here and there, and he and his mother lived very poorly; at the same time in some office next to his name was the sum of a thousand rubles, a fortune. It only needed getting rid of the house. If it weren't for the Acad. Sciences, he would have gotten rid of it in a flash: the house stood off to one side, so there were no neighbors to worry about. But "Property of the Acad. Sciences" held him back for now. It said in printed letters that it wasn't Petrukha's property, and he didn't want to get into trouble. There it was: Petrukha's house, but not Petrukha's property—go figure out who the owner was. They won't give it to him and they won't take it for themselves.

"They'll get theirs," Petrukha would nod threateningly toward somewhere beyond the Angara. "Wood isn't metal, it could go up in smoke on its own. Then go find out whose property it was. They'll see."

So there they were, Klavka and Petrukha, and probably a few other young people who had already moved and some who hadn't, who were glad to see the changes and didn't hide it. But the rest were afraid of the changes, not knowing what awaited them. Everything here was familiar, cozy, tested, even death among your own could be pictured clearly and simply—how they'll mourn you, where they'll bury you, next to whom—but there, it was completely dark in this world and in the next. And when Pavel would come for a short visit from the sovkhoz and Darya began asking questions, he would answer unwillingly and almost guiltily, as though afraid of scaring her, afraid that the new would not fit in with her old ideas.

"You say there's only one steambath for everyone?" she gasped, trying to imagine what kind of bathhouse that could be. "How could that be! One for so many people? . . . Can't we set up our own?"

"Where?"

"God! I think I'd rather be overgrown with dirt then go to a place like that."

And then the latest news: the cellars were full of water. If it was there now, it would be there next year—this wasn't even a damp summer. That meant they'd have to raise the cellar, if there was room to raise it, and turn it into a hole with a wooden floor. But a hole would be enough for a garden on a plot that was a hundredth and a half. That wasn't a lot of land—the chickens could dig it up and clean it up.

Oh, you'll miss Matyora, you will . . .

6

AND WHEN NIGHT CAME and Matyora fell asleep, from the bank
on the mill canal came a small animal, slightly bigger than a cat
and not resembling any other animal—the master of the island. If
houses have poltergeists, then the island must have a master. No
one had ever seen him or run into him, but he knew everyone and
everything that happened from one end to the other, from one
side to the other on this isolated piece of land that was surrounded
by water and had risen from the water. That's why he was Master,
to see all, know all, and interfere with nothing. That was the only
way he could remain Master—if no one met him or suspected he
existed.

Earlier, peeking out from his lair, from his old den on the bank
of the mill channel, he saw that the stars had come out and then

gone out. Perhaps they were somewhere now, because a gray, dusky light was filtering down from above, and it had to be coming from somewhere, but even the Master's sharp eyes couldn't see them. And he didn't like looking into the sky, it led him into a vague, causeless anxiety and frightened him with its awesome bottomlessness. Let people look up there and find solace, but what they think of as dreams are merely recollections, even the most distant and delicious projections—only recollections. No one is given to dream.

The night was warm and quiet, and somewhere else probably dark, but here, under the huge river sky, it was translucent. It was quiet, but in the drowsy, living quiet that flowed like the river, you could easily distinguish the murmur of the water on the upper, closer, promontory and the tide, hollow and unsteady, like the wind in the trees, far on the unfamiliar left bank and the infrequent, brief splashes of a late-playing fish. These were the superficial sounds that the ear could hear, the sounds of the Angara, after which you could also hear the sounds of the island: the heavy, strained scrape of the old larch in the pasture and the hollow steps of the cattle there, the juicy slurp of cud chewing, blending into one low ringing sound, and in the village, the constant rustle of everything that lived in the street—chickens, dogs, animals. But these sounds were crude and loud for the Master; he took particular pleasure in listening with particular sensitivity to the sounds of things in the ground and close to it: the rustle of a mouse climbing out to hunt, the muted movements of a little bird sitting on its eggs in its nest, the weak, faint creak of a swaying branch that didn't seem comfortable to a night bird, the breathing of the growing grass.

Leaning out of his den and listening, recognizing everything that went on around him with accustomed ease, the Master started his rounds of the island with the same accustomed unhurriedness and care. He didn't keep to one path; today he might come from the left, tomorrow from the right. He could turn back at the middle, somewhere near the pine grove, or he could run to the end or even go over to Podmoga and stay there for hours, checking its life, too, but he never missed the village. Most often the changes that he had to know about occurred there. And even though he sensed, he knew that soon in one fell swoop everything would change so radically that he would no longer be Master, would no longer be at all, and he had come to terms with it. What would be could not be avoided. And he had come to terms with it also because after him there would be no other master here, there would be nothing to be master of. He was the last. But while the island stood, he was the Master.

He ran up the hill, near the spot where the old woman Darya had sat in the daytime, and raising his head, looked around. Matyora lay peaceful and motionless: the forests were dark, the young grass stretched watery-silver across the ground, and the village lay in dark, spreading spots, where nothing hammered or clattered but seemed to be preparing itself for hammering and clatter. The daytime heat had abated, and the earth gave off cool, bitter smells. A weak and heavy gust of air tore out of somewhere, sighed, and settled, like a wave sucked into the sand. But the old larch creaked longer and more anxiously, and a cow mooed in its sleep for no reason, sounding like a cat. Deep in the shoreline scrub a gooseberry bush, pushed down by another bush, finally freed itself and stood up with a lurch. The water slurped—either a foam bubble that had been floating since the evening burst or a fish shuddered, dying; an unfamiliar shimmer raced across the grass in a narrow strip and disappeared; and only now the last leaf of last year fell from the birch that stands next to the larch in the pasture.

The Master headed for the village.

He began the check, as usual, from the shack on the cape where Bogodul lived. Long and narrow, like a barge, the shack had long reeked of disuse and rot, and Bogodul's presence didn't help. Things thrown together in a hurry age quickly. Matyora had buildings that had stood two hundred years and more and didn't show their wear, and this one hadn't served half a century. And all because it never had a single owner, because everyone who lived there only hid from the cold and rain and planned to move as soon as possible to somewhere better. And Bogodul was no owner, even though he wouldn't be moving anywhere.

Bogodul slept in the room closest to the village. His two-voiced snoring, there and back, carried through the window and walls, and listening to it the Master was convinced once more of what he had sensed earlier: it was here on Matyora that Bogodul would finally meet his death, and he was living out his last summer, like the Master.

Once upon a time the channel stretched through here in a single straight and even stream, but gradually the turn from the tip of the island dragged in rocks, and the lively, fast water went off to the left, and beyond the promontory there was a stagnant pool with a silt bottom and swaying aquatic plants. Lower on, the channel righted itself, stretching out in its full breadth, and the bottom was gravel and sand again, leading to the ravine on which the village was built. The first house, standing low, as though too tired to climb up the ravine and left behind, was Petrukha Zotov's house. The Master knew that no museum would come for it, just as it wouldn't take the other marked buildings—the *mangazey* and the smithy—and that Petrukha would soon take care of his house himself. It gave off that special, barely perceptible—and then only by the Master—worn and rancid smell of a played-out fate that was unmistakable. The entire village from one end to the other gave off a similar scent at night, but it was fresher here. The land and the silent buildings upon it were preparing themselves for whatever would come.

The Master sat down and leaned against the old sturdy wood house. Creaking bumps dripped down the logs. "Bump-bump-bump," the house groaned. "Bump . . . bump . . . bump . . ." He listened and then pressed closer, relaxing, to the warm logs. Someone had to start the final truth, they had to start with someone. Everything that lived on earth had one meaning only—to serve. And every service came to an end.

He rose, stepped back a few steps toward the road, and looked back at the low window under the beautiful, lacy carving. Low—not because the house had sunk, but because the ground had risen during its lifetime. There, beyond the windows, Petrukha slept a murky, tortured sleep, and his mother, Katerina, slept on the Russian stove, warming her old bones even in the middle of summer. Katerina, Katerina . . . Who could say why worthwhile people have worthless children? The only solace is that your years are coming to an end.

There, where the village began its orderly growth, the Master slowed his pace, stopping frequently, sniffing and listening. He wasn't afraid: neither dog nor cat could smell him, and he didn't want to miss any changes that might have occurred overnight. Last night he didn't dare enter the village until early morning, but even then the old people were tossing and turning sleeplessly, frightened and ennervated by the incident at the cemetery, anticipating punishment with hope and fear. Today, it seemed, the village had quieted down and gone to sleep.

The village slept: dogs didn't bark, like yesterday, doors didn't squeak, and feeble, anxious noises didn't escape from the houses. The houses with cataract eyes stood silently, not giving away the life inside, but when the Master approached a house, it sighed its own long sigh, showing that it knew all, felt all, and was prepared for anything. There were young houses among them, built twenty and thirty years ago, still not blackened or grown into the ground, but they too stood docilely in their rows, knowing their fate, taking another step toward it in the short summer night. Patiently and silently, like stone, they would go on to the last, final say, determined long ago, and patiently they would be executed, showing in farewell how much warmth and sun they had contained, because fire is nothing more than absorbed and saved sunshine that is forcefully torn out of the flesh.

The night was growing, but it was still pale and shadowless. Waves of stagnant dampness rolled in from the nearby water, and when the waves fell, a strong dry odor of disuse and rot took their place. Running up to the buildings, the Master could feel the warmth, gathered over the day, escaping from the wood, but it was weaker and more controlled today—truly, the sun wouldn't come out tomorrow.

The village Matyora slept. The old women dreamed dry anxious dreams, which came down to them secondhand, but the old women didn't know about that. Only at night, casting off from solid land, the living and dead meet—the dead come to them in body and word and ask for the truth in order to pass it on even further, to those who they remembered. There is much that the living say when they are unconscious and unencumbered and that upon awakening they do not remember and seek random answers to the last visions they saw.

Now those dreams blazed pale beyond the windows, like very distant dawn lights, and these lights alone were enough to let him know where there were people and where there were not. No one was bypassed by dreams that night: the old women complained bitterly, telling about the last few days.

Having run from one end of the village to the other, the Master turned left past the street to the naked high bank above the river. The visibility was better here, and the dark distance flickered in layers in the opened space; the water in the lower shoals sparkled like glass, and like glass it rang in the shoals. The Angara rolled on with a stringlike, extended hum; in the middle of the island the hum separated into two strings, hung over the water, until the river flowed into one again. The Master liked listening to the streaming, tumbling sound of flowing water, which was drowned out by the day's extraneous noises, and which turned purer and clearer at night. It carried him up to eternity, to the order of the universe, but the Master understood that the sound would soon break off and only the wind would howl over the silenced water. Remembering this, the Master turned back to the island's interior.

It was as though the night had stopped and no longer flowed across the Angara toward the west, but had filled space from horizon to horizon, circling over Matyora blindly and warily. The breeze bumped blindly from one side to the other without blowing itself upward, falling asleep as it went, dropping into the grass, and getting stuck. The grass was damp and aromatic, and from it the Master could tell that by midday tomorrow there would be a brief shower.

The island continued its usual and fixed life: the wheat and herbs rose, roots stretched in the ground, and leaves grew on trees; it smelled of wild cherry blossoms and the dampness of vegetation; bushes discreetly bending low to the water on the right bank; night animals and birds hunted.

The island intended to live a long time.

7

AND THE DAY BECAME LONG AND SLOPING, with no end or boundaries in sight, the deadline set by Grandpa Egor for leaving came
with it, so soon that they really hadn't had a chance to realize
where the last two weeks had gone. And Nastasya had gotten
three more days after Pentecost—and now they too had passed.

They were leaving on a Wednesday. It made no difference
when they left, but she somehow felt that it was better in the
middle of the week, so that by some miracle they would be
brought back here, to the same shore. Nastasya preferred Thurs-
day, it seemed luckier, but it was closer to the end of the week,
and that meant closer to the other shore, the other life, from
which it would be harder to get back.

Nastasya didn't sleep the entire night, burning the lamp—the electricity had been turned off in the spring, and the machine that had generated it was taken away, and the villagers had reverted to kerosene. And how could she have slept the last night, where could she find the peace for sleep? Where do you find no thoughts, no remorse so as to fall asleep? She kept realizing that she had forgotten this or that, rushing to look for things and not finding them, muttering to herself as she ransacked the corners for the tenth time, looking in the porch and storeroom, going with a candle into the granary, untying and taking apart prepared packages, finally coming across the lost article—and immediately starting in on a new one. Even if she hadn't lost anything, she still walked around and looked, afraid to leave something indispensable behind. The house was empty and hollow, and Nastasya's footsteps, as though striking metal, echoed in the walls, and the unshuttered windows piteously rang with each step. Also, they hadn't closed the shutters so that they wouldn't oversleep, missing the dawn, so that they wouldn't be late. How could they oversleep! The time was long past when they slept late, and certainly there was no chance of that tonight!

In the midst of her pointless bustling Nastasya froze more than once: where was she—home or not home? Bare walls, with white patches from the removed framed photographs and a big circle between the windows where the mirror used to hang, a bare floor, open doors, the sleeping space over the stove without curtains; empty hangers, empty corners—everything was empty, naked, over. In the middle of the entry like a robber's booty were piled a huge metal trunk and three bundles, containing all their goods. Only the windows were still curtained. At first Nastasya had removed them, but when she saw how utterly naked and shamed the house looked, she couldn't stand it and hung them back up. Then she got out an old rug and put it back in its former place by the doorstep, with a gentle word: "How can you, dear thing, go to the city and change your life? Stay here where you used to lie, stay home. You don't need Egor and me, and you need to stay by your own doorstep. That's so. Stay, no one will touch you here. You'll be like you're retired." After that she began talking to almost everything she touched. "And you're going, you're going, don't hide. I won't leave you behind, without you I'm without my hands. And don't beg, don't hide. I'd like to stay myself, but it's impossible." Or "Oh, I forgot all about you. You get in there, too, there's room. Go on, get in." Or "I'd be happy to, but how? How can I take you? It would be good, but it won't work. Stay—what can we do? I'll come back, we'll see each other."

Nastasya planned to come back in September to dig potatoes.

Grandpa Egor watched the old woman suspiciously: she hadn't dropped a tear since Pentecost, as though she had finally understood that they had to go, that there was no turning back whether she cried or not. Before that she walked around with wet eyes, sobbing, and the closer it got to their departure, the more she cried. She'd stop in the middle of doing something and stare at Egor. He'd turn to her and she'd say:

"Maybe we won't go, Egor? Maybe we'll stay? We could just stay ..."

"Shoo, you damned woman!" he would roar. "How many times do I have to repeat the same thing?! Who needs us here!? Who?"

"But how will we live there?" And tears. And an hour or so later, it would start all over.

A week ago the first river store of the summer had come by, they supply the buoykeepers; Grandpa Egor heard that he was there and ran down and bought some makhorka, homegrown tobacco, and two bottles of red wine. They opened one on the holiday. They sat together, the two of them—the entire family. Lately Grandpa Egor, as though trying to wean himself gradually of Matyora and accustom himself to loneliness, started avoiding people—he just stayed home. Nastasya drank, mellowed, and something clicked in her poor brain.

"And you and I, Egor, we'll be like this together over there. What else now ... where could we go?"

"About time you've come to your senses," he said happily, but not trusting the old woman's mood, wondering how long her understanding would last.

"We lost the children ... where could we get them back now?"

she continued dreamily and docilely. "And the two of us . . . maybe it'll be all right . . . After all, there are people there too. So what if we don't know them? We'll get to know them. And if not—we'll be just the two of us. What else? . . . Don't cry, Egor . . ."

He accepted that: as long as the departure would be easy. And from that moment she stopped crying. Only once in a while, when Nastasya couldn't stand it, she would lift her large swollen face to the old man and, biting her disobedient, trembling lower lip, repeat:

"Don't you cry, Egor. Now . . . maybe it'll be all right."

The last night in Matyora passed, the last morning rose. Only just before the light, when Egor yelled at her, Nastasya lay down for a bit, spreading a jacket on the trunk, and not reaching sleep, not even immersing herself in it, she rose immediately. Egor was still lying down. Nastasya went outside, stood on the porch, warming herself in the just-risen sun and looking around, seeing her Matyora before her, the village and the island, and then she sighed, thought a bit, gathered a pile of logs, returned, and lit the Russian stove. Egor heard her and grumbled.

"What's the matter, old woman, have you gone completely mad?"

"No, Egor, we have to light it for the last time," she countered quickly. "Let the warmth stay. While we get ready, it'll burn out. How much longer does it have? How long will it need? That's as it should be. How can we leave a cold stove behind us—what's the matter with you, Egor?"

And she lit it, warmed up their last food, and swept the coals into the hearth.

The day promised to be beautiful; the weather was good on the day the old people had to leave Matyora. Not a mote or a wrinkle in the vast, bright, and dry sky; the sun sparkled and burned. A wind from the upper end did its duty and ran along, but quieted down before it could raise a wave, lulled by the peace in the air; the current crumpled up and immediately smoothed out again. Everything under the bright sun had been gleaming since early morning, every tiny thing became visible, exposing itself. Matyora's lands were lush and rich—the forests, fields, and banks all blazed with raucous greenery, and the Angara rolled on in full regalia. Life was so good at this time of year, you soothed your soul just by looking around and estimating the harvest—wheat, vegetables, berries, mushrooms, and every kind of wild crop. Waiting for the mowing, then the haymaking, quietly getting ready for it and quietly fishing, doing the day's work every day as it came along—and it turned out that they had lived this way for many years and didn't even know that it was the life.

They finished tea—Nastasya lit the samovar for the last time. But the tea had been rushed, without pleasure, because they were in a hurry and there was no time to sit around. Nastasya poured off the remaining boiling water, tossed out the coals, and set the samovar on the floor near the door, close to the exit, ready for the journey. Egor brought out the wagon from the lean-to; they took hold of the trunk, strained and grunted, and let it down—they couldn't lift it. Grandpa Egor, confused and angry—it was all right here, here they could get help, but what would they do there?—in a fit of temper decided to leave the table behind, even though he had planned on taking it no matter what. Besides the table, the other furniture that they were taking was a metal bed frame with springs, two stools, and a hutch. The chicken coop, benches, cot, another table, the Russian stove, cellar, and doors remained. Many things remained in the barn, yard, sheds, cellars, stalls, hayloft, and porches—and they were all things that had been passed down by fathers and grandfathers, things that were indispensible here every minute of every day but worthless over there. Oven prongs, skillet handles, dough trough, churn staffs, cast iron pans, wooden jars, earthenware pots, tubs, kegs, pliers, loom . . . And also pitchforks, shovels, oars, saws, axes (of the four axes, they were taking only one), whetstone, iron stove, wagon, sled . . . And still more: traps, snares, wicker muzzles, skis, hunting and fishing gear, and all kinds of carpentry tools. Why go through all of it, why torture yourself! And you can't sell it or give it away, everyone has the same problem: what to do with his worn things. It's a sin to throw them away, but you can't go into a new house with old stuff, and besides, you won't need it there. Nastasya kept adding things to their baggage, until Egor shouted: "What for? What for?" And some powerful swear words.

"No, Egor, you look: this is a good trough. Like new. We can keep water in it."

"Drop it where it was and don't touch it again. Keep water . . . What do you want to keep water for?"

But he did take his gun, an old Tula-made, sixteen-caliber gun, and all the things that went with it, even though it was doubtful that a gun would be any use at his age in a big city. But a gun's a gun and not a trough, and there was no way he could part with it. Nastasya for her part didn't want to leave her spinning distaff. Seeing it in the old woman's hand, Grandpa Egor shouted again: "What for? What for?" But Nastasya turned him down with determination.

"No, Egor. When I have to spin tow, how will I do it without the distaff?"

"Damn you! You know what use your distaff will be? What about the tow? Where will you get it?"

"No, Egor." She resisted stubbornly and won the right to take her distaff.

She set it up next to the table for the first run, holding it down with a bundle. Grandpa Egor took the wagon down to the shore, where a large freight rowboat he borrowed from the buoykeeper was waiting. The old people were to take it to Podvolochna, to the pier where the ship would dock in the evening, and from there, leaving the rowboat with the local keeper, continue by ship. Pavel Pinigin, Darya's son, offered to tow them with his motorboat so that they wouldn't have to row, but Grandpa Egor refused.

"Across the Angara, all right, you can tow us, but then we'll go under our own steam. What's the rush? We'll get down to the ship in time. At least we'll see the Angara one last time."

As soon as he had left with the wagon, Darya came by. She stood in the yard, listening and looking around with pity, walked up to the porch, and carefully pulled on the door.

"Nastasya!" she called, not knowing whether she was in or not.

"It's all right, Darya," Nastasya called out. "Come in. Egor and I are going. People live here . . ."

"Are you ready?" Darya asked, coming in.

"Uh-huh. Egor is crying and crying, he doesn't want to go. I say: 'Don't you cry, Egor, don't cry.' " Her eyes rested on Darya, as though she only now recognized her and stopped talking with a shudder—she was fully aware now.

"It's all right, Darya," she whispered guiltily. "You see . . . it's like this . . ." and she pointed at the bundles on the floor, the bare walls, meaning that she would be glad to remain aware but she couldn't. And she asked pitifully: "Darya, don't speak ill of me . . ."

"And you of me." Darya said in a trembling voice, wiping her eyes with her kerchief, asking forgiveness for her long life with Nastasya.

"Remember, we had children?"

"How could I forget?!"

"And where are they now? Nowhere. I said to Egor: 'Let's go, Egor, there's nothing to wait for, let's go.' And he . . . "

She blanched and slumped down on the bench. Darya came over and sat next to her. Sitting in the empty, ransacked house was uncomfortable—they felt guilty and bitter sitting in the house they were leaving to its death. And they couldn't help, there was nothing that would help, and it was unbearable to watch the walls go blind and the light that no one needed anymore pour in through the windows.

Nastasya remembered: "I wanted to ask you, Darya. I almost forgot. Take our Nunya. Take her, Darya."

"Who's Nunya?"

"Our cat. Remember our cat?"

"So?"

"She ran off somewhere. When we started packing, she ran away and won't come back. Take her and feed her for me."

"But I have two of my own. Anfiza stuck me with hers when she left. What will I do with them?"

"No, Darya, you have to take Nunya," Nastasya grew excited. "Nunya is a gentle cat, you don't have one like her. I wanted to take her with me, I'd never leave her in my life, but Egor says they won't let her on the ship. And if they don't, then Nunya will be lost. She won't be any work, she doesn't even eat anything, just throw her a crumb once in a while . . ."

"God . . . you and your Nunya . . . If she comes my way—I'll take her, but if she doesn't, it's her fault. I'm not running all over the island after her."

"No, Darya, she'll come on her own. She does everything on her own. She's such a smart cat. And when you look at her, you'll think of me. She'll be a memento from me. And when I come back, I'll take her back . . . You just have to keep her alive, so that she doesn't starve."

"Will you really come back?"

"How will we manage without potatoes? What if we live through another winter—how can we do it without potatoes?" It seemed as though Nastasya was talking to someone else—for to Darya, her voice dropping to a moan, she said:

"Oh, what am I talking about the winter for! I can't see one day ahead for me. Oh, Darya . . ."

Grandpa Egor came back, the wagon rattling, and the old women stood up. They tried the trunk again, three-strong this time, and let it down again—they weren't strong anymore. Darya had to call Pavel. He came and looked in surprise at the trunk, not intended for travel, made in the olden days to stand for centuries immobile in one place, but said nothing about it to the old people. But when they hauled it up into the wagon and strapped it down, he did say:

"Look, Uncle Egor, when you get to Podvolochna, go see Mishka right away. Don't even think of trying it yourself."

"Never alone . . ." Grandpa waved the idea away. "I don't want a hernia. The fool stuffed it full." Grandpa Egor wanted to lay the blame for the trunk on Nastasya.

"It's all right, Egor, it's all right," she said, not hearing what he said, nodding her large head and looking around.

Pavel took the trunk; Grandpa Egor walked alongside, holding it steady by the brass ring. Pavel also helped them move the rest of their things and load them on to the boat, then brought the boat out into the water, checking the water level—they weren't overloaded. They brought back the wagon, Grandpa Egor put it in the lean-to, carefully lowering the shafts to the ground, but thinking it over, raised them for some reason and leaned them against the wall.

Clucking away, chickens now sold to Vera Nosaryova walked around the yard. They had killed three chickens: they ate two earlier and boiled one for the road—and four chickens, live and feathered, they sold to Vera for ten rubles. And the silly birds came here, to their yard, not knowing that now it was no longer theirs and dead. They sold the calf for one hundred thirty rubles to the sovkhoz—they got rich! But the calf was out to pasture on Podmoga—that was good, at least they wouldn't see her. And that was it. And yet they had had a household, they had lived a lifetime using things—and it all fit in the boat. Let it all die, too, they would all die.

There were more people in the house; Katerina and Sima with the boy came by. They sat in silence, dejected, having lost all the words that might have fit, and watched Nastasya as she continued running to and fro from one corner to the other, as though seeking and not finding herself—the one who had to go away. When Grandpa Egor and Pavel came in, the old women shuddered in fright and froze, prepared for the final command. But Grandpa Egor got out the second bottle of wine he had bought from the floating store and he and Pavel brought out the table from the kitchen and set it down next to the bench, and the old women sighed happily, glad that they didn't have to get up. And Nastasya was happiest of all, she cheered up, giggled, and started telling them how she kindled the Russian stove today for the last time.

There were only two glasses; Pavel and Grandpa Egor raised them first.

"A farewell toast, I guess?" Pavel asked uncertainly. He had to say something else, and he added: "Live long, Uncle Egor and Aunt Nastasya."

"We will!" Egor swallowed the words so that they squeaked out.

Pavel drank and went to get ready. The old women fell silent again, drinking the wine in small sips, like tea, grimacing and suffering, blocking out one form of suffering with another. Grandpa Egor also rose, lit up under the eyes of the old women and, as he walked out, warned: "Not for long, neighbors. Time to set off."

The old women sniffled and talked, all of them apologizing to Nastasya, but what they were guilty of and what they were explaining away they didn't know—an unknown sin needs all the more expiation. Nastasya, not hearing or understanding, agreed: if you're being swept away, off somewhere, then why count the pebbles on the shore; they're on the shore, after all.

"Are you taking your samovar?" Sima asked, pointing at the polished, gleaming samovar on the doorstep.

"Of course!" Nastasya nodded. "It won't squash us. I didn't let Egor drive it, I'll carry it in my hands. And you can't wrap it up in the house; I'll wrap it in the boat."

"Why not?" They had to talk about something, so they talked.

"So that it can see where to return. It's a superstition."

"No superstition can help us now," Darya said. "We don't exist for them now. And you'd think that somebody would have thought to put a samovar into someone's grave. How will we manage without one?"

"What will you need one over there for?"

"To drink tea—what else?"

"Well, Egor and I are going," Nastasya said, interrupting what she considered an empty conversation. "Maybe it'll be all right. We're going right now, all our things are at the shore."

And, as if he had been eavesdropping, waiting for the right moment, Grandpa Egor knocked at the window, showing her it was time to go.

"There, we're off," Nastasya bustled happily and jumped up from the table first. "I told you . . . Let's go, Egor, let's go!" she called out, suddenly changed and frightened. "Wait for me, Egor, don't leave."

She grabbed the samovar and rushed to the door, turning back to the old women, silently urging them on. Darya rose and majestically crossed herself in front of the empty corner, and after her, saying good-bye, Katerina blessed herself. Holding back, they were waiting for something from Nastasya, some action appropriate to the moment, but she was completely lost and didn't remember anything or do anything. On the porch she set the samovar in its usual place by the wall—where it always came to a boil—and when the women finally came out of the house, hurrying, she spent a long time trying to get the key in the padlock and locked the door. She turned—Egor was going out the gate—and shouted at the top of her lungs: "Ego-or!"

He stumbled.

"Egor, where docs the key go?"

"In the Angara," Egor said and spat.

And stopping no more, he stalked into the alleyway, moving his feet with the attention that accompanies preparing and memorizing every step. Nastasya, her face contorted pathetically, watched him go away without understanding.

"Give it here," Darya said, and took the key, covering her mouth with her kerchief to keep from crying. "I'll keep it. I'll come by here, keep an eye on things."

"Keep the gate shut," Nastasya remembered—she seemed to be smiling or smirking, her face, forgotten and left to fate, drooped first on one side, then on the other, "or the animals will get in and dirty things. That's so."

"I'm right nearby. I'll look in every day. Don't worry about it."

"Egor and I are going . . ."

The morning was high up in the sky, but it was still morning when Nastasya and Egor pushed off from Matyora. The sun was blazing away, the greenery on the island had faded, and the rocks on the bottom glistened lushly through the water. The Angara played and burst into hot, sparkling stripes, and swifts darted into them with a whistle, getting lost in the showering sparkles. There, where the current ran clean, the high bright sun went deep under water, and it was as though the Angara was flying through the air.

The loaded boat stood at the planked walk where they drew water. The old women followed Nastasya down to the pebbles, and they could no longer see the village over the high ravine. And you couldn't hear Matyora next to the Angara. Nastasya settled the samovar at the bow and returned to the old women to say good-bye. They were sobbing uncontrollably. Frightened by their tears, Sima's boy bawled loudly. Nastasya shook hands with the old women in turn—she didn't know how else to say good-bye—and shaking her head, repeated: "It's all right, all right . . . maybe it'll be all right . . ."

Grandpa Egor hurried her.

Looking down at her feet and waving as though waving them off, her arm straight behind her, she went up on the wooden walk, looked back briefly once more, and stepped into the boat.

"Egor keeps crying and crying . . ." she began, pointing at the old man, and stopped. Grandpa Egor faced the shore and bowed from the waist three times—right, left, and straight ahead—to Matyora. Then he quickly pushed off the boat and scrambled into it.

"Nastasya! Nastasya!" the old women cried.

"It's all right, all right," Nastasya muttered, standing up in the boat and wiping away her tears. And then, as though mown down, she fell on the bundles and wailed.

Grandpa Egor quickly used the oar to push away from shore. There, in the deep water, Pavel was waiting in his motorboat. When the current lifted the boat, Grandpa Egor tossed the tug line to him; Pavel started the motor, and the boat with the old people lurched and followed, faster and faster, further and further down the Angara.

For a brief moment at the turn, the village of Matyora revealed itself, then immediately disappeared from view.

8

AND THE NIGHT CAME TOO, the first hot and bright night on Matyora. There would be many of them later; closer to the end, the nights would blaze one after the other and the Angara would be visible for long distances, accompanied by huge fires, seemingly set in the river's honor. But this night was the first, and it happened on Matyora long before the others.

That night Petrukha's house burned. Petrukha, who was there from beginning to end and who had the presence of mind, despite the hullaballoo, to watch the time, later informed the villagers that a good, dry, long-standing house burned for two hours. There were few in the village who doubted that the house went up for any reason other than his own desire. Before that Petrukha had gone off somewhere, sniffing something out, and on his return, ordered his mother, old Katerina, to move out: he said that the museum would be coming for the house any day. There wasn't very much to move; Petrukha was one of those rich men who have as much to move as you would need to take a steambath. They had sold the cow two years ago; their last livestock, the pig, they killed in April, when their table had gotten really bare. Old Katerina gathered her simple things and carried them in her arms to Darya's. She moved the day before the fire: Petrukha was drunk and insisted, almost forced her out, and Katerina moved away from sin, to keep from arguing with him. Darya had invited her before, telling her it would be easier for them to live out their last days in Matyora together. It really was easier, and the old women gathered in a circle around Darya every day anyway. Darya lived with the same fear as the others, but she lived more confidently and seriously, she was respected by her son, not the least important man in the sovkhoz, and she had a place to lay her head after the flood, even with a choice: if she wanted, she could go in one direction, and if she wanted, in another; and besides, Darya had a temper, which didn't mellow or weaken with the years, and if it came to that, she could stand up for more than just herself. In every village of ours there always was and is one, or sometimes two, old woman with a temper to whom the weak and suffering come for protection; and it is inevitably that if one such old woman lives out her days and dies, her place will immediately be taken by another woman who has grown old, strengthening her position among the others with her firm and just temperament. In the special situation that Matyora found itself, Darya could be of no help to the old women, but they came to her, to be near Darya and thus feel stronger and braver. It's a fact that even death looks good in company, and if you were to offer them death at the same time, next to one another, hardly any of them would think twice—they would agree gladly.

That night Matyora had settled down early. Late-night things happen to young people, and there weren't any left in Matyora except for visitors from the sovkhoz. They went to sleep before dark, when the light was quieting down, setting behind the Angara, following the sun. It was an uncomfortable time, not like life among normal people: on one hand they wanted to slow down the summer and put off the unwanted that awaited them, and on the other they were getting impatient, they wanted to put an end to the torture of being neither home nor visiting, not sure that they were alive or just dreaming about themselves in a long, bad dream. They went to bed, as usual, early; Katerina was out of her house for the first time, and even though she had prepared herself for it a long time ago and had anticipated this small move before the big one, she was extremely bitter and sad, and every word seemed inappropriate and unnecessary. Darya, understanding, didn't bother her with conversation; in the evening Bogodul came by, but you can't have a conversation with him either; they grunted and sighed, so as not to be completely silent, and then Darya saw the old man out. She made her bed on the Russian stove—she usually slept there summer and winter—she climbed up over the partition, and Katerina settled down on the cot in the front corner. There was still a wooden bed left for Pavel when he came to visit.

They lay down and grew still. Katerina didn't know whether she had fallen asleep or not; praying with hopeless thoughts, she was just creeping up on sleep when there was a banging, first on the window and then on the door, and Bogodul was at the door (Bogodul brought all the bad news) calling out hoarsely and loudly.

"Kater-rina!" And then the usual string of swear words, without which he couldn't put together two normal words. "Kater-rina, you're burning! Kur-rva! Petrukha!"

The old women jumped up. Flames danced in the two windows that opened on the upper end of Matyora, and the fire seemed so close that half-asleep Darya reacted in fright.

"Oh God! Is it our house?"

But Katerina knew right away what was happening. And struggling with her clothes, she shrieked vehemently and weakly, as though beating her forehead against the wall.

"What a devil! What a devil! I knew it! I knew it! Mother of

God!" She took herself off as fast as her legs would carry her—home, to the place that just that evening had been her home. Bogodul started out after her, but stopped halfway and turned toward the lower end of the village to wake up the rest.

When Katerina got there, the house was blazing mightily. There was no opportunity to beat down the flames, nor was there any need. Only Petrukha rushed around among the people who stood silently and watched the fire intently, trying to tell them how he almost burned to death, how he awoke at the last minute "from smoke in my lungs and heat in my hair—my hair was crackling." "Or it would have been the end," he repeated with a laugh. "I would have burned to a crisp, and you couldn't tell what had been what on me." Ducking his head he would look into people's eyes: did they believe him or not? They moved away from him as though from a leper but Petrukha didn't really count on their believing him. He knew Matyora and he knew that they knew him inside out and that's why he admitted his unwitting fault. "I lit the stove in the evening and then went to sleep," he persisted with his unwanted and unnecessary explanations. "Maybe some damn coal or other jumped out and made all this trouble." And then he would tell about his escape again. That was the only thing that was important to him—that he himself might have burned and survived only through a miracle—and he had convinced himself so that he even managed a tear and a tremor in his voice as he told the story—an artful touch of truth. He sometimes forgot about the stove and the coal and threatened: "If I find out what bastard set the fire, I'll . . ." And he sharpened his fists, striking them against each other the way people sharpen knives. Either the fire intoxicated him or he hadn't dried out from the evening before, but Petrukha didn't seem sober and he lurched and stumbled; shaggy and dirty, he wore a sleeveless undershirt, which had slipped off one shoulder, and boots—he somehow did find the time to pull on his boots properly. And Petrukha also managed to save a few things from the fire: a cotton patchwork quilt, and old fur coat, and his squeezebox, his *podgorna*, lay on the ground. In Petrukha's hands his *podgorna* knew only one tune: "You Podgorna, you Podgorna, a broad street, no one walks on you—not roosters and not chickens ..." Petrukha kept picking it up and moving it away from the heat; the people moved away too when the heat grew more intense, but they didn't leave or take their eyes, anxious and trying to make some sense of it, from the fire.

Everyone left alive in the village was there, including the children. But even they didn't make noise, as usual; they stood stunned and oppressed by the terrible power of the fire. The old women with their harsh, bitter faces didn't stand together, but were scattered throughout the crowd, wherever each had first come upon the site and had been transfixed by the fire. As never before, their motionless faces in the light of the flames seemed sculpted, waxen; long, ugly shadows danced and waved. Katerina screamed when she reached the house, wailed, arms outstretched before the burning house, bending over in sobs, bowing in its direction. They turned to her to see who she was and why she had the right to scream, recognized her, pitied her silently, and went back to staring at the fire in silent thought. Darya came out of the darkness and stood next to Katerina, and the rest felt better knowing that Darya was there, that if necessary she would keep Katerina still by her side, and that they, therefore, could stay where they were. But Katerina, falling under the spell of the horrible and attentive silence, soon quieted down, raised her eyes, and kept them on what had been her home from her earliest days.

People forgot that they weren't alone, they lost one another and didn't need one another now. It's always like that: at an unpleasant shameful event, no matter how many people are there, each tries not to notice anyone else and to remain alone—it's easier to rid yourself of the shame later. In their hearts they felt bad, uncomfortable, that they stood motionless, that they hadn't tried when it was still possible to save the house, and that there was no point in trying. The same thing would happen to the other houses—soon—and Petrukha's was just the first. And they watched and watched, not missing a thing, to see how it was, to know how it would be, the way a man pierces a dead man with his gaze, trying to picture himself in the same situation, which he cannot escape.

The fire illuminated the future of each of them so brightly, without any mistakes, the fate that could not be shared with anyone, waiting nearby, that they couldn't even believe in the reality of the people around them—it all seemed to have happened a long, long time ago.

The flames had engulfed the entire house and were shooting straight up; the house burned strongly and evenly, and everything burned, heated by the flames: the walls, the roof, the porch —sparks showered and exploded, making the people back off; glass burst and melted; long, boisterous tongues of flames lashed out as though someone was splashing gasoline around inside. The flames blocked the sky. The hot evil glow lit up the area for a great distance—it showed the closest houses, on the beginning street, and they also seemed to be burning, caught in the flashes that raced through the wood; it illuminated the Angara under the bank, and there, where it was lit up, it gaped like an exposed wound with pulsating flesh; the knoll beyond the dancing glow seemed dark brown and burned out. Behind the burning walls things fell and thudded, as if in the aftershock of explosions; heated coals were thrown out the windows; sparks flew up high and disappeared in the stars; the inferno hissed on top and turned to faint smoke. A board on the roof suddenly stood up on end in the fire, coal-black but still burning, and then bent in the direction of the village: there, there's where the fires will be, look that way. And at almost the same instant the roof collapsed, the fire dropped, and the top row of logs fell in flames, and the people screamed and jumped aside. Katerina began weeping again, bowing blindly to the destroyed house, which was briefly enveloped in smoke while the flame rested, catching its breath and belching, then redirected itself with new strength. The Russian stove showed through the fire, seeming to dance in the flames. The fire crept through the fence into the yard, but they didn't want to stop it there either—what use is a yard without a house? Who would try to save feet left without a head?

When the top collapsed and there was no more house, the people's attention weakened. As though on precise signal, they all turned toward Petrukha. They glanced at Katerina, too, who was sobbing, and felt even sorrier for her, but their gaze remained on Petrukha. How was he? What was he doing? What was he feeling now? Was he happy or frightened? Petrukha was standing, rubbing his bare chest with his hands and nervously twitching his head; the curious stares made him angry. Petrukha had been going crazy since the moment his mother had arrived, angered by the fact that she hadn't come up to him, hadn't asked him, hadn't scolded him, shamed him; she seemed to have forgotten him completely, disowned him, and therefore Petrukha was itching to go over to her and remind her of his presence to see how she would behave. And now, angry, he decided to do it, and coming up to her, he spoke and said something so arrogant and crude and in such a tone that he frightened himself.

"Mother, give me a light."

She raised her face toward him, uncomprehending and still sobbing.

"You sniff tobacco, I know that. You must have a smoke," Petrukha persisted.

Darya heard him.

"I'll give you a smoke!" she threatened, quietly but severely and insistently. "I'll make your face smoke! I'll take you, you arsonist, and rub your face in what's burning over there. And he dares mock his mother, as though he hasn't done enough! You get yourself out of here before I latch on to you!"

"Ho . . ." was the only repartee Petrukha could come up with as he stepped back into the darkness.

But the dark was noticeably lighter, drooping, and light was streaming from the sky. Now, when the flames had died down and were only getting at the remaining wood below, there was a stronger smell of burnt wood and large cinders floated in the air. Firebrands that had flown off smoldered on the grass and the road. The barn burned steadily, without passion or turbulence, listing to one side. The gathering morning light made the fire lighter, too.

The crowd began dispersing. They left, uncertainly, cautiously looking around: the order on Matyora had been disrupted, the village was exposed on one side, and now that side was defenseless. Truly, the fire would move on from here, there was nothing, no unity that could save them from it . . .

That's what Darya was telling Katerina as she comforted her and led her away from the fire. Everyone would experience the same thing, no one would escape that fate. Katerina was first, and it would be easier for her later; she wouldn't suffer and torture herself in apprehension of her fire and she wouldn't watch it, singeing her heart. She had passed her turn.

And truly, a house doesn't burn long, two or three hours, but it smolders for many more days, without cooling off, giving off an acrid, bitter smell of habitation, scorched but not burned out, indestructible.

The Master came on duty early that night, to his chosen post on a nearby knoll, from where he could conveniently and safely observe the fire. And he saw it all from beginning to end. He saw the burst of the first match, a special, unneeded flare-up that the house immediately discerned and sensed; it stretched taut and sank, creaking painfully. The Master ran over to it, pressing himself close for the last time to its dry, dead wood, to show that he was there and would be there to the end, and went right back.

He saw the house flickering light from within, at first with an interrupted, weak glow, which grew and grew until the windows were filled with playing color. The Master watched and could see inside through the walls. The fire kept trying to grab the solid floor, scuffed smooth over the ages, but couldn't, slipping off, and suddenly it saw the thin plank wall and ran up it easily. The walls cracked as they heated, and either the heat or outside interference made the glass break softly, as if being poured, in the window that opened on the Angara. A gust of fresh air splashed in through the window and the fire, breathing freely, roared and roamed over the house, picking up every flammable trifle and continuing to heat up the ceiling and walls.

The Master saw people running, saw Petrukha bustling in front of the first ones on the scene, waving his arms in the direction of the flame-engulfed house. All the life that had been in the wood had been cooked by then, and it burned without suffering. The flame forced its way outside and attacked the building from both sides. The roof burst into flames with a mighty roar, the light reaching even the Master, who had to draw back into the darkness.

And while the house blazed at its peak, the Master looked at the village. In the generous light he could easily see the fires, pale for now, above the still-living houses. Only he could see them and could tell the order in which fire would take them. And he saw strangers near them, many people. And raising his eyes even higher, the Master saw smoke over the forests of Matyora, and the smoke moved without wind over the island in farewell circles.

Podmoga was burning . . .

He saw smoke over the cemetery, the very fire that the old women interrupted a month ago . . .

He saw, looking over at Petrukha's house once more, how tomorrow Katerina would come here and walk until nightfall, looking for something in the hot soil and in her memory, and how she would come the day after tomorrow, and after that . . . and after that . . .

And he saw even further . . .

9

PAVEL CAME LESS FREQUENTLY, and when he did come he didn't linger, quickly taking care of his business and heading back. The constant back-and-forth traveling wore him out, and he came up from the bank weary and sullen; he had never been much of a talker anyway and now his tongue was completely dried out. In the kolkhoz Pavel had worked as a brigade leader and then as head of the garage and did his work well, but he didn't know yet what position he would have in the sovkhoz, nor did it seem that anyone did. One of the difficult problems facing the new management was where to stick the former kolkhoz brass, the people from the middle and top ranks, who had come to know at least some form of power and who had learned to command, and naturally, had forgotten how to obey. Pavel was ready to take any job, he didn't have an overexaggerated idea of himself, but he saw how the men seeking power checked one another out and how they talked distractedly and less than candidly with the big and the small, not knowing whether they would end up with the former or the latter. Pavel for now was in vehicle repair, as brigade leader, and at first he was alone, but then a second brigade leader appeared, and now there was a third one scrambling up. That meant that no one would be held accountable, and there was much to answer for: the vehicles, both new and old, broke down for lack of roads and care; there weren't enough spare parts, as usual, and there were plenty of orders put in and often enough the order was followed by a refusal, and then by a countermand. And the same thing was happening with them, the leaders, and their workers— the workers didn't know which one to obey. It wasn't a job, it was a nerve frazzler. And there was nothing better in the offing, until the time when the sovkhoz completely extricated itself from the Angara, until it gathered all the people and labor, and the new life took root and flowered.

Once Katerina moved in with Darya, Pavel felt better, too: it would be easier for the old women together and he wouldn't have to worry about his mother so much. Katerina could help around the house, she still moved around, and she could hold up her end of a conversation. Pavel, of course, had asked to be released to come to Matyora for the last months, the mowing and harvesting, to clean up and to prepare the island with familiar hands for its watery grave—he got the usual farsighted foggy answer: "We'll see when the time comes," and he didn't have great hopes of getting permission. But he didn't insist too much, fearing that after the harvest he would be forced to do another clean-up job— burning down the houses. Someone would have to take on the job, but Pavel couldn't imagine how he would command setting fire to his own village. Twenty, thirty, and fifty years hence, people would remember: "Ah, yes, Pavel Pinigin, who burned Matyora . . ." He didn't deserve to be remembered that way.

Coming to Matyora, he was always amazed at how quickly time disappeared behind him: it was as though there was no new settlement from which he had just come, as though he had never left Matyora. And if you insisted, there was a settlement, it was there on the other bank, but it had nothing to do with Pavel. With someone perhaps, but not with him. He had been there and seen it—it was a fine settlement, but there are plenty of those around. His house was here, and as they say, home is always best. That was what occurred with Pavel as soon as he climbed to the top of the ravine and his village opened up before him with everything that he had known and seen from childhood. He arrived—and an invisible door slammed shut behind his back, and his memory helpfully only prompted him with things that referred to life here, blocking and removing all the recent changes.

And what about the changes? You couldn't alter them or change them—or get away from them. That didn't depend on him or on anyone else. If it had to be, it had to be, but he only understood one half of the "had to be," he understood that he had to move from Matyora, that the hydroelectric power station under construction was necessary, but he didn't understand why he had to move to that settlement, built—though handsomely and richly—with the houses so close together, line by line, and placed so stupidly and without any regard for human needs that you could only shake your head in wonder. And when the men got together to chew the fat and try to figure out what was what, why they had to put the settlement five miles from the shore that would form here and put it on clay and rock, on the north slope of a hill, they couldn't come up with a single idea, not the most ridiculous answer. They put it there—and you can burst if you want! It was as if, the way they did in fairy tales, they shot an arrow in the air and went wherever the wind carried it. The answer was a simple one: they weren't building it for themselves, they were only interested in where it was easiest to build and were least concerned with whether it would be easy to live in it. They thought a site for the new settlement was being chosen, that they had their own man in the commission who would stand up for the interests of the locals—the director of the sovkhoz, but this "own man" had come from the outside somewhere and disappeared immediately, barely staying long enough to sign an agreement. He would have just as calmly signed an agreement to build underground. They said that the head of the construction management company putting up the new settlement, when he came and saw what was happening, what a town he was creating, cursed and admitted that if it were up to him he wouldn't build here at all, but would move it to where it should be. But the deed was done, the money allotted, and quite a bit of money, and it was impossible to change anything. Life was life so that it could go on, it could take everything and survive anywhere, even on bare rock or shifting sands, and if necessary, even under water, but why torture it this way for no good reason, creating totally unnecessary difficulties for people, why worry about small conveniences and create major inconveniences? That's what Pavel thought and tried to comprehend. And he couldn't. And that's why he couldn't totally accept the new settlement, even though he knew that one way or the other he would have to live there and that eventually his life there would come to be all right.

If it has to be, it has to be, but thinking how this soil would be flooded, this soil that was so rich, tended for centuries, fertilized by his grandfathers and great-grandfathers, and having fed more than one generation, his heart stopped anxiously and uncertainly: was this too high a price to pay? Were they overpaying? It wasn't painful only for those who had lived here, worked here, watered every furrow with their sweat. Over there it cost a thousand rubles to dig up a hectare of new arable land, and they had just planted wheat in that golden hectare, and it didn't even come up. The topsoil was black, but when they lifted it, the soil was red, they might as well put up a brickyard. So they sowed alfalfa in keeping with the old saying: a mangy sheep at least yields a handful of wool—but you never know if the alfalfa will take. Who knew how much time it would take to prepare this wild and poor forest soil for wheat, to make it do what it's supposed to. And the old fields, he remembered, in the olden days, fed them and had thousands of tons left over to be shipped to the north and the east. The fields were famous.

"No, I'm getting old, I can tell," Pavel would say, putting himself in his place. "I'm getting old if I don't understand. The young people understand. It doesn't even occur to them to doubt. They accept whatever's done. If they build a settlement here, then here's where it should be and this is its only possible site. Everything that happens is for the best, so that life is happier and more interesting. Just live without looking around or thinking. If the land won't yield bread, then they'll bring you bread, ready-baked in black, white, and gray loaves, just fill your stomachs! If you won't get milk from your own cow, they'll bring you milk so that you won't have to bother with the cow or get scratched in bushes gathering hay. And they'll bring you potatoes, and beets, and onions—everything. And it's no concern of yours where they get it. We have an urban-type settlement—and you can live there like you're in a city, just like it. You'll get money for the fields, for sowing and resowing it, and you can buy things with the money, whatever you need. They've built a big glass store—it's beautiful to look at. And they're putting up another one next to it, and a third one's in the works . . . And if you don't like it here, you can go somewhere else, where it's better, no road is closed to you.

"I'm getting old," he admitted. "I am old—what do I mean! I think that Mother clutches pointlessly to the past, but how different am I? But Mother has lived her time, and I still have to work and live. I understand that you can't build the new on an empty spot and that you can't get it out of thin air, that you have to give up something dear and familiar, that you have to put in no little effort. I understand that perfectly well. And I understand that without technology, the most major technology, you can't do anything nowadays or go anywhere. Everyone knows that, but how do you understand and explain what they've done with the settlement? Why did they demand useless labors from the people who will be living there? How much do you lose of the future when you gain a day's time? And why didn't they think about that ahead of time? Of course, you could live without asking questions, just live the way life comes, float with the current, but I'm crazy that way: I must know why and wherefore, dig down to the truth myself. That's why I'm a man."

And coming back to the settlement, he entered his yard, to which willy-nilly he had grown attached, and he felt better: he could live here. It was unfamiliar and uncomfortable, he felt like a boarder, which he was in fact, because the house wasn't his and he couldn't behave like lord and master, but on the other hand, everything was done for him: he didn't have to chop wood or stoke the oven. He did have to haul water for now, but they promised running water soon. How could you compare—he had an easier life now. You come home from work, wash up, and you can lie around spitting at the ceiling without a worry or care . . . But with all that relief and ease you don't feel you're carrying your own weight any more, without your strength and dependability, as though any ill wind could pick you up and carry you off—and then go find yourself; some disgusting uncertainty kept gnawing at him: is it you or not? And if it's you, then how did you get here?

But he could get used to that too . . .

Pavel was amazed looking at Sonya, his wife: from the moment she entered the house—now he had to say *apartment*, not *house* —she walked in, gaped at the electric stove that gleamed like a toy, the flowers and leaves on the walls that, it turned out, you didn't even have to whitewash, the cabinets that were built in, and the bathroom with tile and a toilet, which for now had no water and didn't work, and the merry green veranda, glassed in on one side, and seemed to have always lived there. In a day she had her bearings, ran to see the neighbors—to see how they set things up—and began getting organized: where to put what, what of their existing furniture was good enough to bring over and what had to be bought, learned where they could dig a basement and how to expand their cellar, and raced around excited, animated, bustling, ever so happy and apparently ready to live forever in that apartment. And yet she was a country woman too, she didn't hang around with princes and nobles, she hadn't tasted the good life, but just look at her, she took to it right away. Where did that come from? As though a fried roaster had pecked her in the rear. It really was a lure for a woman: it was beautiful, clean, she didn't have to run like on fire from yard to kitchen and back again, everything was right there within reach. And Sonya had two sisters in Irkutsk; one of them had married a lucky and quick man who worked in provisions, she lived like a rich lady, her apartment had absolutely everything, and Sonya envied her quite a bit. When she came back from a visit in the city, whenever she managed to get away, she would look with loathing at the oven prongs and cast iron pots, and once she even tried to lure Pavel to the city. They had filled her head with stories about how good and fine it was, how cultured and respectable, and a friend in provisions promised to find a place for Pavel, too—and she melted, gave in, rushed off to pack. Pavel almost fell for it himself, because the rumors about the flooding had just started and they'd have to move somewhere anyway, but he restrained himself. Life in the city is good for people who find the city good, but anyone who was brought up by the village and grew to old age there, well he'd better stay put. And now Sonya could calm down too; before she used to nag her husband. Now they had crawled out of the mud, and were on the way to princehood . . .

Slowly but surely life becomes normal, and a man gets used to it, it doesn't happen any other way. Later they'll divide up land in some old fields for potatoes, for you can't bring in enough no matter how hard you try, they'll realize that it's difficult without a cow—depend on the communal herd, but keep your own cow, too—and as though granting a great gift, they'll say: keep your own cow if you want, fence in plots, mow, knock yourself out from dawn till dusk if you want. And probably not many will want to anymore, the people will have different habits by then.

It was easier for them—Sonya didn't need any more even now, and he would get used to things—but Pavel knew that his mother would never get used to it. No way. It was someone else's heaven as far as she was concerned. If they brought her over, she would hide in a corner until she shriveled up. She couldn't handle the changes. And as though she weren't planning to go anywhere, she almost never asked him what things were like there, and when he brought something up himself, she oohed and aahed and clasped her hands, but as though over some distant and unrelated mystery that had no relation to her. The new settlement was no nearer or dearer to her than, say, America, where they said people, in order not to wear out their feet, walked on their heads. Watching his mother, Pavel was more and more convinced that even as she discussed the move, she did not picture herself anywhere but on Matyora, and he feared the day when he would have to take her away.

10

PETRUKHA, AS WAS TO BE EXPECTED, left Katerina the very next
day after the fire, and he hadn't been heard from in a week. And
he didn't leave his mother a crust of bread; Katerina lived on
Darya's tea. The last grain of flour had burned in the storehouse.
She hadn't thought that she had anything in the house, but when
she began thinking after the fire—this had burned, and that—
Katerina was most upset over her samovar; when she moved to
Darya's she hadn't thought of fire, of course, and she left the
samovar for another day. Later she found a melted brass lump in
the ashes. Petrukha hadn't forgotten his off-key squeezebox, he
brought it out, but abandoned the hard-working samovar that
had brought him up with tea. Without it, Katerina was truly
alone.

She still held on to the hope that Petrukha would come to his senses, find a job, and send for her. And she sighed over the samovar, picturing the house they would have with no samovar in it: they didn't make them anymore, they were nowhere to be found. A table without a samovar at the head was no table at all, merely a feeding place that birds or animals have, it had no coziness or pomp. There were always three masters honored in a household—the one who was head of the family, the Russian stove, and the samovar. The rest tried to suit them, respected them, and usually they didn't start a new day without them, and it was on their orders and whims that things got done. And now in one fell swoop Katerina lost a house, a samovar, and a Russian stove (the stove hadn't burned, and it protruded, cracked and open, from the ashes like a monument—but was she going to heat the air with it?). Katerina hadn't had a master since her father.

Darya simply couldn't understand how you could burn down your own house ahead of time; she kept castigating Petrukha over and over again, demanding an answer: how, how could he have raised his hand to do it? Katerina, hiding, didn't reply, looking down guiltily, as though it was she who was being shamed and when Darya came up close to her and she had to say something, Katerina said:

"He's worthless, you know . . ."

And there was no anger or bitterness in those brief words against her son, who had left her without shelter or bread—only a defensive, all-forgiving meaning: that's the way he was born to me, what can you expect from him?

"There," Darya said, poking her finger at her, getting angrier. "You're like that all your life. You gave him everything all your life, you spoiled him terribly. And now it serves you right. It serves you right. He burned down a living house and he'll bury you alive in the ground. Not in the ground," she suddenly realized sadly. "In the water, he'll throw you in the water so that he won't have to bury you. And you'll ask him to tie a bigger stone round your neck . . . so that you don't float up."

"He could do that," Katerina sighed. "He's worthless, you know . . ."

"Just try talking to her," Darya said in exasperation. "I'm talking about serious things, and she's blabbing. The devil take you and your Petrukha both! Some provider God gave you . . ."

Katerina had never married. She got Petrukha from a Matyora man, Alyosha Zvonnikov, now long dead, killed in the war. Katerina was much younger than him; when they came together, he already had four kids running around, but he had taken her heart so much that she refused to marry anyone else, even though she had many suitors in her youth. Alyosha Zvonnikov was pretty much a bum, and Petrukha took after him a lot, but the old man was a good worker and did have something special if his own wife put up with Katerina and if Katerina, with no hopes for anything, lit up and held her breath when he showed up on her doorstep after midnight. Even now, reminiscing about him, she became animated and her face would change as if from wine, her eyes opened, and she stared happily at the days and nights of forty years ago, and what she saw there warmed her even now. And she spoke of Alyosha as if he were her own, and on Matyora she had the right to do so, because after the war Alyosha's family moved from the island.

It was impossible to hide the relationship between Alyosha and Katerina, everyone in the village knew about her. Then, when Petrukha was born, Alyosha stopped hiding completely and openly took on the responsibility of his new family, and in broad daylight in front of everyone he would bring Katerina logs and hay and raise fallen posts. And he lived that way, with two families, for three or four years, right up to the war, and people in Matyora got used to it quickly and stopped clucking over it. You couldn't cluck and berate Alyosha too much anyway—criticism rolled off his back like water. He was quite capable of making a laughingstock out of anyone, and not many were willing to take him on. "I'm like that," he used to brag, "you can't outtalk me." And ten and fifteen years after the war the villagers would say about a cocky, wisecracking youth or man: "Well, we have another Alyosha Zvonnikov here!"

And it was more than enough of that glibness and conversational ease that Petrukha had gotten from his illegitimate father. But while that one didn't abuse it—Alyosha never chewed the fat when there was work to be done, he did the work first and then whatever else he might have felt like—it was just the other way around with Petrukha. He was an awful worker, whatever he undertook failed, he never did anything right. Where work called for moving your hands, he folded his hands behind his back, and where you had to use your wits, he flailed about doing this and that and getting nothing done. The kolkhoz sent him to study tractor driving; he was there for six months, and when he came back they entrusted him with a new Belarus with big wheels—in a week's time he knocked down half the fences in the village with those big wheels chasing after cats and dogs, leaving flat fields in his yard and the cattle yard. He would drink, get behind the wheel, and start circling, scattering wood splinters in all directions. Katerina would jump out:

"What are you doing, Petrukha? Come to your senses—what are you doing, where are you going?! Do you think the land is fenced off so that you can smash it?"

He would wave her off.

"You don't understand anything, old woman. I'm supposed to be doing this. That's the order of the day." And so on, and Katerina would walk away thinking: who knows, maybe it's true, he had to do it to learn to drive the tractor steady in the fields, to stay in the furrows.

They took the tractor away from Petrukha and set him down on the ground, but by then he was completely spoiled and didn't want to do any work: they moved him from place to place, from job to job, but he was useless everywhere; everywhere they tried to get rid of him as soon as possible and didn't even hide it from him—he would merely laugh at what they said about him, urging them to speak more strongly and openly, as though he derived some pleasure from it. Nothing could hurt Petrukha. And when they switched the kolkhoz over to a sovkhoz, at least as it died the kolkhoz could die happy knowing that it was finally rid of that worker.

The man was almost forty, but he didn't want to grow up, he still behaved like a child: no family (by some miracle he twice managed to lure women from across the river, but after the first month both fled from him back over the Angara), no hands capable of work, no head capable of life. All flimflam. Just get through today, and as for tomorrow—that didn't concern him, his short-range, wandering thoughts didn't reach that far. He had signed up for the sovkhoz at first and then declined, planning to move to the city, and then, as though bitten by a bug, began talking about a hunting co-op, even though in his whole life he had shot a rifle only at bottles and had missed at that. And recently he had been dreaming of the north and big money . . . But you needed patience just to get north, and Petrukha didn't have a drop of it.

So now you judge what it's like being the mother of a man like that. Katerina was afraid: the soul with sin is the one that answers—and so she took the blame for Petrukha's craziness upon herself. She said: "But if he's that way—what can I do with him? Put his head on the chopping block?"

"How else could he be, when you spoiled him rotten?" Darya replied. "He burned down the house, did you at least say one word to him?"

"You said yourself we'd have to burn it sooner or later . . ."

"Not by your own hand! Why hasn't it dropped off, the one that struck the match?! You have to have a heart of stone to do that; he was born in that house, he grew up in it, and he burned it down ahead of everyone else! Well!"

"Maybe it really was an accident."

"What a Christ's fool, what a fool!" Darya was amazed and awed. "Of course, it was an accident. He built it for you himself with his own hands, and then he made a fortune—that Petrukha of yours has golden hands. Why would he go burn it down—what black things they made up about the man. It was an accident, an accident . . ."

Katerina grew quiet.

"But how do these people become like that?" she would try to understand. It wasn't the first time she tried to find out and she already knew that she wouldn't, and still she asked, hoping for short-lived relief and an excuse for herself, when neither she nor Darya could come up with the answer. "He was worthless from childhood. You say I spoiled him. What did I do? There was nothing to teach him. I tried being kind, and every other way—he was just born that way. Even when he was little he didn't want to listen. He would shut his eyes—and talking to him was like throwing peas against the wall. Did you have a lot of work with your children?"

"When did I have time for that? I was busy from dawn to dusk."

"And they're all fine people. Not one of them went bad. I didn't spoil him either . . . I wasn't up to it. Of course, he wasn't abandoned. I tried. When I look at Klavka's kids . . . it really would be better to live with a stepmother . . . She's their mother, but she doesn't mother them. She doesn't take care of them or caress them—they grow up on slops and scraps, poor things . . . And they're such sweet children, gentle and obedient . . . How can that be, when all she knows is being vicious? Did she bring them up?"

"Hah!" Darya harrumphed, totally denying Klavka's ability to do so.

They were talking about Klavka Strigunova.

"Then what is it? One is beaten till he passes out and turns into a human being. Another isn't changed by any amount of beatings —once a robber always a robber. You baby one and it does him good, another one is spoiled by it. Isn't it so? People are going to be what they'll be no matter? And you can break off his arms and cry yourself to death and he'll still be what he is? There's no way to change him. Is that it? You say I don't make demands on him. Mother in Heaven! I wore myself out demanding. And now I really have stopped, because I see it's useless. The way he was is the way he is now. All my anger is gone . . . only pity that he's like that is left. After all, I can't send him to the scaffold, now can I? Let him do what he wants. It's his life."

"But you're not saying all this from your grave. You still have to live too."

"Ah, what does it matter," Katerina shrugged. "We're not living on our power now anyway. We're being dragged. And wherever they drag us is fine with me."

"You're right about being dragged, all right," Darya agreed.

"And then they'll grow up, Klavka's kids," Katerina said, returning to the subject and polishing off the conversation, "and they'll kiss her feet for never having a kind word for them. And they say you get answers in kind . . . aah . . ." she moaned in disagreement, "nothing works that way. It's all written at your birth. You never know what can happen; another mother can raise a dozen children and live worse in her old age with them than she would with strangers. Strangers would be too embarrassed to be like that. But family, you'd think they have the right to be vicious . . . They're kinder to an evil burglar. Why is that? Do you remember old Agrafena?"

"So don't live to be that old," Darya said with sudden anger. "Know your limit," and she stopped, lowering her voice, realizing that it is not given for man to know his time. "Is it for one's sins that God keeps you alive beyond your time? Oh, they must be terrible sins for that . . . Where do you collect them? Man must live only as long as he serves a purpose. No purpose—get off. We're here. Why wear yourself out and others? The living need to live, not keep death in the house, pulling bedpans out from under it. I pulled enough of them, I know. They'll be using them for me soon, I went from potty to potty in a flash, but I remember. I remember my mother-in-law, I remember how I used to look at her," she went on, angry again about something. "I used to look and think: 'When will God take you? You're worse than a burr in the side.' And we got along well, she was a peaceful woman. And I wasn't squeamish. And yet I remember I was so sick of coming close to her at the end. I mean I understood it wasn't her fault, and still I couldn't do anything about my feeling. I just couldn't go near her, I wanted to run from the house. And I thought: what if it was my own mother lying flat on her back like that—would I want her to die too? I said no, of course, but I could hear a voice from far off: I would want her to die too. Not as much, of course, and I would have more patience, but in bad moments, in my secret thoughts, I would give in. It wasn't even coming from me—from something else. No, Katerina, you can't let old age drag on. No one needs it."

"What then—a noose around your neck?"

Darya didn't reply.

"And they bury us and weep . . . they're not weeping for us, the ones they're putting in the coffin, but the ones they remember . . . the way we were," she said. "And they pity us because they pity themselves. They see that they'll get old and won't be any better than us. And without us they get older faster. They've already buried us in their minds before then. And that's the moment to get away, if we could just catch that moment. But we keep holding on to life. And I don't know why—it just makes it worse. If you die younger they'll remember you better, and have prettier memories of you too. The memory will be sharper and more noticeable. But if they put old monster bones in the coffin—they don't even want to look. And that horrible ragbone will destroy all the other memories . . ."

"But how is that our fault?"

"It's our fault that we get used to ourselves, like to a puppy dog, and treasure ourself. We want it to protect us and bark at others. If they told you in your youth what you would put up with as yourself—you'd make the sign of the cross in disbelief. Nothing alive left, everything fallen out or turned bony, no teeth, no horns, no nothing—but you don't think there's ever been anything dearer than you in the whole wide world. And what for? God gave you life so that you would do your duty, leave children behind—and then into the ground with you . . . so that the soil stays rich. That's what you're good for now. But you keep creeping around up here, getting in people's way. Pack up and go away, don't bother others. Let others do their duty, don't take up their time. They're short of time too."

"But what's the hurry?" Katerina argued. "Live on the run and die on the run? Maybe we won't have another chance to live?"

"Maybe even now it wasn't you who lived—"

"Then who? Go ahead and talk, but talk sense. Who would live instead of me?"

"Maybe someone else. And they just tricked you into thinking it was you. And if it is you—then why can't you manage with your Petrukha? Why don't you live the way you want and do what others tell you to? Why have you suffered all your life? No, Katerina, forgive me, Lord, but I wouldn't say that it was me who lived . . . Too much of it doesn't match up with me . . ."

It truly was easier for them together, both with the housework and with conversation. The days were long, and the old women had time to do everything and then, exhausted, to lie down after lunch, but instead of sleeping they talked. And they talked when they got up, ready for the evening chores, and then when they were done—and so time passed, and the long summer days slipped unnoticed from one side to the other. Sima came by for the conversations with her unremovable tail—Kolka; Bogodul appeared, grunting and swearing, and tried to get in a word here and there; hard-of-hearing Tunguska came by with the pipe that she almost never removed from her mouth, and therefore never spoke; and other people who were still on Matyora came for tea and talk. They reminisced about the old, wondered about the new, and discussed this and that, life and death . . . they had never talked so much before.

And there was little left that they hadn't discussed and there was little, despite their long lives, that they understood of it.

And ahead, if you were to look at the remaining days, there was more and more space and freedom beyond them. Ahead, the wind was already roaming in the emptiness.

11

BUT LIFE MANAGED ONCE MORE, splashing up in Matyora—when the mowing began. There wasn't enough feed in the new pastures, for there weren't any new ones yet, and so they advanced on the old ones for the last time. The sovkhoz had to separate into kolkhozes again—people went back to their old places. It was a rare man who wasn't happy to have an opportunity to be in his own village toward the end, almost everyone had a house, cattle, a garden, unfinished chores, and the earth wasn't silent, it called to them, the neither blind nor deaf, to say farewell before its death. There weren't many who were blind or deaf or stuck in an office or busy with demanding work and would refuse to go— a man who's had his own house and land is attached, oh, how attached he becomes!

Half the village returned to Matyora, and Matyora came alive if not with its former life, reminiscent of the old order, with a life that resembled it, and it was as though life had returned for a last look to remember how it was. The horse driven over from Podmoga neighed once more, workers' voices called to one another in the morning, and the mowing equipment rattled and clanked. They found and heated up the smithy to repair the horse-drawn machines, got out the scythes, and Grandpa Maxim got up out of bed, got his hammer out from the rubbish heap, and tied a strap to it so that it wouldn't slip out of his frail hands. When they were needed—just think!—they found the scythes and Grandpa Maxim turned out to be alive. They brought their rakes, pitchforks, wheelbarrows, to him; he fixed and balanced them, sharpened them, and replaced lost teeth. And he seemed to perk up and grow cheery over his work, even though he had just been dying, and he waved his arms and yelled and bossed. They obeyed with a smile and great pleasure—he had yelled at them just that way twenty years ago, and Pavel had assigned them to their jobs just that way, when he was the brigade leader, and he was serving as leader now—as though nothing had changed. And just like then, they managed without much technology: the tractors and cars were on the other side, and were constantly in use, and here they only had one trailer machine and two self-propelling combines, which waited for their turn on a knoll outside the village. But the car, because it was here, almost in punishment for being here, was used for errands: to run down for some cold kvas in the heat or take a woman who was late down to the cattle pasture. They didn't give it any serious work to do. Some whim made them roll out two old carts from the zavoznya and hitch up the horses to them in the morning and go out to the meadows with them, and the car, left all alone, afraid to dash out in front, tailed behind and seemed older and more out of place than the carts. But this really was a whim, a caprice, just a game, which everyone, however, joined, and joined readily.

Later, of course, they wouldn't be able to manage without technology, and they would have to bring over a tractor and maybe more than one when it was time to haul the haystacks to the water—they planned to put them right in the tractor sleds. But that would be later, later . . . for now they managed, as in the past, with scythes, horse-drawn rakes, and they wove brooms for the haycocks.

And they worked with joy, with passion, the likes of which they hadn't felt in a long time. They swung their scythes as though they wanted to prove who knew his work best, the work that would have to be left behind here with the soil forever. Through swinging, they fell on the mown grass and intoxicated and excited by the work, stirred by the feeling that this would never be repeated, they teased and egged on one another with old and new tricks, with what was and what wasn't. And the no-longer-young women grew young before one another's eyes, knowing that right after this summer, no, right after this month, which had miraculously taken them back ten years, they would have to grow ten years older. They made noise and played and fooled like children: drying off from their sweat, they jumped into the Angara with a squeal, and the ones who didn't want to jump were rounded up by the group and thrown in still in their clothes; and there was no shame among your own—following Klavka Strigunova's easy example, the women stripped down to bare breasts, stepping out in front of the men with a daring and dashing air, and even chased the men, whom they outnumbered, to throw them in the water. And then, tackling the work once more, coming to their senses, they would say: "Well, we women went completely mad now that we're finally back on Matyora. It probably doesn't even believe that it's us." But in the next break they happily went crazy again.

The old women crept up to the fields from the village and couldn't keep back the tears as they watched the people work. And they asked: "What more did you need? What did you want, what did you complain about when you lived this way? Well? Ah, too bad there's no one here to whip you!"

And the people agreed, pausing to think.

"No, there's no one."

Klavka Strigunova herself kept quiet and didn't start an argument.

They returned in the evening with a song. And the men, who used to scorn a sober song, joined in, too. Hearing the singing, everyone who had remained in the village came out and lined the street—children, old women, and also outsiders when there were any; lately there was a lot of traffic, what with motorboats zipping back and forth across the Angara. People came not only from the sovkhoz: people who had once lived here and hadn't forgotten Matyora came from cities and distant parts. It was bitter, but it was a holiday, when two people who hadn't seen each other in many years, who had lost and forgotten each other, met in the street and ran to each other, calling out and weeping till they were dry, till their legs gave out. Mothers and fathers, grandfathers and grandmothers, brought children, even brought along total strangers to show them the soil from which they had come and which would soon be invisible and lost. It seemed that half the world knew of Matyora's fate. Beyond the village, on the upper end, where there was higher ground, colored tents appeared, people walked all over the island—some wandered in the cemetery, some sat on the shore staring out sadly into the distance, some picked the first ripe berries in the meadows—and it was hard to tell at first glance whether they were strangers or not.

The mowers came back from work slowly, wearily, and with pomp. In front came the horses hitched to the carts, heads bobbing in unison, seeming to bow as they entered the village, with two or three people in the carts, and several people on horseback around them, and the rest singing and walking behind the carts. They sang one song or another, an old one, then a new one, but most often it was an old, farewell-reminiscing song, which it turned out the people knew and remembered, saving it within themselves just for this occasion. It was easier for the ones who sang it, but listening to them carrying the song like a joint and hopeless invocation was so painful and trying that it made your heart bleed.

July was in its second half, the weather was still clear and dry, the best for mowing. They mowed on one meadow and raked on the other, and sometimes the scythes clicked right next to the horse rakes that bounced jingling with large bent teeth; the mown hay was drying in the sun and wind in just a day. The women came out before lunch with small scythes to clear the spots that couldn't be driven through, damp and uneven, and in the afternoon they took up rakes. The men set the ricks, manning the pitchforks; the huge shaggy piles of hay floated behind their backs like living independent beings that moved on their own feet with monstrous pulled-back heads. By the end of the day they were high on work and sun and, more than anything else, the pungent, tangible smells of fresh-cut hay. The aroma reached the village and the people there breathed it in with pleasure. Ah, how it smells! . . . where else, in what country, could it smell that good!

And they began looking around anxiously: the work was coming along fast, too fast—they'd be heading back soon without having tasted the life on Matyora fully. Why couldn't it rain a little to drag things out, so that they could laze a bit and stay longer? The men began hammering the tractor sleds together—truly the end was drawing nigh, why hurry? The hay was keeping them from bidding farewell to Matyora, from seeing where they had spent their lives, what they once had, and what they had to give up. But they went out in the morning and the work caught them up, rushed them along, and they didn't have the strength to slow down—on the contrary, they hurried even more and hated themselves for doing so. This wasn't work you slowed down; they hadn't turned into spoiled workers yet.

In the evening before falling into bed they went out into the street and gathered either in the meadow or for a sit-around: the main thing was to be together, remembering that there weren't many such evenings left and forgetting their exhaustion. Matyora's fate made it grow still in those hours: the sunset blazed behind the Angara, brightly burning the windows that faced that way; the vast expanse of sky stretched out even more; the water gurgled gently on the near side. The day was fading and life all around faded joyously: sounds and colors blended into a pleasant sleepy rocking, which waned and ebbed; the human emotions in keeping with it also reduced themselves to a single trembling responsibility that stressed nothing. And it seemed that the houses moved closer together and swayed, humming in a single, interior voice; it seemed that the odor of old, long-dead smoke came from somewhere; it seemed that everything that was on the island, whether the work of man or of nature, had moved closer and stood in rows, peering over one another, asking a question in a single whisper. What you couldn't tell, you couldn't hear, but it seemed that this vague and inaudible question should be answered.

They spoke little and softly—and as though trying to answer a question someone had put to them. They didn't think about the life they'd lived and they didn't fear what was ahead; only this cataleptic taste, sensed in dreams and by the heart, seemed important, and only this was what they wanted to feel. But like the devil in church, Petrukha would show up with his squeezebox, unfortunately saved from the fire, and start playing "You Podgorna, you Podgorna . . ." ruining the mood—and they had to get up, had to think about tomorrow, and go to bed.

Petrukha returned to Matyora after a two-week absence in a very merry mood, wearing a new but extremely soiled light suit with red stitching and a leather cap with brown designs, and in that outfit he looked even more like a bum. The first time she saw him, Darya exclaimed:

"Well . . . and where did this ladybug crawl out from?"

"Excuse me for living!" Petrukha was upset—not by the "ladybug" but the "crawling." "I don't crawl, I travel by plane, you know, I fly."

He had picked up the "excuse me for living" somewhere on his latest travels, and he liked it so much, it seemed so beautiful and clever to him, that Petrukha couldn't imagine talking without it. He brought his mother fifteen rubles from the money he made on the burned property and when she dared mention that it seemed very little, he said:

"Excuse me for living! And what am I supposed to live on? I have to travel, look for a permanent habitation. Who'll take me there for free? You don't need any money here."

But he softened and gave her another ten in crumpled bills.

"Did you cash in a lot?" Katerina asked, seeing the worn, torn, colorful bills that seemed to always pass through hands like Petrukha's and never fall into good hands.

"That's my business. I don't interfere in your personal life and you don't interfere in mine. When I find a job I'll send for you, and we'll live together. And meanwhile—excuse me for living."

He hung around Matyora for two days without a liquor store and then dove into the new settlement, swimming there for three days without ever taking off his dirty suit, the pale color of which showed only in spots, the red thread completely invisible. Then he reappeared in Matyora, sleeping wherever he could, sometimes with Bogodul in the Kolchak shack, which was considered the height of homelessness and dereliction, but he kept up his airs, making up stories about being on official vacation, that someone soon would come for him in a cutter and carry him off, an indispensable man! He tied a rope to his old "podgorna" to sling over his shoulder and "torture" it, in his own words, day and night. Once he even came over with it to the meadow, settled down under a birch, and began plinking and plunking, but the hot, happy, and angry workers attacked him with such force that Petrukha, who usually had a quick reply, didn't even try to talk back—he retreated.

But one night after a long and strong spell of good weather, one sky managed to crawl beneath another and the rains came . .

12

ON THE FIRST DAY, when the rain was just gathering, sprinkling manna from heaven for the fields and gardens, company descened on Darya's house—Andrei, Pavel's youngest son. As a father it was Pavel's lot to have no daughters, and his wife, Sonya, gave birth four times to boys, but one died immediately upon opening his eyes, he couldn't stand the world and passed away, so there were three left. The eldest married a non-Russian and went to her homeland in the Caucasus Mountains to see what it was like and stayed on, seduced by the warm life; the middle one, with a knack for education, was in Irkutsk studying geology and was supposed to finish next year; and Andrei had gotten out of the army in the fall and had returned to Matyora, but he only stayed two weeks, amazed by the ever-increasing turmoil brought on by the move and left for the city, where he got a job in a factory. Now it turned out he quit the factory and was on his way to another job and had dropped by his home on the way. Andrei spent two days with his mother in the sovkhoz—Sonya worked in the accounting office and had stayed on in the settlement—seeing her first and then crossed the river to be with his father and grandmother. Pavel, in case someone missed it, had gotten what he wanted and was in charge of the mowing on Matyora and was living there permanently, visiting the sovkhoz the way he used to visit Matyora.

The rain was handy: they could sit and chat without rushing; they didn't dare take a break on their own, so God sent one along for them. Andrei, big and healthy-looking next to his father, not sickened and worn out by his work, was a fellow who had been done some good by the army—he went in stoop-shouldered and gawky and came back hale and hearty, back straight and head held high. Andrei impatiently whizzed back and forth between the house and yard while his grandmother set the table, stamping loudly on the porch, removing damp earth and sticky dust that hadn't had time to turn to mud from his shoes, remembering and asking about the villagers, who was where, and for lack of anything better to do, gently teased Darya:

"Well, Granny, you'll be evacuating soon too?"

"I'll be ekcuating, ekcuating soon," she replied docilely, calmly, without so much as a sigh.

"You probably don't want to leave here, do you?"

"How could I want to? Left in our own place we old women would creep around some more, but now they'll pull us off and we'll all die."

"Who's going to let you die, I'd like to know?"

"We won't ask for permission for that. That's up to us," Darya said, falling into a teasing mood herself. "Nobody's thought of appointing officials to give the order for that yet. So people die any which way without following a precise order."

"Don't get mad, Granny. Are you hurt? I was just talking."

"Why should I be mad at you?"

"Then who are you mad at?"

"No one. Myself. You should be mad at me for beating your rear with stinging nettles so that you would sit still. I see I didn't beat you enough, you didn't sit still, and ran off from here . . ."

Andrei laughed.

"When you're young, Granny, you have to see everything and go everywhere. What's the good of it if you spent your whole life here in one place? You can't give in to fate, you have to rule it."

"Go rule . . . I'd like to see you years from now with your rule. No, fellow, you won't get around the whole wide world. Even if you fly on wings. Don't even dream about it. You think just because you're born a man you can do anything? Oh, Andrei, don't think that. You'll live a bit more and you'll understand . . ."

"Ah, Granny, I have to disagree with you here. You think that way because of Matyora, because you never poked your nose beyond Matyora. You haven't seen anything. Man can do so much, so much that you can't even say it all. He had such power in his hands now—oh, boy! He can do whatever he wants."

"That he'll do," Darya agreed.

"So then what are you saying?"

"That's what I'm saying . . . He'll crumple and he'll flood . . . And death will come and he'll die. Don't you argue with me, Andrushka. I've seen little, but I've lived long. What I have seen I've looked at for a long time, not like you, passing by. While Matyora stood, there was no reason for me to rush. And I saw that people are little. No matter how they present themselves, they're little. I pity them. And the reason you don't pity yourself is because you're young. Strength boils within you and you think that you're strong and can do anything. No, fellow. I haven't met a person yet who shouldn't be pitied. Even if he's Solomon. From distance you might think: well, this one fears nothing, he could scare the devil . . . he's got honors . . . But look closer: he's like the rest, no better. Do you want to get out of your human skin? Ah, no, Andrushka, you can't. It's never happened. You'll just get scraped and wounded for nothing. And you won't do the deed. While you struggle to get out, death will come, it won't let you go. People have forgotten their place under God—and I'll tell you why. We are no better than those who lived before us. And there's no use in us taking on so much. Put no more in the cart than the mare can haul, or you won't have anything to haul with. God hasn't forgotten our place, no. He sees: man is full of pride. The prouder you are the worse it is for you. That melancholic who chopped off the branch from under himself also had a high opinion of himself. And he fell hard and hurt his kidneys—and he fell on the ground, not the sky. You can't get away from the earth. Of course you've been given great power nowadays. Very big! . . . You can see it from here, from Matyora. Just watch that it doesn't conquer you, that power. It's big and you're all as small as you were before."

They sat at the table a long time: father and son drank a bottle of vodka that Andrei had brought, and they didn't get drunk in the least, only Andrei seemed even younger in the face and Pavel seemed older. Darya looked at the two of them side by side across the table from her and thought: "There it is, one thread with knots. It seemed that there were so many years between knots . . . where are they? My knot is going to be stretched out and smoothed over, they'll let the smooth end go so that it'll be invisible . . . so that they can tie a new one on the other end. Where will the string be pulled now? What will happen? Why do I care so much about finding out?"

The rain outside grew stronger and beat down, rivulets appeared on the windows. The earth grew dark; large, iciclelike drops fell from the roofs; foaming, the Angara stood still in the windows. And the smell of the samovar seemed stronger and cozier at the table, the tea that they were all drinking by then appeared more fragrant, and the family conversation seemed more important and significant.

"Weren't you making enough?" Pavel asked, trying to find out why Andrei had quit his job at the factory.

"Enough for myself." Andrei shrugged. He was trying to talk to his father on equal footing, but he wasn't used to equality and kept stumbling, slipping from the right tone, raising his voice or losing it. "Of course it was enough for me. That's not the point. It was boring. The new place is doing construction that's famous the world over. You turn on the radio in the morning—not a single morning goes by that they don't talk about it. They give the weather especially for it and concerts. And the factory . . . there's plenty like them. There's one in every city."

"They don't give the weather for the factory?"

"I knew you'd say that," Andrei replied. "They don't need to give the report for the factory, they give it for the city. That's not the point. The factory won't go anywhere, but they'll finish the construction—and I'll be sorry I missed it. I want to take part in things while I'm still young . . . so that I'll have things to remember . . ."

Andrei frowned, unhappy with his answer: he crumpled it, shortened it, to keep from making grand pronouncements, which he knew his father disliked. Pavel waited in silence and that unclear, creeping silence made Andrei angry.

"These aren't times when you can sit in one place," he said, either arguing or justifying. "Now, you wanted to sit still, but they're moving you, making you move. These are lively times . . . everything is in motion, as they say; I want my work to be visible, for it to stand forever, and how can I do that in a factory? Weeks go by that I don't get out of the site . . . and that's with the car. I move iron beams from to place to place, from one shop to another, like an ant, circling around. Any old man could do that. The plant is for middle-aged people, family men, so that they can retire from there. I want to be with young people, like me, where everything is different . . . new. When they finish the hydroelectric power plant, it'll stand for a thousand years."

"Well, you're a little late," Pavel said, nodding thoughtfully. "They managed to finish the power plant without you, if the flooding's about to be started."

"Ah! there's still plenty of work left! Enough for me. The most interesting part starts now—"

Darya listened warily.

"Wait a minute, you mean—are you planning to go work over

where they're raising the Angara?" She had only now understood.

"Yes, Granny."

"Oh-oh, if that's not the—," she began and didn't finish, the confusion making her forget what to say, and she stared at Andrei with intense incomprehension.

"Why, Granny?"

"Why couldn't you find some other job?"

"Why another one? I want to work there. They'd flood Matyora either way, Granny, with me or without me. I have nothing to do with it. They need electricity, Granny, electricity," Andrei explained, his head low on his strong neck and his voice raised, as if addressing a child. "Our Matyora will go for electricity; it'll also help people."

"And what was it doing before, hurting them by being here?" Darya replied softly, almost to herself, without any desire to enter an argument that had been decided without them and stopped, withdrawn, listening without great interest to what they were saying, actually watching how they spoke, how their faces changed in the course of the conversation, whether words came easily or not, what voice they turned into. But what she had just learned would not give her peace and forgetting herself, she said it again, not even asking, but confirming for herself—she just couldn't accept it. "So that means you're going to let loose the water on us? . . . Well, well . . . just look at what's going on!"

"Why do you say 'me'?" Andrei laughed. "Everything's ready to go over there without me. Don't you blame sins on me that aren't mine, Granny."

"I wish you wouldn't go there . . ."

"You know," Pavel carefully picked up his mother's thought. "Why don't you stay here. We need drivers. You'll have a new car. There's more work here than your whole plant could do."

He said it and laughed without hope, looking down: he shouldn't have brought it up—he wouldn't stay. And sure enough, after a silence, as though giving it thought, Andrei shook his head:

"No. I leave the city and come here to you?"

Pavel could have been incensed: what right did Andrei have, born here, raised and turned into a man here, to talk that way about his homeland, but Pavel didn't become incensed. He had brought up the subject to hear what his son would say, what he had become in the last years of independent life away from home, what he lived by and what principles guided him. And no matter what Andrei might have answered, everything would be taken calmly and thoughtfully. And really, why not look for reason in his words—he was an adult after all and not a bad person, and he was the one who would soon replace his father on this earth—no, better say in the world, not on the earth. He had left the soil and it looked like he would never return. And if Pavel went on talking, it wasn't to convince his son, but to find out his answers.

"You're wrong, you know. Things aren't so bad here. It's not this old village where we're sitting now." Pavel glanced over at his mother, afraid of hurting her feelings unintentionally; he didn't have any love for the new sovkhoz settlement, but what was true was true. "It'll be just like the city there, things are moving that way. You were there, you saw what was going on."

"I did. It's terrific, of course. But still, it's boring."

"What kind of excitement do you need?"

"I told you . . ." Andrei grimaced at the thought of repeating what he hadn't been able to put well in the first place, something that he didn't know how to express, that made his head spin and therefore was hard to state. "Later I'll have a family and then, maybe, I will move here. But while I'm young, unmarried, I want to go to the frontier, as they call it . . . I don't want to miss it. All the young people are there."

"Is it a war: the frontier?" Pavel asked, not missing the point.

"The frontier . . . I don't know how to put it. People call it that. You know, the hottest spot, the most necessary construction project. All attention is there now. People travel to work there from really far away, to participate, and I'm right nearby and—I miss it. It's almost embarrassing . . . as though I'm hiding. Then later maybe I'll be sorry the rest of my life. That power plant must really be very important, they write about it so much. So much attention . . . How am I worse than anyone else?"

"When they finish—there'll be no more attention. Then what? Will you look for another place that's in the center of attention? If you get used to being on display, you'll get spoiled, one sun won't seem enough. So, do you think you'll be there long, in the center of attention?"

"I'll see when I get there." And sensing that that wasn't an adequate reply, he talked faster and more confidently, with a new, sad, and slightly insulted intonation. "Why don't you understand? Granny doesn't understand, but she's old, I can see that. But you?" Andrei stumbled, not daring to say "father" but unwilling to return to the former "papa," which seemed childish to him now. "Why don't you understand? You work with machinery, you know the times are different now. You can't run a farm on foot, as they say. You won't get far. Unless you hang around Matyora . . . What's the good of Matyora? And they're building the power plant . . . they must have thought things out, what's what, they're doing it not off the tops of their heads. That means that they really need it now, right now, not yesterday, not the day before yesterday. That means it's the most important thing now. And that's where I want to be, where it's the most important. You seem to think only of yourselves, and you think with your memories, you have lots of memories, but over there they think about everyone at once. It's too bad about Matyora, and I'm sorry too, it's our homeland . . . but there's no other way. In any case it wouldn't have lasted long the way it is, this old, I mean. It would have to change, be rebuilt for a new life anyway. Even people don't live more than a hundred years, others are born to take their place. Why can't you see that?"

Pavel looked at his son carefully and in surprise, as though only now realizing that there was a truly grown-up and completely rational man before him, but a man from the next, future generation, not his own.

"Why don't we understand?" he said thoughtfully and not right away. "We understand a bit. I'm not talking about whether or not the power plant is necessary. There's no question about that. I'm just saying that someone has to work here too."

"So you go ahead and work. Work is sort of divided by age too.

The new construction, where it's hardest—that's the place for youth. Where it's easier—the rest work there ..."

"Why do you think it's easier here?"

Addressing no one, looking at no one, Darya said: "In the olden days, here's what they said . . . A mother that spoils one child and doesn't want the other is a bad mother."

"What are you talking about, Granny?" Andrei laughed merrily, happy that she had stirred and interrupted the disagreeable and somehow insincere, embarrassing conversation between father and son—it was as if they had been talking about women. When there's a thirty-year difference and one has hot blood coursing through his veins and the other's blood is barely warm, how can they agree?

"Nothing," Darya said, clamping her thin, sharp lips together.

"The rain seems to have stopped," Andrei said, looking out the window; he felt he had to say something to dissipate the tension and misunderstanding.

They looked at the rain—how it struck the ground, collecting in puddles in the hard ruts; how it dripped in rushing streams, rather than drops, from the sheds; they listened to the uneven, pattering gurgling, which found resonance as a pleasant and true peace in the soul; and they felt that they could breathe easier and fresher, that the air, renewed by the pure smells of heaven brought down by the water and the rich smells of the earth brought up by the rain, had penetrated the house. And they believed that they had sat too long at the table and that their talk had divided them who were related in the closest way, and that a minute's empty watching of the rain had brought them back together. But getting up, Pavel asked his son a question that he should have brought up long before.

"When are you leaving?"

"I'll stay here a while," Andrei shrugged, smiling for no reason, showing that he had no firm date in mind. "What's the rush?"

"If you're staying, maybe you could help me mow some hay?" the father suddenly suggested. The idea had just come to him that second and sprang from his lips; he hadn't had time to think it through to see if it should be said and if he was prepared for what he was urging his son to do.

Andrei agreed heartily.

"Let's. What else is there for me to do here? Of course I'll help."

"Good," Pavel said, happy to have reached a decision. "Together we'll mow enough for the cow, we'll be able to keep her all winter. While you're here, it won't take long. We were getting panicked, we didn't know what to do. I couldn't manage alone . . . I'm working. Your mother's over there. And Granny isn't much help."

"Three farts away from death," Darya added.

But that light and meaninglessness mention of death reminded her of what had been torturing her almost without stop all the time recently, and raising herself up, stretching herself, Darya pleaded in a taut voice: "The graves, Pavel. You promised. When will there be time later? . . . You could do it at the same time . . ."

"Aha," Pavel remembered. "We should move the graves. She's been asking me to do it for a long time."

Andrei was surprised and waited silently, eyebrows arched quizzically, to see if they were serious, but he agreed to help with the graves as well.

13

THE RAIN SOMETIMES GREW STILL, turning into a hazy, dustlike drizzle that hung in the saturated air, and then came back lashing the earth with renewed strength. Everything was soaked, swollen, soggy, and no longer absorbed water, filled to the brim; the water spilled over and spread and spread . . . There was standing water in the wheat fields. The street, rutted by wagons and cars, looked like a river with rows of houses on its banks; you could walk along the length of these rows but to get across the river you needed help, you had to maneuver and plan. For several days in a row there was an uncanny stillness in the air. High above the earth the heavy, swollen sky still had the strength to move, seeming to push aside the used-up, rainless clouds, but below there wasn't even a hint of a breeze and the motionless air knew only rain. The tree branches drooped, huge white drops resembling snow fell from them; the unmown grasses fell, hiding their sharp points and spreading themselves into flat waves—which the rain struck now harder, now weaker, but with steady noise. After the first three days the Angara started rising, its merry mumbling stopped, both at the promontory and along the spit; jetsam came downstream, and the water that rushed by was noticeably fuller and foamy—the foam was pushed out to the shores, to the flooded quiet water, but gathering in white ragged rolls made its way out to the fast-flowing water in sneaky, indirect circles, rushing head-long, showing off.

They lit the ovens to take off the dampness; the smoke rose in the morning above the houses as in winter—jointly and seriously, pushing through the thick air. Nastasya's chimney smoked, too, for Katerina had moved there as soon as Darya's grandson had come to visit. It looked as though she was glad for an excuse to move there because she could arrange for a dry corner for Petrukha, who was still hanging around the village without care or duty, like a dandelion: whichever way the wind blew, he went. Hearing that Andrei was going to the power plant, Petrukha showed up and asked a lot of questions about the conditions: what the pay was, how they lived, what the "grease" was—by "grease" he meant profit.

"I need a real apartment and not a dump," he said, showing off, always overdoing it as usual. "I have my mother, I want to create a spiritual life for her. She's had enough wear and tear. Of course, she's too old for a komsomol, and you say there's one there . . . But she might come in handy, very handy. She can tell about her old, unenlightened life." Petrukha relished saying the word *life* stretching it out.

Andrei couldn't tell him much about the construction because he only knew what he read in the papers and what he heard from secondhand stories, but Petrukha decided to go with him. He started coming over every day to talk about it, picturing himself there as a long-time and needed worker, and spread the word around the village that he had already gotten a job there and was practically receiving a salary. Knowing Petrukha, people asked him with some malice: "Do they send the paychecks here?"

"How could they? We don't have a post office, now, do we?" He was amazed at how silly people were. "They would be sending it, but I told them the situation and they're holding them for me. Later, when this spell of bad weather ends, I'll go up there and get it all in a lump sum."

"I guess they won't even take taxes from you since you haven't been working?"

"What?!" Petrukha stood for complete justice. "If that's the way it worked, I'd have to sign up for the orphanage because I don't have kids. You say I haven't been working. So what if I haven't? They're paying me so that I don't go work anywhere else. They want to keep me for themselves. And according to the law I can't go anywhere else. The law is sneaky. Excuse me for living, but you can't fool with the law."

"What a liar! What a liar!" people would exclaim, amazed and appreciative, right to Petrukha's face, and pleased that they had nothing else to say, he would answer with overweening confidence: "You have to understand these things . . ."

In those days unsuited for work, through boredom and lack of something to do, and more likely from some vague throat-grabbing anxiety, people got together frequently, talking over many things, but the talks were anxious too, viscous, with long periods of silence. Either it was the weather, or it was the realization: the mowing with its fast and furious work, and the singing, and the get-togethers in the evening, and the entire living here in their native village with almost the whole kolkhoz, like a gift, or rather something stolen for a farewell—it was all a delusion to which their weak human hearts had succumbed. And the truth was that you had to move, you had to willy-nilly start your life over there and not seek and try to figure out how you had lived here. If they had lived without knowing how they had lived, then why find out as they left, leaving nothing but a blank spot behind them? The truth wasn't in what you feel in the work, the songs, the thankful tears that come when the sun sets and the light cools and your soul is filled with confusion and love and the desire for greater love, which comes so rarely—the truth was in taking care of the haystacks. That's what they were there for. But doubts crept in: that might be true, but there was more. They would harvest and take away the hay, and the cows would eat the last blade by spring, but the songs after work when it seemed that it wasn't them singing, not people but their very souls uniting into one— they believed so deeply and with holy fervor in the simple lyrics and raised their voices so strong and united—that sweet and troubling awe in the evening before the beauty and horror of the coming night, when you no longer remember who you are and where you are, when it seems that you're gliding silently and smoothly above the earth, barely moving your wings and following a blessed path revealed to you, acutely aware of everything that floats below; that quiet profound ache that appears from nowhere, the ache that comes when you realize that you didn't even know yourself until this very minute, didn't know that you were more than what you carry within you, that you were also what surrounds you, the ache that isn't always noticed and is sometimes more terrible to lose than an arm or a leg—all this would be remembered for a long time and remain in their souls as an unsetting light and joy. Perhaps that was the only constant, the only thing that could be passed, like the Holy Spirit, from person to person, from father to children, and from children to grandchildren, exciting and protecting them, guiding and purifying them, eventually bringing them to the reason for which generations of humans had lived. What would it be? A quiet universal song over an empty, renewed earth at dawn or something else? No, it wouldn't be an empty earth. Let there be a child, stumbling on bare feet, crying, looking up into the sky in fear and enchantment: where are they singing—and let him fall, and sleep under the singing that descends low over him and the ever-brighter evening sunset—a rebirth for you, too, man, begin all over again, you won't go far without this.

So why shouldn't they fall into prayer at the end of the life that had existed on Matyora for so many many years and look around with surprised and saddened eyes. It had been. And now it's gone. Death seems terrible, but it sows the most kind and useful harvest in the souls of the living and from the seed of mystery and decay develops the seed of life and understanding. Look, think, and have ceremonies and rites! Man is not alone, there are many countrymen in his skin, like men in a boat rowing from shore to shore, and the true person appears perhaps only in moments of parting and torment—here he is, remember him.

But why the anxiety and trouble—was it only from the extended cool weather, the enforced indolence when there was more work than they could do, or was it caused by something else? Go figure it out. Here stands the land that seems eternal, but now it turns out it was just a figment—the land would be no more. The air was filled with the scent of the herbs, the scent of the forest, separate scents for leaves and for needles, every bush had its own scent; the lumber of the houses, the cattle—it smelled of life, of the manure pile behind the barn, of cucumber soup, of old charcoal from the smithy; the rain had washed up sharp smells from everything, liberating everything. Why would all this disappear from this land while they were still alive—not before and not after? Was there more to it? Was this good? How will they find comfort, in what? And when talk turned to it, and talk in those days went everywhere, Darya as usual waved it off with a determined and hopeless gesture.

"Aah, I'm not sorry about anything anymore . . ."

The weather tried to clear up in the morning, the clouds brightened and danced, there was a breath of different, clean air, and it seemed that the sun would dive through the clouds and the people believed in the possibility and started moving too, gathering at Pavel's house to find out if there would be work. And while they were there, it grew dark once more and started pouring. They didn't feel like leaving, so they sat and rehashed the same old talk. Darya boiled water in the samovar, but they didn't want tea, they were still wet from the tea they had had at home. Only Katerina took a glass and set it on her lap. On the bench by the door Afanasy Koshkin, or Kotkin, as you prefer, leaned against

the door and raised and embraced one knee. Petrukha used both
his names together and ran around the village shouting "Kot-and-
Koshkin, hey, Kot-and-Koshkin!" Afanasy had been a Koshkin all
his life, but when they were moving to the sovkhoz the whole
family changed their name to Kotkin: if things were going to be
new, then everything should be new; beautiful, then everything
should be beautiful. They teased Afanasy and he laughed it off
good-naturedly and explained.

"What do I care! Koshkin, Kotkin, it's all the same to me. I
went around as Koshkin for sixty years and then some, and no one
spat in my face. It's the kids. The daughters-in-law, the bitches,
made trouble. Especially Galka. What do they care, it's not their
own name anyway; it's like a head scarf—wear one today and
another one tomorrow. They nagged; do it, do it. And then they
got me drunk . . . and I thought: 'They say Koshkin is like there's
a woman over you, but Kotkin it's like you're over a woman.'
Look what the bitches used on me . . . I thought about it and
said: 'Give me another pint and you can do it.' They hustled me
so fast, on all fours, it was unbelievable."

"So you sold your name for a pint?"

"Looks that way. Galka went to the district center and filled
out the documents. And I did it myself. I crossed the letter. Who's
going to know if it's *sh* or *t*? If I sign my name I'm careful to
scribble that letter so no one can tell. I was Koshkin and I'm
still Koshkin .They can do what they want."

Vera Nosaryova, Darya's neighbor from below, sat next to him.
Vera had tried to get up and go home several times, not even
home but to work—Vera would run over to her field and mow
some hay quietly for herself—but she didn't want to leave the
warmth and company, and the rain had gotten worse and
sounded like a tidal wave. Klavka Strigunova twisted and turned
on the cot as though on pins and needles—she would have run off
long ago, but the rain kept her put. Out of boredom, Klavka took
up with Andrei, asking him about city men and what kind of
women they preferred—plump or scrawny? Andrei, embarrassed,
shrugged. It got dark in the middle of the day, the rain was

whipping around like a madman, and the merry talk sagged and turned low key, slowly moving back to the same old thing—to Matyora, its fate, and the fate of its inhabitants. It was then that Darya said: "Aah, I'm not sorry about anything anymore . . ."

"I'm sorry, how can you not be sorry . . ." Afanasy began and stopped.

"Oh, you old farts, is there no end to you!" Klavka attacked, jumping into the conversation and letting Andrei off the hook. "You've really found something to weep over! And you weep and weep. Your Matyora stinks through and through of manure, you know that? There's no air left. What happiness have you found here? A new life has come everywhere, but you, you're like dung beetles clutching the old, looking for some sweetness in it. You're just fooling yourselves. It's more than time to pluck out your Matyora and send it down the Angara."

Afanasy was the first to reply, thoughtfully containing his voice as though he was answering his own doubts and not Klava.

"Whether you like the new or the old, you still can't live without bread—"

"So are we sitting without bread? We're even giving pigs pure grain!"

"For now we have bread—"

"What a loudmouth you are, Klavka!" Darya came in, suddenly aware of the conversation. "What a loudmouth! Where did you come from? We didn't have gals like you on Matyora before."

"Now you do."

"I see that, I'm not blind. How come you haven't gotten together with Katerina's Petrukha? Don't listen, Katerina, I'm not talking to you. How could you be living apart so long? He's just like you. Two shoes make a pair."

"I need him like a dog needs a fifth leg," Klavka sassed.

"And that's how much he needs you," Katerina butted in.

"What do you have to be sorry about here, to weep over?" Darya attacked. She sat alone at the table, as though in the chairman's seat, and shook with injury and excitement, pecking it looked like, her faded blue kerchief creeping down on her forehead. "Your legs have been dancing a long time: where to now? Matyora is like the plague for you . . . You didn't take root here and you won't take root anywhere, you'll never be sorry about anything. That's what you are . . . fruitless seeds!"

Klavka, having upset the old people, began arguing lightly, with a smile.

"Auntie Darya, you're the ones who are like that. You're inhaling incense and you want people to live like you. But life is moving on, why can't you see that? I'm sick and tired of your stinking Matyora, the settlement on the shore suits me fine, but for your Andrei who's younger than me, the settlement isn't enough. He wants the city. Right, Andrei? Tell me, are you sorry at all about this village?"

Andrei muttered.

"Come on, come on, say it," Klavka insisted.

"Yes," Andrei said.

"What for?'"

"I lived eighteen years here. I was born here."

"You sissy! What do you need your childhood for now that you're out of it? You're grown out of it. Look how tall you are! And you've outgrown Matyora. I'd like to see someone make you stay here! You're just saying that because you're afraid of your grandmother. You feel sorry about your grandmother, not about Matyora."

"Why?"

"Because, that's why. You can't fool me. And your grandmother feels sorry for herself. She won't get any younger, and so she's mad, she's afraid to go where there's life. Don't be mad, Auntie Darya, I'm telling the truth . . . You don't like hiding it either."

But Darya had no intention of being mad.

"I've thought about that too, girl," she admitted, nodding to confirm that yes, she had thought about it, and poured herself some tea. "Sometimes you get to thinking and you think about everything. Well, all right, I think, say that I am like that. But what about you? Why are you behaving like this? Does this land belong to you alone? We're all here today and gone tomorrow.

We're all like migratory birds. This land belongs to everyone—those who were here before us and those who will come after. We're only on it for a tiny time. Why are you treating it like that mare that plowed for seven brothers—you, like one of the brothers, throw the bridle on it and sell it to a gypsy for twenty rubles. It's not yours. And we were given Matyora only to take care of . . . to treat it well and be fed by it. And what have you done with it? Your elders entrusted you with it so that you would spend your life on it and pass it on to the younger ones. And they'll come asking for it. You're not afraid of your elders—but the younger ones will come asking. What are you birthing children for? Just try fooling around like this and you'll see. We only live once, but who are we?"

"Man is king of nature," Andrei prompted.

"Yes, yes, king. Just reign a bit and you'll be sorry."

And they fell silent. The downpour eased up and a fine drizzle fell along with the last drops that were being shaken off. The darkness that had fallen like night, as though someone had put a lid on Matyora's sky, was dissipating—it was gray and washed out, the sky was just as gray and washed out, and the eye could make nothing out but watery depths in it. And it was gray and foggy in the house, where they all sat in silence for a moment, like stones.

"Well, well, well, it's time to go to hell," Afanasy broke the spell with the ditty and rose. "Pour me some tea, Darya. Our work has floated away today, we might as well sit around and drink tea."

Tunguska came. Whenever people congregated, she always dragged herself over, silently sitting down, silently taking out her pipe from inside her shirt, and smacking her lips, puffing on it. And if you don't touch her, she won't say a word the whole day, and perhaps she doesn't even hear what is being talked about, always in a deep and sleepy daze, and if you got through to her and asked what she was thinking about, she would beat her fist against her chest and say: "Me Tunguska."

"You're an Evenka," they tried to teach her at first. "There were Tungus under the tsar, now they're Evenki."

"Me Tunguska," she would insist. "You know Tunguska River. Me. Evenka—uh-uh." And she would wave her hand vaguely into the distance.

And that's how they knew and called her: Tunguska. She wasn't a local on Matyora, but no longer a stranger, either, since she was spending her second summer here. Sometimes, when she was stirred to talk, Tunguska would explain, more by gesture than by word, that this was her land, that the Tungus came here in deep antiquity—and that was probably so. But now the old woman had moved here for a different reason. The sovkhoz was planning to start an animal farm, but for now all they had was the director—and that was Tunguska's daughter. Last spring, when they had arrived, they were still building houses in the new settlement, there weren't enough apartments, and someone suggested that the daughter bring her mother to Matyora, where houses were becoming available. And Tunguska stayed. She sits at the shore and spends the whole day staring out into the distance, north. She didn't bother much with her garden—just a row or two, and she let them go to seed—either she didn't know how or she didn't want to, wasn't used to it. What she lived on, no one knew: her daughter didn't visit very often from the settlement. She joined the others for tea, but no one could remember her ever taking a single crust of bread. But she lived on, managing somehow and sensing where people were gathering and setting off to join them right away. She was late today, she usually arrived earlier.

Tunguska went into the front corner and settled near Katerina's feet on the floor. They had gotten used to that by now—that she sat on the floor and you couldn't lift her by force into a chair. The old men would sometimes settle down on the floor to smoke, too—and that's where it came from, that habit: from the ancient Tungus blood.

"You're here?" Afanasy asked, looking up from his tea.

Tunguska nodded.

"Now here's a person who's living," Afanasy noted philosophically. "She lives on.'"

"She's kind, let her live," Vera Nosaryova said with a smile.

"Of course, let her. Are you going to the sovkhoz?" he called to Tunguska, yelling as though she were deaf.

She nodded, still not drowsy, and this time the pipe was in her mouth.

"See, she's planning to move. But it will be really bad for her there."

"You keep harping on the sovkhoz," Klavka started in again. "Like a cataract in my eye. But if they were to chase you off the sovkhoz tomorrow, you'd sing a different song. People are so spoiled: whatever they take away you want back, even though you don't need it, and they're giving you something a hundred times better, but no, you're picky: this is bad and that's no good. Take what they give you, they won't offer anything bad. Look how happy other people are. What's wrong with life there? Aunt Darya aside," she waved her hand in the old woman's direction, "you can expect about as much from her as from summer now. But what more do you want?"

Vera Nosaryova, unusually quiet, tired and lost without her work, confused by the conversation, sighed deeply.

"If they'd only let us keep a cow . . . and let us mow . . . otherwise what? It's a different life, and unaccustomed one, but we'll get accustomed. There's a school there, up to the tenth grade, they say. And here it's just torture for the kids with a four-year school. What would I do with Irka now? But there she'll be in school and with me. I don't have to send her away from home." Vera looked up guiltily at Darya and tried to bring things together in a dream that she must have had more than once: "If only they could bring the settlement here on Matyora . . ."

"Is that all?! No, I don't agree with that," Klavka shouted. "Then we're back stuck in the middle of the Angara, between the devil's horns! Can't go anywhere, can't drive anywhere—like a prison."

"We'll become accustomed," Afanasy said, finding the word he wanted his own way, in his own time. "Of course, we'll get accustomed. In a year or two . . . Klavka was right before. In a year or two if we had to move, we'd be sorry to leave the settlement. Our work would be in it. It's our work that relates us to the soil. You don't mind leaving here, Klavka, because you weren't very attached here. Don't jump on me, don't jump on me," he stopped her, "we know all about it. While your mother was alive she raised your kids. You just hopped around from store to store and the reading rooms—"

"I'm literate—"

"I'm not saying anything against it. I'm talking about the soil. And over there it'll take a lot of work to make the soil good. Inside everything's perfect, everything's done. You don't have to ever go outside. But if you do go out and look around—oh, so much work, you don't even know where to begin. If I could get hold of that commission that picked out the land, I'd rub their noses in it . . . Ah, their mothers are so-and-sos . . ."

"Maybe that's why they're sending you there, so that you can put in more work and attach yourself more firmly."

"Maybe so. We'll manage. Turn the wheel. Be patient, be clever. We'll lose some, win some. As long as he has strength and people don't interfere, the peasant can get out of any mess. Aren't I right, Pavel? Why are you quiet?"

Pavel was smoking, listening, and getting more and more lost, not understanding and hating himself: when his mother spoke, he agreed with her; now Afanasy spoke, and he agreed with him, not finding anything to argue with. What is this? Pavel asked himself. Where's my own head? Do I have one? Or is it full of sand that soaks in whatever's said without distinction? And where's the truth, why is it stretched out so far and wide that you can't find the beginning or end? There has to be a single, root truth, doesn't there? Why can't I find it?

But he had a feeling and had secretly agreed with it a long time ago, and if he hadn't turned it into a firm conviction that would do away with any doubts it was only because of the pain of parting with Matyora and the bitterness and the bustle of moving —he felt that the words of Klavka, even though it should have been someone far wiser than she to say them, and that Andrei's reasoning that day when they met and sat around the table, did contain today's truth, which could in no way be avoided. And the young seemed to understand it better. Well, that's what they were young for, they had longer to live. And everyone who had to live had better understand that truth. Andrei was right—and you had to agree with him whether you wanted to or not—you can't keep up with today's life on shank's mare and stuck in old Matyora at that.

"Right," Pavel confirmed.

"What do you think, will we get bread or not from that land?" Afanasy asked.

"We have to. Science will help. And if we don't, we'll feed pigs or raise chickens. There's that . . . specialization everywhere now."

"So what will do with my combine—tickle chickens?"

The women perked up.

"They'll make an adjustment and you will. What's wrong with that?"

"You've swallowed enough dust, you're all black from it."

"The feathers will fly and clean you up."

Darya slipped away from the conversation, heard and saw no one, and concentrated totally on one thing only, sipping tea from the saucer she held in her hands and, as usual, nodding quickly and agreeably.

"Well, women," Afanasy directed, "let's bring the meeting to a close. We've sat too long. Darya is finishing up the samovar. What resolution shall we pass? To move or not?"

"It's been decided without us."

"Let's move! There on big land we'll have bigger attention on us."

"Just shake out all the fleas and roaches!"

"How about you, Tunguska? Shall we move?"

Tunguska took the pipe from her mouth, licked her lips, and raised her cloudy eyes, which had been wandering somewhere at the voice, and nodded.

"You get ready, too, Darya. We won't go without you."

But Darya didn't reply.

"Look," Vera Nosaryova suddenly said. "The rain seems to have quieted down. We've been sitting too long . . . Sift water and all you'll have is water. I'm off. Call me, Pavel, if something happens. But don't call me today. Today I'm off . . ."

Rain, rain . . . But its end was in sight, the intervals from rainfall to rainfall were getting longer, a high wind began blowing and with an effort and a heave-ho it moved the wetness stuck to the sky and dragged it north. Only passing clouds, floating by, threw down their remaining rains. And then they stopped and the weak sunlight, bent into many angles, fell again without the sun; but then it got cloudy again and the rain came down—out of meanness and spite, so as not to give people hope that it would ever finally clear up. And people, unwilling to give in, grew angry and cursed the sky and themselves for living under it.

On such an unsteady day, still rocky—neither rain nor good weather, neither work nor rest—Vorontsov came over with a representative from the district capital responsible for clearing the land to be flooded. The people were called together in a dirty camp building with half its windows knocked out, the former kolkhoz office. There were no benches and the people had to stand, and there was no table for the visitors to sit behind, so they created a distance of three paces or so between them and the people and stood by the far wall. Vorontsov spoke first—about how they had to finish the mowing with an extra effort and the people didn't interrupt but looked at him as though he had fallen from the moon: what was he talking about, there was rain outside the window. And sure enough, the rain poured again, pattering on the roof, but Vorontsov, wrapped in a poncho, heard and saw nothing, and went on with his speech. The representative from the capital, by name of Pesenny—a simple-looking man with a tan, high-cheeked face, like all the locals, and with blue childlike eyes—when Vorontsov introduced him, began a long speech, harking back to Adam, but saw that the people were stepping from foot to foot and huddling from the cold and damp and draft and stopped short. After a short silence he said why he was here: Matyora had to be cleared of everything that stood and grew on it by mid-September. On the twentieth of the month a government commission would be arriving for the ceremonies opening the reservoir floor.

"But we won't have time to dig up the potatoes. We won't harvest all the wheat. If the weather keeps up . . ." someone countered timidly.

Pesenny spread his hands; Vorontsov answered.

"I don't care about private potatoes, you can forget about it for all I care. But the sovkhoz harvest must be done. And it will be. If necessary, additional manpower will come from the city."

But the people, exhausted by the weather, accepted the announcement of the date of the destruction of their native village rather calmly and simply. They couldn't believe that anything would ever burn now that the place was waterlogged. And the middle of September looked as far off as the middle of December. They merely noted that they'd have to start on the potatoes earlier this year. And their thoughts went off on a tangent: all right, we'll dig them up, but how do we get them over, and where do we store them? Where do we get so many sacks? They usually dug up seventy or eighty bags, and this summer they planted no less than usual. Here it was so easy: if you had to you could drag the entire harvest in one sack—for the garden was right there—but how to get it all the way over there? And so they thought: what to do, how to go about it.

They also remembered from the meeting that Vorontsov instructed them not to wait for the final day, but to gradually to burn off things that weren't desperately needed and used Petrukha as an example, a man who cleared off his territory first. Petrukha had never been praised in his life and he beamed and looked around like a hero, and after the meeting he went up to Vorontsov and Pesenny for a chat. What they chatted about, no one heard, but they saw Vorontsov point at Petrukha and talk at length to Pesenny, who took a pad from his pocket and scribbled on it with a pencil.

And it was only in their houses, after they warmed up, that the people began talking: the middle of September. Six weeks left. Just six weeks—you won't even notice them pass. And it was strange and terrible to imagine that the days would go on without Matyora village. They would rise, as usual, and stretch out over the island, which would be deserted and cleared, and no human eyes would look up from it, seeking the pretty sun. The autumn days would pass and wander over Matyora island, peering down to see what had happened, why there was no smoke rising and no voices calling from the island until one fine day, on whichever one it would fall, they wouldn't be able to find the island in its usual place.

And from then the days would go past without a stumble, past and past.

14

ANDREI HAD ALSO GONE TO THE MEETING for lack of anything better
to do, and also stood around, leaning on the doorframe, away
from the rest, like a stranger, and listened to what the leadership
had brought. And back home he told Darya in detail what had
been said. She sank onto the bench by the wall, her hands lowered, sat in silence, and then seeming to have thought it over and
come to a conclusion, she said: "Well, well."

Her voice amazed Andrei: with that one sound it managed to fly
to a truthful majesty, as though no one knew or believed, only she
believed and knew and the truth was with her. And there was
something else in it as well, something like a warning, like we'll
see how it will be. Be it would, there was no getting away from
that, but how would it be? What if the rest of the land, watching

Matyora, went up in flames? But Darya added in a quieter, more docile tone: "That's how it should be for man. If they told you when you would die, you'd know and could get ready . . . you wouldn't worry for nothing . . ."

"Don't be silly, Granny? Why should you know?"

She didn't reply, maybe because she agreed with him that there was no reason for man to know and scolded herself without admitting it to him. But Andrei was caught up in it, and began imagining.

"It would be amusing. Say you're alive and well, and there in your passport next to your birth date is your date of death." He laughed a false, put-on laugh. "You hand over your passport and they don't look at your name but at how long you have left. That's what's interesting. If it's a short time, be on your way, you're no worker; if you have a long time—come here. And if, say, you want to get married: come on, sweetie, let's see how long-lived you are. And the first thing she'll say: let's see . . . No, Granny," he said, frowning thoughtfully, "no. Let it be the way it is. Your God had a reason for keeping it from man."

Pavel came and Darya got up to set the table but Pavel said that he wanted to go down to the meadow to look at the haystacks first. It cleared up toward evening, bigger and broader than the previous brief promises, the sky raised itself high above the earth, and the clouds hung in it like mountains, turning white around the edges. There was a cold wind blowing, the first sign that good weather was coming. The sun peeped out from time to time, falling in a ribbon on the river, or floating, surfacing by the village, along the pasture, fields, and meadows and then falling off somewhere. The roosters, which had been quiet the last few days, gave voice—and they could tell what was coming, they weren't just crowing for nothing; sounds were more audible and clearer; a clink a verst away sounded as though it were right by your ear. And Pavel believed it: this was it, the end of foul weather, and believing, he decided to check what the rain had managed to do—did the raked grass blacken, did the stacks burn —so as to know where to take up the work.

After Pavel left, changing from his raincoat to a jacket, Andrei, embarrassed and prompted by private considerations, brought up the conversation that took place on the day he arrived.

"Granny, you said then that you felt sorry for man. All of them. Remember, you said that?"

"I remember. How could I forget?"

"Why do you feel sorry for him?"

Darya was cleaning house; she had lost the ladle and was circling the house in search of it, and she didn't take his question seriously.

"I'm sorry for him because I'm sorry. How could I not pity the poor thing? Man's not a stranger, you know."

"But why do you pity him, I want to know. You said he's little, man. You mean he's weak, impotent, or what?"

"Lay off it. I said it and that's all. Maybe I just said it like that."

"You didn't say it like that."

Darya finally found the ladle, got some water from the tub out on the porch, and came back to the kitchen. And unable to avoid the conversation, she spoke from there, bustling at the same time, taking care of overdue chores.

"And he's not little, is that it?" she asked, easing into the conversation, getting ready to say what she could say. "He hasn't changed. He's just like he used to be. He had two arms and two legs, and more haven't grown. But he's boiled up his life . . . it's frightening to see what a life he's boiled up. But he did it himself, no one made him. He thinks that he's the master over it, but he hasn't been master for a long time. It got out of his hands a long time ago. It's got the upper hand, it makes demand on him, it makes him run around like mad. He just barely keeps up. He should hold things up, wait awhile, look around, see what's left and what's been blown away by the wind . . . No, he's against that. He pushes on, and on. And he's overstrained already, he won't last long. He's overstrained!"

"How can he overstrain himself, when there are machines? Everything is mechanized now. If you only knew what kinds of machines they have now. You can't even imagine what they can do. More than any man. There's no work left anymore that you have to do yourself. How can he overstrain? You're barking up the wrong tree, Granny. You're telling me about the old man, who existed a hundred years ago."

Darya looked up angrily from her pots and straightened.

"I know what I'm talking about. A hundred years . . . a hundred years ago people lived in peace. I'm talking about you, I'm talking about the people who are living now. You don't strain your belly-button nowadays—that goes without saying! You take care of it. But you've wasted your soul and you don't care about that. Have you at least heard that man has a soul?"

Andrei smiled.

"They say there is such a thing."

"Don't laugh, there is. You've taught yourselves that if you can't see it or touch it, it doesn't exist. He who has a soul, has God, my friend. If you don't believe it, that's fine—He's still in you. Not in the sky. And He'll bless you, and protect you, and show you the way. And more than that, He treasures the man in you. So that you were born a man and stay a man. Have goodness within you. Anyone who kills off his soul is not a man, no-o-o! One like that will go in for anything without a second look. There are so many of you who got rid of it like that—and it's easier without a soul. That's what you want. I do what I want. And nothing inside will ache or hurt. No one will ask you anything. Machines, you say. Machines work for you. Oh, no. For a long time now it's not them working for you, but you for them—you think I don't see! And they want a lot! They're no horse that you toss some oats and send out to pasture. They'll pull out all your sinews and ruin the soil as well, they're good at that. Look how fast they run and how much they rake. You're impressed and you want more. You reach out after them. They're not running after you—you chase after them. And whether you catch up or not, those machines have made other machines, they do that without you now. Or give birth to them, iron from iron. And the new ones are even worse. And you have to work harder to keep up. There's no time for yourselves, for man . . . you'll lose yourselves completely on the road. You'll only keep what you need to run fast, and you'll leave everything else behind. People worked in the olden days, they didn't sit around with hands folded, but they worked peacefully, not like this. Everything's on the run now. Run to work, to eat—no time for anything. What's going on in the world! They even give birth on the run. And the poor babe, just born, unable to stand, hasn't said a single word, and he's out of breath. What good is a baby like that?" Darya stopped briefly, setting the potatoes that she cooked in the morning for the cow on the floor next to the bucket. Then she went on: "I look at your father. Do you think he'll live to be as old as me? Matyora has to do with that—it's quieter here. I was in the city, I saw—oh, how many of them running around! Like ants, like gnats. Back and forth, back and forth. Like a bottleneck. They push each other, run ahead . . . Heaven forbid! You look and think: where do you find enough land to bury them all? There won't be enough land. And you're just like that. You gallop off in one direction, take a look or maybe you don't and you're off in another. Heaven forbid you should stand still in one place. There's more excitement there, hah, it's excitement you want."

"What are you saying, Granny? Gallop, run . . . We live, that's all. People live as best they can." Andrei stood in the kitchen doorway and, amazed by Darya's words, looked at her attentively and mockingly.

"Live . . . You live however you want, whatever comes to mind. I'm no example for you. We've lived out our time. But you, too, Andrushka, you too will remember my words when you're exhausted. You'll say, Where was I rushing, what did I do? All I did was increase the fire and steam around me. Nothing else. That's all the good you did. Live . . . Your life has big demands: give it Matyora, it's hungry. Do you think Matyora will be enough?! It'll gulp it down, purr and snort and demand more than that. Give it some more. And what can you do. You'll give it more. Otherwise you're through. You gave it the reins and now you can't stop it. It's your own fault."

"I'm not asking about that, Granny. I asked why you feel sorry for man?"

"And what am I telling you?" Insulted, she stopped and sighed, realizing that she really wasn't talking about that. It would have been better to talk about nothing—what was the use? They went and announced when they would take Matyora away, turn it to ashes, and instead of getting her soul up and ready for that day and deed, she was talking about something that couldn't be talked about, pouring from one empty pitcher into another. Oh, how much time is wasted on that! People think that the mute are pathetic because they can't speak, but how pathetic were they, taking their long, uninterrupted thoughts? But Andrei was waiting, he needed her answer for some reason, and sighing once more, searching for where to start, her voice so low it was almost lost, she said uncertainly: "Well, I'm sorry for him . . . Just look at him . . ." Stirring the mash in the bucket, lowering her voice, trying to find it in her work, then raising it freely, waving it about, jumping from one thing to another, Darya began explaining: "He gets everything mixed up terribly, your man. He confuses others—all right, he'll have to pay for that. But he's confused himself so much that he can't see where right is and where left is. He does everything backwards. He does what he doesn't want. I'm not the only one to see this, I don't have special eyes, and if you look you'll see it too. Look close, take a good look. He doesn't feel like laughing at all, maybe he needs to cry, but he laughs and laughs . . . And talks . . . he's clever at every turn, that's not what he meant to say . . . And what needs to be said, he won't say, he'll keep quiet. He has to go one way, so he'll turn in the other direction. He'll realize it later and be ashamed and angry with himself . . . and if he's mad at himself, then he's mad at the whole wide world. And there's nothing more miserable than that. And you can't live that way, you have to control yourself. You live almost nothing, why not live a good life, why not think what memory of you will remain. Because memory, it remembers everything, it saves everything, not a single grain is lost. And later you can plant flowers on the grave every day and only brambles will grow there. Ah!" Darya sighed once more and suddenly Andrei didn't trust that sigh, something that never would have happened to him before—did it come out on its own to relieve a built-up pressure or did Granny use it cleverly to fit her words? But he didn't interrupt his grandmother, and she went on: "Do you think that Katerina's Petrukha isn't tired of acting the fool? He's not a stupid man, you know. He knows that he's not living a real life. But he won't turn around, out of spite. He marked out his path and he'll go down it to the end, the very end. But why bring up Petrukha? There's no asking of Petrukha. Look at a serious man, who seems to be living smart, and he's even worse. He doesn't appear as himself with people, he pretends to be someone else. Why is someone else any better than you? Because you, the way you are, you're not living, you're trying to pretend. Tanya's daughter-in-law, married to her Ivan, had a sister-in-law, Gutka, a pushy kind of girl, who pretended that she was cross-eyed, making her eyes jump for nothing. Well, this Gutka always hid a hammer in the toilet. And if someone saw her go in there, she'd grab the hammer and start hammering. As if that's why she went in there, to nail a board. But who doesn't go there? Why be ashamed? And we're all like that. We hammer nails in boards. Man is created, let out to live, and he wants another self. He's confused, so confused, he's playing out the end."

"And you too, Granny?"

"Why not me? I catch myself doing the wrong thing. And it doesn't cost anything to do it right, but no, my feet go the wrong way, my hands take the wrong things. As though the devil prompts me. If it's him he's managed to do a lot while people were figuring out if there is a God or isn't. Forgive, merciful Lord forgive me, a sinner," she said, crossing herself through the door, beyond Andrei. "Why not me? It's not for me to judge people. But my eyes still see and my ears still hear. I'll tell you something else, Andrushka, and you remember it. Do you think that they don't understand that they shouldn't flood Matyora? They understand. And they're still doing it."

"That means there's no other way. It has to be done."

Darya straightened up in front of the stove, where she was about to lay logs for the morning, and turned to Andrei.

"If there's no other way, then go and cut off Matyora—if you can do everything, if you have all these machines—cut it off and take it over to land, and put it next to it. When God was putting the earth down, He didn't give anyone an extra inch. And now it's extra for you. Bring it over and let it be. It'll serve you and your grandchildren. They'll thank you for it."

"There aren't any machines like that, Granny. They haven't invented ones like that."

"If they set their minds to it, they would."

But then, either scared or embarrassed by what she said, she spoke in a conciliatory and tired manner, while putting the logs into the Russian stove with a wooden shovel:

"You say why do I pity him? How could I not? If you don't look at his honors, he was born a babe and stayed a babe all his life. And he has fits and is silly, like a baby, and he cries like a baby. I can always tell who cries secretly. No power over himself, no nothing. And there's so much directed at him, I'm afraid to look. And he just runs to and fro . . . And for nothing. Where you can walk, he runs. And then there's death . . . How he fears it, poor man! That's reason enough to pity him. No one fears death like him in the whole world. Worse than any rabbit. And the things fear makes you do . . ."

She put the shovel in the corner and turned. Behind Andrei's back, in the entry, where the window faced the Angara, was the sun. Her face brightened.

"Lord!" Darya whispered guiltily. "And I'm going on about death. I must be out of my mind. I must be."

It was the real sun, pale and tired, pushing its way through the clouds with great difficulty. Just before setting it rolled out into the narrow clear strip and, proclaiming its liberation, it shone out, promising that it would set just for the night and come out in the morning and do its work.

The roosters crowed drunkenly; the cattle mooed loudly; and somewhere iron thumped resonantly and majestically.

15

IT HADN'T FOOLED THEM, the sun. The next day it came out with the dawn: there were clouds still holding on in the sky, dried out and wrinkled, tired of themselves, but the eastern morning side was clean, and the sun rolled out without any mistakes. And while it was rising, the clouds, growing thin and transparent, retreated from it, and finally, like icicles, they melted away. By lunch the sky was completely free and the sun blazed forth, seeming in its joyous impatience to swoop over the earth, sending down generous color in one wave after another. Birds threw themselves into the sky and played, gliding, unkinking their wings, crying out in their deep dives with joy that they were able to fly. The wet earth gave off a white, milky steam that burned off in the sun; the puddles prepared to ferment, and chickens peered into them carefully, as though they finally decided to learn to swim, and piglets wandered through them but didn't lie down, only picking out spots for later. The green in the forests and grasses was so rich and thick it was dark, but even after a week of bad weather the leaves weren't touched by yellow—that meant the summer would be a long one. Distinct in the rain, the sharp and pungent odors blended into one mighty aroma, like a river, where it was impossible to tell which water came from which stream.

After lunch, it had barely dried out. Pavel took the people out to toss over the stacks, to dry out the hay. The rain had done enough damage, but the worse part was that it had washed away the passion and broken the stride of the mowing. Redoing and going back over work is never fun, but the people felt that even when they caught up and went on they would still be working only because the work had to be done and not because it was a pleasure. And at first it had been a pleasure. Now they just wanted to get it over with, set up the ricks and go home. They had had enough of living in a straddle: one leg here, the other there; it was time to attach themselves to solid land. Now, in the sun, the middle of September seemed so close you could reach out and touch it, and there was so much more to do, so many things to organize for the move—where would they find the energy and time? There was the cow grazing, no sense of impending trouble—what to do with the cow? And the ones who had decided to mow for themselves thought: When? Wouldn't it be easier to kill the cow now and worry no more?

"You could have gone mowing a little in the rain, you know," Darya reproached herself and her menfolk, sighing in dissatisfaction, poisoning herself with the knowledge that wisdom only comes with hindsight.

"We could have," Pavel said, looking away nervously. "But we didn't know how long it would rain; the hay could have rotted."

Only Andrei didn't give up hope.

"We'll mow, Granny, what are you so upset about? The weather will settle down and we'll mow. I can start tomorrow.

We can set up thirty stacks in a week. Will thirty be enough for the cow?"

"If the potatoes come up, it'll be more than enough."

"Of course they'll come up, where will they go?"

Pavel was cheered by his son's confidence.

"Maybe I can make an arrangement with someone else. Three pairs of hands work faster. There won't be work in the kolkhoz for a while now." He still said "kolkhoz" out of habit.

"And then the graves, Pavel, the graves," Darya reminded him. "Until you move the graves, I won't let you off Matyora. And if you don't, then I'll stay here myself."

Andrei shifted his gaze in surprise and distrust from his father to his grandmother and back again. Could it really be, as they said, that they would have to open the graves and dig out what was left of people buried long ago, before he was even born? What for? The pending work both scared him, seeming eerie and evil, and lured him, teasing: it would be interesting—interesting to see what a man turns into after lying in the ground for thirty, forty, fifty years, and not just some stranger, but someone from your clan and family, an uncle or a grandfather. Would it elicit special, never-before-felt sensations? He would probably never in his life have another opportunity to see anything like it. This was a special case, a special incident that would never be repeated.

But everyone knows that man merely proposes. The next day, as sudden as a snowfall, Pavel was called back to the settlement by a messenger. One of his workers, either drunk or careless, stuck his hand into the machinery and ended up crippled for life. Pavel ran home from the meadow where the messenger had driven to get him, changed quickly, and hurried off without tea or packing. Darya called after him.

"When should I expect you?"

"I don't know," he said brusquely as he ran.

Andrei mowed that day. The Pinigin meadowlands were located on the same spot for fifteen years now, on the right far bank beyond the fields and hummocks; Andrei hadn't forgotten the way and went off alone in the morning, packing a lunch (in case he was too lazy to come back to eat), a pot and a whetstone to sharpen his scythe. He took two scythes: his father was supposed to come by in the evening, early, right from the meadow. But he didn't come, and Andrei learned about what had happened when he came home at twilight. He listened to his grandmother and said confidently—so confidently that she believed him: "He'll be back in the morning."

But Pavel didn't come in the morning. Darya waited and waited, and when the sun had gone down, she ran impatiently to Andrei on the meadowland. There was water in the hummocks; you would have to make a wide circle to go around, it would take too long, and she unwisely continued straight ahead, dropping into cold, sticky mud above her knees, crawling out as dirty and wet as a witch, still having to make the detour. She was exhausted by the time she got to the spot—and Andrei wasn't there. The scythe, stuck in the ground, protruded by the shelter, an old, decrepit hut, roofed with tanbark back in the first year that they were assigned this parcel of land, and still usable and handy in moments of rest or sudden rain. The other scythe was hanging on a birch, one of the three that the hut nestled under. It was in the shade, and Darya moved away from it and sat in the sun on the mown grass—her legs refused to warm up. She took off her shoes and massaged her feet, looking around.

Andrei hadn't mown as much as he had made trouble—she could tell that he had lost his peasant's habits, had forgotten and lost what he once knew. The mown grass bristled unevenly, the growing, surviving grass stuck out through it, and the swaths were wavy. Looking closer, Darya saw that the mown grass was wilted and dry—that meant that Andrei hadn't mown at all today or had just made two or three short turns. And a bitter, unpleasant feeling enveloped Darya: no, nothing that she had hoped would come to pass. Nothing would happen, there was no point in hoping. It was all for naught.

She called out Andrei's name, then again and again, until she got an answer. Andrei crawled out of the willows a half verst upriver from her, and he was holding the pot with something bright red in it. And she guessed: he was picking berries! God, he was still a child! If you don't keep an eye on him, he runs off into the bushes to pick berries . . . How did he live alone?

But she had come to take him away from the work. She had reached the end of her tether over the course of the day, and when she learned that they were getting a boat ready to go over to the settlement for groceries, she thought: let Andrei go over, let him find out what his father was doing. The hell with the mowing; if Pavel came he'd do it, and if he didn't, Andrei couldn't do it alone, anyway. But she had little doubt now that this year's mowing would end right there. Why "this year's"?—there would probably never be another one for her. That was one job that was closed to her forever. And was she alone in that? . . . Not listening to Andrei who wanted to hide the scythes in the bushes, hoping to return and continue mowing, she determinedly took one scythe on her shoulder, shoved the other one at him, and started back, thinking that she would have to pick a good time to come back here to say good-bye. All the land on Matyora was her own, but this was the most personal—how much work had been put in here, how much sweat was spilled, and how much was taken from it, how much joy!

Andrei took off and disappeared. In order to pass time while waiting, Darya puttered in the garden. The weeds were thick after the rain, the soil around the potatoes was washed away, and the greens were pushing up stupidly like thin reeds. It had to be raked all over again. After a week's downpour and then hot weather, the cucumbers came in thick and heavy—you could pick them twice a day. And Darya picked them, sorry that there was no one to eat them, remembering the days when her children and then her grandchildren stood watch over almost every cucumber, picking out their favorites while they were still on the vine: that's yours and that's mine . . . Was it so long ago? Yesterday. She had told Andrei when he was pestering her with questions that man lives almost no time at all. And it was true—before you knew it, life was over. There were only three days that you could count on: yesterday, today, and maybe a little of tomorrow.

Now that there was something to peck, the chickens appeared in the garden, and birds from the sky came down too, and so Darya decided to set up a scarecrow. She put her old and worn dress on two crossed sticks; she couldn't find an appropriate hat so she tied an old rag on top, and stepping back so that the stick was covered by the greens, she was struck by the thought: but that was she! She, she . . . If she were to stand in the middle of the garden and extend her arms, not a single chicken would walk over, not a single bird would fly down. And she had wondered, asked herself what she was like . . . Lord have mercy!—was this the way it was supposed to be?

Andrei returned only four days later and said that his father was making the rounds of various commissions, and that the whole situation would drag on. They decided not to mow. But Darya was no longer thinking about the hay. She was frightened.

"But what does he have to do with it? He wasn't there. He was here. Why does he have to go?"

"He's responsible for safety measures."

"And what will happen to him now over that safety?" In her lifetime Darya had come to the conclusion that man's justice was often indiscriminate: whoever they point at is the one they blame and try, and human guilt is often assigned blindly.

"Nothing will happen," Andrei replied confidently, as usual. "They'll interview him, drive him batty, and chew him out, just in case. And that's all."

"Did he say that?"

"He did. And I know it myself. That's the way it is."

He was planning to leave, but for some reason felt compelled to justify himself before Darya, saying that he couldn't drag it out any longer, that soon loads of soldiers would be coming out of the army and it would be harder to find work. But Darya didn't try to hold him back, didn't remind him about the hay or the graves—it was all happening as she had guessed. Bogodul came by that evening and stayed a long time, snarling at Andrei, who in his turn gave the old man challenging and dirty looks. The three of them drank tea in silence, and Andrei quickly jumped up from the table, whistling and humming to himself, and began packing his bag, not bothering to hide his happiness at leaving. Before, Darya would not have tolerated whistling: "Who are you whistling, you so-and-so, who are you whistling out of the house?" But now she didn't care. Everyone would be whistled out, no one would be left. Bogodul creaked and spluttered, incensed by her silence, why she put up with it, but she made believe that she didn't hear him, didn't understand his hints.

Later, when the grumpy and angry Bogodul left, Andrei asked indignantly: "Why do you receive him, Granny? Why don't you chase that animal away? He's not human, he's an animal."

"Why isn't he human?" she replied with an unbearable spiritual weariness and pain. "He's human."

"He's not! Just take a good look at him, at his face. He's terrifying. He doesn't even talk like people do, he just grunts and groans."

"I can understand him without unnecessary words. And he understands me. Nowadays, Andrushka, I seek out people who are my equals. Am I any better? There's nobody left who can understand me."

In the morning, when he was leaving, Andrei hurt Darya's feelings by saying good-bye in the house and not letting her see him off at the boat. She went anyway. But even greater and more painful was the hurt that she couldn't express because there was no word for it. She could only suffer from it, the way you suffer from depression or aches when you can't tell what hurts or where. She remembered well: from the evening when he returned until today, Andrei didn't go out further than his own backyard. He didn't take a walk around Matyora, he didn't grieve in secret that he would never see it again, he didn't stir his soul. There was something there to stir it, the land where he was born and raised, but he just picked up his suitcase, took the shortest path to the bank, and turned on the motor.

Farewell to you, Andrei. Farewell. God forbid that your life should seem simple to you.

And soon after, Petrukha was off somewhere again without a word, and Katerina moved back in with Darya.

It was August already, the month of ripening. The gardens, the fields, the forests were ripening and the Angara had ripened like a woman, playfully, and no one swam in it after St. Ilya's day, as after a wedding; because "deer had pissed in the water," you couldn't anymore. The sky was fading and seemed heavy and fleshy in the midst of a sunny day. The weather had settled down, it was fair and dry, but you could feel the time now. The nights were cool; the stars burned bright and shiny, falling frequently, extinguishing in flight, streaking the sky with farewell fiery stripes that made something anxiously tear in your soul when you saw them, made your heart contract in loneliness. In the morning, after particularly clear nights, gray, murky fogs crept in, hugging the shore for now and not covering the Angara; the days, noticeably shorter but retaining their strength and power, seemed full and stuffed to the limit, as though they had absorbed much more than they could possibly carry. And sure enough, an overload seemed to build up, and two or three times, always toward evening, somewhere in the distance, beyond the sky, thunder rumbled grumpily, but it was only a threat, it never came to rain and rampage.

The mowers had done their work: there were eight large stacks in the meadow. Only two houses out of the entire village had dared to mow for themselves: the Koshkins, or Kotkins, who cut for a cow with their whole large family in no time; and Darya's neighbor Vera Nosaryova. She was an amazingly reckless woman: in rain and at night, never straightening up, she cut and cut alone, without any help, and cut enough for her cow. And almost alone, because her ten-year-old girl wasn't much help, she raked it up into ricks, and the villagers helped her bale it after their common work out of respect and amazement for Vera's stubbornness. And even though the woman had put out food after the baling, it was clear that they did the work not for the food but for her, who decided against all odds, as a silent reproach and to show them all that she wouldn't give up her cow, to fight for her right to her own and not store-bought milk for her kids. And looking at her, Darya reproached herself for not having tried to take up a scythe once more. And then, maybe things would have been different, maybe Andrei would have stayed on and that incident wouldn't have happened to Pavel. Maybe it did happen because they ruminated too long, waiting on the shore for the weather to change. They got theirs . . . And there she was, old as the hills and knowing better, and she just sat around like it was her birthday instead of urging the men on: Why not go cut hay in the rain? It wouldn't do a damn thing to the green grass. By the time she thought of it, it was too late. Ah, what was the point of living eighty and more years if she couldn't even have thought of that!?

They were digging up new potatoes and frying them with the boletus mushrooms that dotted the land in countless numbers—as though to make up for all the years that would not be. Even lone pines and firs had a thick carpeting of these mushrooms beneath them. The agarics came up, too, both the fir and birch varieties, but they grew slowly and cautiously, without rushing or clamoring. In general this final summer, as though it realized that it was the last, was a good one for berries and mushrooms. After the wood sorrel, black currants grew on the banks; once after her chores Darya went down and picked a big bucketful in a minute, dragged it as far as the cemetery, and left it in the bushes by her family's graves. In the evening she and Katerina did the second lap and got it home. In recent years they had begun picking "crow's berry"—honeysuckle, which, according to rumors, was good for high blood pressure, but the old people, who didn't know what pressure was and what you ate for it, didn't start eating the rather bitter berry, which probably did grow just for crows who liked to eat leftovers and garbage. And the fact that it pretended to look like bilberry and didn't have its own appearance did nothing to improve its reputation. And it was a strange name, it seemed murky and runny, they hadn't known it before on Matyora. Now, black currants, wild cherry, or whortleberries— that was a different matter altogether; you couldn't suspect them of poor lineage in any way. Whortleberries, actually, didn't grow profusely on either of their islands, just enough to pop in your mouth, and they used to go over the river for them, to the old slashings. But it wasn't even whortleberry time yet. Now that was the berry's berry, and no one ever dared call it crow's or bear's berry.

Darya was expecting Sonya, her daughter-in-law; she thought that maybe Sonya could go down and pick some and then she would cook them up. But no, there was neither hide nor hair of Sonya—she must have really liked the new place. She couldn't be working all the time . . . Well, let them live as they want.

More than a week after he was called away, Pavel came back, finished with the whole business and with his position as brigade leader; he brought the old women tea and sugar and said that he would be working on a tractor now, loaded up on garden vegetables, and without spending the whole day, puttered away on his motorboat. Darya walked over to the promontory outside the village and watched his motionless, hunched figure in the boat, fleeing some outside force, and she thought wearily, heavily: no, Pavel isn't his own master. And Sonya wasn't his boss, either—he wouldn't allow that—they were all swept up and carried off somewhere, without a chance to look back. There weren't many who set their own pace. Should she go to Ivan, her second son, at his lumber town? What was there? Even though it wasn't far, it was alien, and the people would be strangers, the things would be strange, and who knew, maybe her son would be a stranger too. Maybe she should just go for a visit, see how things were? No, first she had to see Matyora off. See Matyora off and then join her kin—go where she had ten times more kin than here. With a superficial, skimming memory Darya began remembering, counting those who were there, and suddenly thought of her old man— Miron. She remembered him and froze in shame: she had begun forgetting him, he came to mind rarely, so rarely. God, how easily a person parts with the people dear to him, how quickly he forgets everyone who isn't his child: wife forgets husband, husband wife, sister forgets brother, brother sister. When he buries them, he tears his hair out in grief, can't stand up on his own feet, and six months later, a year later, it's as if the one he lived with for twenty or thirty years, with whom he had children and never

imagined a single day without, had never existed. What was it?—
is this the way it was meant to be or had people turned to stone?
And he suffers more over his children, laid to rest before him,
only because he feels guilty: he should have protected them and
failed. And as for everyone else, he met them, accidentally or
not—sharing the same parents—spent time, talked, played at
being related, and parted, each his own way. No, man was wild,
crazy, even an animal wouldn't behave like that. A wolf that loses
his mate refuses to live . . .

Darya had only one excuse, and even then you really had to
look for it. Miron, her old man, didn't have a grave where she
could sit and, releasing her soul, grieve, and cry, and remember
what was and imagine what might have been. He left in the fall
for the taiga beyond the Angara and disappeared. He left and
didn't come back, the earth seemed to swallow him up. And there
was no one who could say what happened to him. When the time
for which he had enough food doubled, Darya got really worried
and ran around the village, getting the men to set up a search
party, knowing where Miron hunted, but they found no traces.
Two dogs disappeared with him—go figure out what kind of
death took all three. He wasn't even an old man, it was now when
she thought of him as being her own age that she said "old man";
then he was just over fifty, in his prime. About Pavel's age now.
But there was no comparison: the father was stronger, livelier,
with more of a temper. Or did it just seem that way now? Many
things were different from the way they seem now, mown down
by time and hope, exhausted by memory. So Miron came to mind,
but peacefully and smoothly, without touching her heart. It had
grown cold. It was cold and only ached for nearby things, things
that were close to today—Matyora for instance. Could it be that
the people who remained would remember Matyora no more than
last year's snow? If you even forget your relatives so quickly . . .

"Forgive me, Lord, for being weak, and not remembering, and
being bankrupt in spirit," she thought. "You won't blame a rock
for being a rock, but you will a man. Or are you tired of asking?
Why don't your questions reach us? Forgive me, forgive me,

Lord, for asking. I feel bad. And you won't let me leave. I don't walk the earth anymore and I'm not in the sky, I'm suspended between heaven and earth: I see everything, but I can't understand what's what. I judge people, but who gave me that right? It looks like I've moved away from them, time to take me off. It's time . . . Send for me, Lord, I'm begging you. I'm a stranger to everyone here. Take me to my kin . . . the ones that I'm closer to."

The Angara flowed on in the sun—and time flowed under the weak upper wind with a light rustle. Behind her back lay Matyora, washed by both flows; the sky soared high above her head. If you were to stop the Angara—time wouldn't stop, and what seemed like a single movement would break up into parts. When Matyora went under water the sky would still glow and celebrate the clear day and the clear night. What does the sky care for Matyora? Darya corrected herself. "That's for people. It's in people's hands, and they're the ones who rule it." And still something in Darya's brief, unconscious arguments, which washed over her from the side and broke off, was missing to make a complete and understandable whole. And a short, obstinate, fragmented thought floundered and struggled: the Angara flows, and time flows . . . And it made her want to argue with someone, to prove her point, even when she knew that she was wrong.

In the evening, as they were going to bed, Darya asked Katerina:

"Has it ever happened to you that there was no one there but it seemed that someone was talking to you?"

"Who?" Katerina asked in fright.

"I don't know. Today I came to and I was talking out loud. As though someone was next to me, asking me questions, and I was talking to him."

"Mother of God! What was he asking you?"

"Upsetting, difficult things . . . And I couldn't say what. I must be losing my mind. I wish it would happen soon . . ."

16

BUT THESE WERE THE LAST, not exactly peaceful but at least quiet, homey days. Then a horde of some thirty people descended for the harvest—all men, except for three young but already used women—and the men were young and rowdy. On the very first day when they took Matyora and sensed freedom, they got drunk and brawled among themselves, sending two to the doctor in the morning. And they argued the next day, figuring out who was to blame, who was right, and sent a boat over to the store for some more liquor, had some more that evening (but not as much) without brawling. It only took one day to frighten Matyora to death; there weren't many who stuck their noses out beyond their gates unless they really had to and they stayed at least a verst away from the office where the horde was based. And when two fellows knocked on Darya's door, she was ready to fall to her knees: spare me, don't kill a Christian soul. But the fellows asked for some onions and even pressed money on her for them and left; later, Darya picked them out from the rest of the troops. Only Bogodul, who feared neither the devil nor the deep blue sea, went over to the office for spite, staring at the newcomers with hostility, and they, even though they picked at him and mocked him, were afraid of him: he wasn't a man, he was a forest demon, and you never knew what might come into his head. Barefoot, shaggy, and red-eyed, with long apelike arms and a catchy, frightening gaze, he inspired respect, and when one of the villagers hinted that he had been in prison for a killing, and maybe several, they stopped picking on Bogodul. But they did add a nickname to "old man" for him—Abominable Snowman, at which he roared and cursed as befits a snowman who had come down from the mountains.

Whether it was for better or worse, at least the newcomers were active, doing something, and the wheat was harvested slowly. They couldn't have worked well—when you don't harvest your own, you don't wear yourself out. After all, they had bread anyway, and this soil was giving birth to grain for the last time anyway, and it might not have had this harvest at all, so it didn't matter anyway. Some left, others replaced them: the boat traveled to the settlement and store almost every day. And they had sown much less than in previous kolkhoz years, they could have managed on their own, but for some reason they turned it over to these people. And the locals, finished with the haymowing, went back to the settlement until potato time and the final moving day, leaving the old women in charge of the village. Before going out on the street, they peeked out through cracks in their fences— was everything quiet out there? They crept along the streets; they sat quietly at home and locked all the doors at night.

And time passed. Day followed day, and with each day autumn came closer, ever closer. The morning breezes were cold and lazy, the dew and fog dried late, and the sun didn't show until it was high in the sky. Voices from the office rang out in loud arguments, there were curses and laughter, their started car hummed for a long time before they finally got in it and drove off. After that the women bustled in the kitchen behind the office, and it was hard to tell them apart; all three were saucy and loud, dressed in men's trousers, and all three, like sisters, were short and beefy. But they said that one of them belonged to someone, to one of the men here, that she was his wife; the other two were single and had a lot of hard work during harvest. By lunchtime some fellow who had stayed behind would come out the door, either hung over or sick, scratching and yawning, squint in the sunlight, and go off to do his business and ponder what to do next—go back to sleep or start living? But the women, lying in wait, would take him in hand and set him chopping wood, hauling water from the barrel, helping them in the kitchen, and then scuffling, slaps, and laughter would come from the kitchen.

It was hot in the daytime, the heated air streaming before your eyes, tasting bitter from the ripe, dry scent of the herbs, grains, and everything that the harvest had brought. From the fields came the pleasant, almost nonmechanical chirr of the combines; a local boy from the Koshkin family worked one of them, and the other was run by a city fellow. A barge, which had brought a second car and tractor to the island and onto which they loaded the wheat from the combines, was docked at the right bank, for easier loading, next to the Pinigin lands. By late summer the sovkhoz had acquired a cutter, which had hauled over the barge, and now they used it to carry food for the newcomers and for communications between Matyora and the settlement. And the women, worried by the presence of strangers, slowly began evacuating the small livestock from the village—chickens, pigs, sheep —on the cutter. It was like that—just let one start, and they all go. There was clucking and cackling and squalling every day. The cows were grazing for now. For them, and for the hay, the men were felling trees and making a raft, a heavy-duty one for freight, two levels high with posts.

The end was in sight; the deadline would not be delayed and the people would get it done—look how they were working, all those hands!

Another crew landed on Podmoga, where there were no fields, only pastures and forests—from the lumber camp. All the cattle there had to be herded to Matyora in one day—luckily the water was low in the channel. And Podmoga went up in flames—the few old structures there for cattle caught first, followed by the forests. There was a low wind and all the smoke from Podmoga was blown onto Matyora—there were times when you couldn't see the sky and the sun would surface, looking like a pale disk. The cattle huddled in their stalls, mooing; the sovkhoz cows, left over from the kolkhoz, ran around the island bawling, forming groups, stampeding, and foaming at the mouth: the horses—there were just a few left—were calmer, but they feared the land and stayed closer to the water. The local people were incensed.

"What are they doing? What? Could they wait just a little? Matyora has to go up in flames soon enough. It's so dry . . . There are haystacks, and wheat . . . Just one spark . . ."

And the nonlocals—who else—set fire to the windmill in response, either following a secret order to start the cleanup, or without it, just for the hell of it: it has to burn anyway, so let's see it happen. Why swallow strange smoke!—we'll make our own with crackling and fire! And they did. In the evening Darya came outside and gasped, seeing the high red color in the sky not from the lower side, from Podmoga, but from the upper end too, to the left of the village. There was nothing there but the mill that could burn. And hurrying back in the house, Darya roused Katerina, who had already gone to bed.

"Let's go say good-bye to it. Otherwise it's all strangers there. Think how it is among strangers—no one will say a kind word; let's go, Katerina."

"Where? What are you talking about?" she asked in fear: they were all frightened all the time now, freezing at every sound, shuddering at every unexpected word—was it bringing trouble, would it tell bad news?

"They've set fire to the mill. It was in their way. Think how much bread it milled for us. Come on, at least we'll be there. Let it see us as it goes down."

In the roadway leading up to the burning mill there really were only newcomers. What does a consuming fire do to people, why does it affect them so terribly? They were like crazy people: they jumped and shouted and ran into the heat—whoever ran in closest and stayed longest and played hero would then, no longer able to stand the heat, fall on the dark brown scorched earth and roll back with a shout. The women squealed—there were two of them here—when the men pushed them toward the fire to scare them; they brandished their fists at the men, pounding them on the back, and were happy and satisfied and merry. One young man, still very young and stupid, made crazy by the fire, climbed up on a birch and, dangling his legs, sang at the top of his lungs. A little dog, also mad, affected by the madness around it, barked at him as though he were an animal—and they all pointed at the fellow and the dog and rolled on the ground laughing. The dog, knowing that it was pleasing them, tried even harder. How funny . . . the leaves on the birch rolled up as they burned, and heavy branches fell from the fire side, and the tree in the bright blaze seemed colorless, transparent. The people's faces seemed transparent, incorporeal, too.

The mill burned with a horrible howl that came from inside; the tall flames were bent above by the wind and torn off; the big flakes of ash flew on. Darya and Katerina stood to one side, opposite the side wall, hidden from the strangers by bushes, so that they would not be seen, so that only the mill would see them. It was lost in the fire, which seemed to lift it up playfully and then set it down; they could even believe that the whole blaze could tear away and fly up high over the Angara, frightening the people who were celebrating their satanic pleasures.

The old women didn't hear the strange man in a loose checked shirt, one of the newcomers but no longer young, come up to them—how could they have heard with all the crackling and howling! After a while, the man asked—and there was sympathy in his voice: "Was it a good mill?"

"A good one," Darya answered without fright.

"I understand," he nodded. "It served its function, I guess." And then he drawled: "It's going!"

That expression—"it's going"—stayed in Darya's mind and became the important phrase that explained everything that was happening around her. A piglet squealed in a sack, dragged on someone's back over to the cutter, and Darya watched and thought: it's going. When they drove the sovkhoz cattle to raft it over to the far bank to the pastures near where the settlement was, Darya went to see them off, watched them drag the reluctant, obstinate cows and calves onto the large, fenced-in raft, tie them to the crampons, and take off. "They're going." Acrid black smoke came from Podmoga, seeping into the houses and making them dough, and Darya thought: Podmoga's going, it's going. Klavka Strigunova turned over her bull calf to the sovkhoz for meat—he was going, poor thing. They hauled the stacks of hay to the shore—they're going! More and more of the familiar things were going, everything was in a rush to leave, to get far away from the dangerous island. And the village was lonely, empty, bare, also ready to leave; the voices of the strangers sounded hollow, as if in a barrel, and the native ones were lost, disappearing. And your eyes could see far, through the village—Matyora was emptying, your gaze could travel freely.

Klavka Strigunova, who had become friends with the city people through her bull calf, talked them into burning down her house—she couldn't wait to get her money. And of course, they set fire to it with great pleasure; at least they didn't burn down the neighboring structures. But now a black, smoking hole gaped in the middle of the village too, and the eye, finding no support, fell through and plummeted, as into a well, into the distant expanse of the Angara. Matyora was separated, divided into two parts . . .

The evening that the mill "went off," when Darya and Katerina came home in the darkness from the fire, they found Sima and the boy on their porch. They were sitting in front of the locked door: Kolka was whimpering and Sima muttered soothingly in his ear. She got up quickly to meet the old women, and as she always did when she was worried, she rubbed her cheek and entreated: "Let me stay with you tonight . . . we're afraid. He won't sleep, he just cries, and I can't either. I'm so scared . . . so scared . . ."

They put them in the bed, and the bed didn't stay empty anymore; in the daytime Sima went to her house, puttering with garden and household chores, but at night she returned to Darya's. Frightened once, she couldn't get rid of the fear. But Sima wasn't the only one who was sacred. Even Bogodul once noticed the Berdan rifle hanging under a fur coat in the porch at Darya's and said happily: "Give it to me. Kur-rva! I'll kill them!"

"Who will you kill?" Darya grew flustered. "How can I give it to you? What if you do kill someone? What's the matter? Who is it?"

"Threats, kur-rva! Burn the shack. I'll . . ." And he smacked his lips soundly, like a gunshot.

"I don't think you can use it. I can't remember when it was last shot. When himself was still alive . . ."

But Bogodul took down the rifle and took it away—probably to scare someone, because he didn't think of the cartridges or ammunition. Darya wouldn't have considered giving it to him loaded: he just might shoot if he got angry—he was Bogodul after all. That's all they needed now. There was nothing they could do to him, and Darya couldn't really be held responsible—that meant Pavel would bear the brunt again.

And so with overnight guests, Sima and the boy, they kept together, not two now, but four. There were plenty of potatoes and other vegetables, they had flour left over from the old kolkhoz stores, and Pavel either brought tea and salt or sent it over with someone—he was working on a tractor now, turning forest into fields and it wasn't easy for him to get away. They had their own milk; Darya was glad that there was finally someone to drink it and she gave Kolka milk in the morning and evening and told him to come home for some during the day. She slept on the stove, Katerina was still on the cot, and they turned over the bed to Sima and the boy. Now that Andrei had gone Bogodul dropped by more often—he, on the contrary, spent most of the day there and spent the night in his shack, worried that they might set fire to it. In order to show off his rifle he walked past the office with it several times, grunting and coughing loudly, calling attention to himself. The newcomers piled out onto the porch and shouted.

"Hey, you! Partisan!"

"Snowman!"

"Turk!"

"Who are you going to war against, hah? What model is that, your cannon?"

"Better ask what model he is! Maybe he served under Peter and Great?"

"Try Ivan the Terrible!"

"That thing doesn't shoot."

Bogodul was waiting for those words.

"Come here!" he nodded off to the side and started taking the rifle from his back. "Come here, kur-rva!"

But there were no takers to try out the rifle on their own hides; Bogodul grunted triumphantly, tossed it over his shoulder, and to the sound of laughter and catcalls, no longer turning to look, walked away.

17

AT DARYA's they stayed up late talking. They got into bed at twilight without lighting the fire and at first talked about whatever they had gone to bed with—after a lengthy tea session and leisurely bedtime chores. As usual they complained about their old bones, tossing and groaning, getting more comfortable to help them; briefly, almost like a signature, they mentioned the day that had passed to confirm that they knew it was there, that they had been in it. But as the light beyond the windows faded and died, and the noises abated, their minor worries fell aside and the conversation quieted down, clambering out into freedom, turning meditative, sad, sincere. The old women no longer saw one another, only heard one another; the boy puffed soundly in his sleep next to Sima, the windows shone icily, the house seemed huge, as big as the world, and the teasing, slightly sour smell of glowing embers in the samovar stood in the air—and the words came up on their own, effortlessly, their memories were easy and docile. What did they talk about? What could they talk about? Wherever the conversation led them, that's what they tried, but they rarely turned far from Matyora or themselves; it was the same old thing in different keys.

This time Petrukha's ears must have been burning: they began with him. Klavka Strigunova, who had gone to the district capital to get the money for her house, ran into him at the wharf in Podvolochna. Petrukha, she said, was working there: he burned down emptied houses. People can't do it to their own houses, that was easy to believe, and Petrukha was an old hand at it, it was a snap for him. Klavka maintained that Petrukha was paid for every burned building, and paid well, he didn't complain. "I'm full, drunk, and have a noseful of tobacco," he supposedly bragged to Klavka, and true enough, while she didn't know whether he was hungry or not, he was drunk and was on his way to buy another bottle. He offered to treat Klavka, but she supposedly refused because the man who was with Petrukha seemed untrustworthy to her, and she had the money.

Katerina, who had come to terms with the loss of her house, couldn't forgive Petrukha for burning down other people's. The whole day after her conversation with Klavka she gasped in shame and fear.

"Oh, what shame! Oh, what shame! What's the matter with him, has he lost his head completely? How can he look people in the eyes after that? How does he plan to walk on this earth? Oh, oh!"

In the daytime, Darya, who was also upset by Petrukha, added fat to the fire.

"Some work he found for himself. He couldn't find any before. Well, burning isn't building. Just stuff some straw about, strike a match, light your cigarette with the same match, and get warm— what a snap! Podvolochna is a big village, three versts or so, it's all stretched out. There'll be plenty of work for him."

But Katerina couldn't get over it and in the evening when they were in bed, Darya said in response to her plaint: "Why are you upset? Why are you torturing yourself? You didn't know, is that it, what your Petrukha is like? Or do you think that he's the only one like that in the world? We went over to the mill, didn't you see how many of them there were? You keep harping, 'shame, shame' . . . If not him, someone else would burn them. A holy place doesn't stand empty—forgive me, O Lord!"

"Let someone else do it. Why him? He's earned himself a reputation to his dying day, he'll never wash it off."

"Why should he? He'll live with it no worse than anyone else. He'll even brag about it. Don't worry about him so, Katerina. You feel sorry for yourself. What does he care: when this job is over, he'll find another one just like it."

"Am I his mother or not? He's shaming me too. And people will point at me too."

"Don't exaggerate. Who's going to point at you, who needs you? No one even knows you. How long are you planning to live anyway—a hundred years?"

"Maybe I should go there"? Katerina cautiously suggested without answering Darya's question. "Set him straight? Say, what are you doing?"

Darya jumped on the idea.

"Yes, go ahead. See which houses burn better—the ones in Podvolochna or Matyora. To celebrate the occasion of your coming he'll set off two or maybe even three houses at once—oh, what a sight. Then you can tell us which village the sun warmed better. Get going the first thing in the morning, don't put it off. They'll take you in the cutter for that. You set him straight. Why is he burning strangers' houses when not all of ours are burned down yet. Ah, Katerina, why did we miss that? We've lived and lived and we haven't gotten any smarter. Are we infants, are we? . . . Well?"

And they stopped talking, dropping a useless conversation. Katerina knew that she wouldn't go anywhere and that there was nothing she could do to teach or correct Petrukha: he always was and would be Petrukha. It looked like he would be that way to the end of his days, that was his fate. And her fate was to be Petrukha's mother. She had to bear it wordlessly, accept it, and not complain. People . . . Katerina started thinking whether she should feel shame before people, acquaintances and strangers, for herself and for Petrukha, since he didn't know the meaning of shame. And if she was useless now, unneeded by her son and even less so by strangers, was it as if she didn't exist? Maybe she should pretend that she didn't exist and that whatever was inside her skin wasn't good for anything—not conscience or shame. Why suffer and feel shame if no one needs your shame, no one expects it, and there isn't a single soul before whom you feel guilty and who would respond to your feelings? Why bother? Darya—she understands everything. Darya wouldn't judge her. She would lie low and live for herself . . . and there was so little left to live . . .

And Darya thought about how she would feel in Katerina's place, what words she would defend herself with. Probably she would feel the same thing and say the same thing. And Katerina would answer the same way if she were in Darya's place. What did it mean? This was the first time that Darya gave any close thought to a person's position in life, to the place in which he stands. She didn't have to be ashamed of her children and so she took it as a right to make Katerina answer for Petrukha, to lecture her, to practically blame her. And Katerina would treat her the same way if Darya had been Petrukha's mother. But then where was a person's character, his own personality, so unlike anyone else's, if so much depended on whether you were lucky or not? What happens to the human being if his position says so much for him? And if Darya were in Sima's position, living in a strange village, without kin or defenders, with a little grandchild on her hands—would she also be lower than grass and quieter than water? What could she do?—she probably would be. How little there turned out to be of one's own in a person, given to him at birth, and how much in him came from fate, from where he happened to be, and from what he carried with him. Could she really have been like Sima?—they were completely different people.

Sima was quietly whispering to Kolka, who was falling asleep. The evening light had gone out and after a brief darkness and night light started: the windows showed more brightly, the murky air trembled with a dead glow, objects floated, swaying out of the invisibility, and weak, shimmering shadows appeared. Somewhere at the other end of the village a dog barked without letup, as though it was its job—tiredly, without anger, just so no one forgot it was there. Individual, unrelated words sounded from Sima's whispers—like shadows of real words, they were so quiet and lonely. And then Katerina began again, quietly and sadly.

"And it's not as though I'm asking a lot . . . Heavenly Mother, listen. All I ask is that he find a job, the shiftless son of mine . . . doing human work. I guess I could live without Matyora then. If they gave him a corner somewhere, then a cot like this would fit for me, too. I would wake him in the morning: 'Wake up, Petrukha, time to go to work.' Pack a lunch for him. Let him yell at me, whatever—I would bear it. I'd bear a lot more than that if I knew that he was on the right path."

"Marry him off," Darya said grumpily: Katerina was going on about Petrukha again. "If you can't handle him, then find him a wife who'll hold him with hedgehog mitts. Or he'll never come to any good."

"Who'd marry a no-good like him? . . ."

"If he only took himself into hand a little, why not marry him?"

"He is kind," Katerina said, happy that even Darya didn't think that he was a total loss, that even she saw salvation for him no matter how weak and undependable a salvation it was. "He has a soft heart . . ."

Darya harrumphed up on the stove; it certainly was soft—couldn't be any softer.

"No, really. I wouldn't brag about things he doesn't have. But this is true. We used to have a calf—and he'd give it all our bread. He'd cut it into pieces, salt it, and give it to the calf. She knew him: she'd come by the gate in the evening and bellow. She was calling him. I'd chase her away—she'd come round the other side and yell even louder. If I fed her with my own hands a piece just like his, she'd eat it but keep calling for him to come out. And when he gave it food, then it went away. And before, we had a cow . . . he'd see that she had eaten everything that I gave her, and he'd secretly throw her some more hay, so that I wouldn't yell. He fed her too. And all the puppies he brought home!— where did he find them all? Especially when he wasn't sober— he'd always have a puppy inside his jacket. One time we had four; that's plenty of dogs. I started yelling at them. Each one had to be fed a piece, and we didn't have enough pieces for ourselves. No, he just didn't understand a thing."

"Hah, how kind!" Darya couldn't resist. "He fed stray dogs, took pity on them, but he abandoned his own mother. Just live however you can. No business of his."

"Worthless. I tell you he's worthless," Katerina replied matter-of-factly. "He gave the cow more without thinking about whether she'd have enough to last till spring. I parceled it out, specifically, to make it stretch, but he fed her any old amount. And then, by springtime, there was nothing to give her."

"What are you telling me about the cow for again? What are you going to do, poor thing, when they throw us out of here? She's telling me about the cow, when the cow's been dead a hundred years at least."

"I'm telling . . ." Katerina had nothing to say and her voice sounded hollow, without firmness or hope. "If he got a job somewhere . . . a corner for me . . ."

Darya sighed loudly, loud enough for the whole house. "Ah, if only the frosts didn't hit the flowers . . ."

But apparently that's the direction the conversation was taking and there was no turning off: Sima joined in after putting Kolka to sleep, and she led it in the same direction.

"To each his own. You, Katerina, would like to live near your son, take care of him. See your grandchild, take care of him—"

"Oh, don't even say it, Sima," Katerina sighed, not even daring to hope for such happiness. "Don't."

"I can't expect any help from my daughter, either. I don't know where to lay my head. At least I have Kolka. I have to keep on living for him. But how? I keep thinking night and day, night and day: how will I live? Where should I go? If I could just find some old man . . ."

"Lord!" Darya pleaded. "What else! Her ass is down to her knees, and she's going on about an old man! Well . . . What would you do with an old man, forgive me, Lord, you're a bride with seventy-seven holes. With sand falling out of every one. What would you do for an old man?"

Sima maintained an insulted silence.

"Well, what do you want with him? What the hell do you need one for?" Darya persisted. "Why won't you tell us?"

"I have nothing to hide, Darya Vasilyevna." If she was using "Darya Vasilyevna" then Sima was really hurt. "Anyone can dream, you know. Katerina dreams of living near her son, and I have my dreams. I want to have my own corner too. I'm not so old, I'm still good for housework. No one would be sorry to have me in the house. I don't need much, Darya Vasilyevna. At my age people don't come together to have children, but to get through old age together more easily. And Kolka would grow up, I have to worry about him. I don't dream about just anything. And what I'm good for, I am good for. I could do the wash and the cooking."

"You're good for that . . ."

"And if you have nothing to dream about . . . well, that's not our fault. Your children are in the world, and they still respect you. It's us poor lonely people . . . And we can't cry all the time."

"And would you sing the old man a song?"

"If he was a nice old man, I'd sing him a song. He would listen."

And now Darya retreated into silence, embarrassed by the forgotten word *dream*. Was it for Sima to say it? And Darya to listen? You dream when you're a young woman, preparing for life, knowing nothing about it, and once you get a man and start a family—you only have hope left. And with each year hope lessens, and it melts like snow until it's gone, absorbed by the soil—

and now instead of hope all you have is a memory steaming up from under the soil. All right, Sima—what could you expect from her? She was down to dreaming! She was all alone, and not too bright. A free bird with no place to perch, all the places were taken. And her wings weren't as strong as they used to be for flying around. "She was Sima, but she missed!" Darya remembered how they teased her. She would miss, that was for sure. But thinking about it, Darya realized sadly that Sima was probably right when she said that Darya didn't need anything for tomorrow. Not dreaming—certainly not that!—and not even hoping, and she didn't seem to have the simplest desires left either. It was all off somewhere. What did she have to hope for that was certain? Death? That was inevitable, no point in wasting hope on that. What else was there? Nothing. That meant she would be dying soon, since she had nothing to live with. Sima and Katerina would hold on and live some more, and not because they were younger, for she still had some of her strength left, but because there was a reason for them to be here: Sima had to raise the boy, Katerina had to worry about Petrukha, hope for his rehabilitation. They were needed by someone, and they would function from that need of them, but no one demanded anything of her. Here she was a guard, but once she moved that wouldn't be necessary. A person can't live without a reason, without being needed. That's the end of him. And people who weren't in her postition and people who weren't as old as she, left without being necessary, without use, just folded their hands to their chest. Someone watched over that carefully.

It grew lighter and more unsettling—the moon appeared in the window. The crazed dog rattled on with its metallic voice—that miserable barking was ear piercing. To disrupt the stifling anxiety that sprang up from nowhere, Darya wanted to get up—and she wanted to so much, it seemed so necessary that knowing that it was pointless, she nevertheless hurriedly lowered her stocking feet on the step, walked down to the floor, and went over to the window. Half the garden was flooded with bright, full moonlight, the wooden walk by the porch bathed in it like water; half the garden lay in the heavy, solid shadow of the barn. It looks boiled, Darya thought with a shudder about the moonlight and turned from the window. Sima, watching Darya, raised her head from the pillow, and Darya—she had to say something—asked: "Is the boy asleep?"

"He's asleep," Sima replied cordially. "A long time ago. What are you doing?"

"Nothing. My back got tired on the stove. All the bricks. I just stretched my legs a little, wanted to see if it was you who talked to me or not. I'm going back up now."

"Well, and who talked to you?" Katerina asked. "Was it us?"

"Who knows? It sounded like you, but the words belonged to young women. Oh, what's our Nastasya doing now—sleeping or not? Maybe she's lying like us, remembering us. She doesn't even know that we're living in one house now. Oh, Nastasya, Nastasya! I wish she'd get here soon, so we can see her again and gab. If Nastasya lay here with us—that would be a commune, we wouldn't need anyone else. She'd have plenty to tell about. She's seen more now than I have in my entire life. She saw enough for herself and for us. We could listen till morning."

She clambered back up on the stove with groans and creaks, and resting after her climb, finally spoke about herself.

"Oh, if a new person took a look at me: I really am like a witch. No skin, no face. And worse than that, I've become angry. That's not good at all. Before I didn't seem mean. But now, I don't like this, I don't like that. It's time for me to die, there's no other way. I guess they'll bury me all right, they won't leave me on top of the ground, and I don't need anything else. Am I right, girls?"

The "girls," not knowing whether it would be good to agree, said nothing.

"Are you asleep? Well, sleep if you're asleep. It'll be light soon. And after the dawn, it'll be day—we'll spend time then. Maybe that's the way it's supposed to be. So you sleep, too, Daryushka. There's no reason, people say, for your heart to ache. Then why does it ache so? It's all right when it aches for one thing—it can be healed: but when there's no reason, or all reasons? It's on fire, the poor thing, aching and aching, burning and burning. No relief. I guess I'm very guilty. I know that I'm guilty, but I wish someone would tell me what I'm guilty of, what I must repent for, sinner that I am. How can I live without repentance? Oh, sleep, sleep now . . . The sun will come in the morning, it'll tell you many things. When there's nothing else in the world, it's still worth living just for the sun."

18

THEY HARVESTED THE WHEAT, and rain came for three more days. But it was modest and helpful—it took away the dust, softened the tired, hardened earth, rinsed the forests that had wilted and turned gloomy in the long sun, chased out the red mushrooms, which were late this year, and doused the smoldering smoke and acrid bitter smells of the fires. And the rain fell radiantly and quietly, without congesting the air, or blocking out the distances, or giving too much water—the sun managed to seep through the incorporeal, melting clouds with a secondary, thin light. It was warm and muggy all three days, the rain caused no commotion falling to the earth, it didn't leave any puddles behind, and the ground dried quickly. And when it did dry out, they saw that the time had come to dig potatoes.

The strangers, done with the wheat, were gone, thank God—the cleansing, blessed rain came after them. It was easier, more peaceful, you could go outside without fear, take a walk on the island. But they had a noisy farewell party, fighting again, chasing one another and yelling all over the village; the women bustled about, soothing someone, and that meant that they were poisoning him against someone, adding more anger; they rampaged all night, like madmen, all night they kept the village a-tremble, and in the morning, before sailing off, for a hot keepsake, they set fire to the office where they had stayed. As soon as they had gone, another of their troop came out from the bushes on the upper canal—a scabby, dirty, and terrible-looking man with fresh tears and gashes in his clothes, who had some reason for hiding from his own gang. Seeing the fire, he rushed over to the village—and still running, without the slightest hesitation, he raced into the office door, behind which he must have left something, and by some miracle he managed to turn around inside and leap out empty-handed. He hopped and hopped around, doing a charred jog, then relaxed, and stepped back to watch the fire.

It burned for an amazingly long time, letting up only toward evening, but the high pile of coals—all that was left of the office —still released waves of heat in the darkness. No one had the presence of mind to watch that mound of coals, and in the morning when they woke up the stables next to it were burning. But they couldn't blame the fellow who stayed behind the rest because he had left during the day. The manure in the horse yards, pressed down by many feet, caught and smoldered. Then the rain came, but it couldn't knock down the smoke—the smoke never did leave Matyora.

They began bringing over schoolchildren to dig the sovkhoz potatoes. The noisy, restless tribe, spilling out on shore, immediately rushed to check the chicken coops and pens for feathers. Heaven forbid that they spot a live chicken—they chased it down and plucked it. Vera Nosaryova barely rescued her rooster: two kids had him trapped between their feet and were finishing him off. After that the marvelous-voiced rooster didn't cockle-doodle-

doo anymore, he just quacked pathetically—he was scarred by
the near-fatal fright. The workers stuck the feathers in the potatoes and threw them into the air—the playthings flew down with
a whistling, beautiful spin. The most fun was hitting your mark,
someone's bent back. Simply throwing around potatoes was hooli-
ganism, but if they had feathers, it was a game. And they played
—that's the kind of people they were. What could you expect
from children? But scattering across the field, they would now
and then bend over for something and pick it up, and eventually there would be enough for the truck to make a trip to the
shore. Probably the older ones among them watched and yelled at
them. Darya once watched them from afar: they played, and lit
bonfires, and circled them to make sure they didn't get out of
hand, but the ones who were working moved quickly, pulling up
potato greens like hemp. And what was left behind in the ground,
only the soil knew. Before, protecting and cleansing itself, preparing
for a new crop, the soil would have pushed up the poor work
itself, but now, before its death, it didn't care either.

To help the children, women were taken off various duties in
the settlement—office, hospital, kindergarten, cafeteria—wherever they could be spared. The sovkhoz directors, not without
some pressure, of course, felt that distant and inconvenient Matyora had to be cleared first and that's where they sent people.
And they did clean it up fast: in other years this would have
been the big push, the height of the harvest, but now it was the
end anyway, it might as well be a party. They didn't care about
big fields: whatever they came up with would do, as long as the
land was cleared. No one asked them about centers. The new
sovkhoz was permitted to function at a deficit the first few years
—so why bother cleaning up wheatears and digging out the very
last potatoes in the ground in doomed, soon-to-be-flooded fields?
It was time to do without the land's full yield.

Few of the Matyora women went to work on the sovkhoz potatoes: they were busy with their own. It was the last time that
all the people were gathered in the village. But now, as opposed
to the mowing, they didn't get together, didn't sing songs, didn't

talk about the pending disaster—they rushed, each one lived in his own house, in his own garden, with his own problems, and the coming flooding grabbed them by the throat without any conversation. They pulled the children out of school, hired workers: the fourth sack is yours, but hurry, hurry . . . The people will finish and the cutter will stop ferrying, and if you have to transport it under your own steam, you'll hop and shout for the boat. The sovkhoz crops were already sent off, the fields were empty and bare, and Matyora was getting emptier and draftier. How could they think of songs?—half the village was burned, and the remaining unchained houses, broken down into links, were so wasted and shriveled into the ground from fear, seemed so pathetic and aged, that they couldn't understand how they had ever lived in them. What songs!—the Matyora forests were burning, and there were days when the island, enshrouded in smoke, could not be seen from the far shore—they just sailed for the smoke.

The fire setters from the lumber town finished up on Podmoga and quickly moved over to Matyora without much ado. There were five men sometimes, sometimes seven—not like the ones from that other horde, they were middle-aged, dignified, quiet. They moved into the Kolchak shack, on the other side of the wall from Bogodul—there was nowhere else on Matyora for them. In the morning they walked through the village from the upper end to the lower one, to work, and in the evening they came back from the lower to the upper end. They seemed terrifying because of their work—that final, last work that would close Matyora for centuries on end. They walked silently, talking to no one, looking at nothing, but firmly, in the middle of the road, with an owner's self-confidence, and their very appearance, their very presence, made people rush: hurry, hurry, before they set fire to us. They won't wait. The dogs could sense what kind of people these strangers were and skulked in doorways, tails tucked in, when they saw them. And then there was the rumor that the "arsonists," as they called them, were prepared to burn down the village along with the forests. And Bogodul had noticed that Vorontsov and someone from the district leadership had come to see them in the shack and talked for a long time. After all, they were arsonists. And even if you were mad at them, there was no reason to be if you thought about it, because if they didn't do it, someone else would, because it had to be done; but naturally, there was no one in the village who cared to talk to them: whatever they did, their eyes were straight ahead.

The potatoes in a farewell gesture grew not simply abundantly but crazily: two bushes—a bucket, two bushes—a bucket. And the buckets weren't the market kind, but your own. And so everyone who had cared for it the least bit had plenty to pick and clean and store. But even as they oohed over the potatoes, white and clean in the sand, as big as piglets, they also oohed over the sacks that they had to drag over and over before they could ship them from the island, not to mention how they would get them home. Drag them from the garden to the wagon, from the wagon down the ravine, from the shore to a ferry or cutter, and you had to wait for the cart because there was only one little mare left for the whole village and all the cars were gone. And the ferry wasn't exactly waiting at the shore. They suffered with their great wealth! But the greatest worry was: Where would they store the potatoes in the settlement? Many had water in their cellars since spring, and pouring the potatoes into these was like throwing them in the Angara. Of course the sovkhoz, to help out, had offered the use of its vegetable cellar, which was barely half full, but that was unthinkable for a housewife: throw your own potatoes, which seemed better, more familiar, and tastier than any other, into a huge common hole and then get who knows what. And the running you'd have to do with your bucket or pot to God knew where, and where would the devil with the key be, by the door or home asleep on the stove? There was nothing to talk about!—if it isn't at home, it's not your own. And there was no underground big enough for twelve villages.

But that would be there, over there, in the future. Here they had to dig it out in a hurry, so that the water wouldn't sweep it away.

The Pinigins managed with their potatoes in three days, with just a few left over for the fourth. Pavel had begged off from work, Sonya came out for the first time that summer; but she didn't come alone, she brought a hired hand with whom she shared an abacus at the office, a yound red-haired laugher named Mila. When she laughed, Mila threw back her curly cap of hair and rolled her eyes, and well, since she laughed almost nonstop, her eyes seemed white, blind. No matter what you said, she thought it was funny, even when she didn't know where she was or whether this was a good place to brush your teeth. That's why Darya didn't like her at first.

"What, what did you say her name was?" she asked Sonya, loud enough for the newcomer to hear.

"Mila."

"Mila? 'Mila' always meant 'darling.' Are they using it as a name now?"

"Yes," the newcomer laughed. "There is, Granny, there is. Why?"

"It makes things hard! Before, a fellow could call any girl that. They were all darlings. They used to make up songs about them. Haven't you heard them? And now they call calves that."

"Calves?" The hand laughed even louder. "You know how to put things, Granny. You mean I'm a calf? Do I look like a calf?"

"Well, you do," Darya agreed with pleasure. "Then you really are Mila."

The hand dug for two days, and dug hard, and so Darya came to accept her constant laughter that rarely stopped even over work, and her frivolous, also laughable name. And she really calmed down when her questions revealed that Mila was married and had, like any normal woman, a child. That meant that the man had put up with the noise for years—let the poor thing get a short rest. By the end of the second day, when Mila was preparing to leave, Darya said:

"You really ought to trade with some calf or other. Some have nice names. We had a Zoya once, I recall—that's a good name! You'll see, you might laugh less, too. What's so funny all the time?"

Mila roared and while Sonya walked her to the shore, as long as Darya could hear, she laughed without stop, as though some incorrigible fool kept pulling a rope and the bell pealed and tinkled. And Darya thought: maybe that's good, maybe that's the way it should be, knowing no worries, no sadness. If they exist, *ha-ha*, and if they don't, *ha-ha!* With people like that, sorrow can come and they won't recognize it, they'll laugh it off like a suitor who didn't please; no sorrow would stick to the heart, everything would be taken lightly, life was a joke. And really—what was wrong with that? Where do you learn to be that way?

Pavel took the potatoes away on the third day. They filled up fifteen sacks, all the bags they had, but the pile in the garden was barely touched. There were so many more! That meant they would not be able to bring it all. Darya hinted they should help Katerina, take five sacks of hers, too; they couldn't count on Petrukha—he might show up, he might not—but the old woman had to live somewhere and eat something.

"Where will I put them?!" Pavel asked, not refusing but really not knowing what to do with them, and shrugged.

"Where will you put ours?"

"What won't fit will have to stay on the veranda for now."

"Won't fit"—that meant in the cellar. Pavel worked on it a whole month: he brought sand from the Angara, built a floor, and got rid of the water (it was lucky that his house happened to be on higher ground: the ones below couldn't get rid of the water), but it became noticeably smaller, and you couldn't stuff too much in it. Digging out to the side meant work: the cellar was cement, and if you dig out beyond it you might hit water again. Better keep away from trouble and settle for what you had.

Sonya, who had dug for two days with a bent back, sank to her knees on the third. As though in payment for their lodging, Sima and Katerina came to help Darya and Sonya. While the family stayed with Darya, the women slept in Nastasya's house, but as soon as Sonya left, they came back. Sonya left in the evening with a groan: she had gotten soft in the office and it was obvious that she had overextended herself. There in the new settlement, she had changed so much over the summer that Darya looked at her like a stranger sometimes: she got fat and fleshy, cut her hair in the city style and curled it, which made her face look bigger and rounder, and her eyes were closed by fat and seemed squinty and small. She learned to be interested in diseases and spoke of them with great knowledge, naming them and remembering what treated what. They didn't have time for diseases on Matyora, even paramedics didn't stay: they'd come see that there was water all around, that the people were busy and healthy, and they'd go back.

"So, do you like it there?" Darya asked Sonya carefully.

"It's not like here," she replied angrily, without explanations. Whether "not here" was worse or better, go figure out for yourself.

And Darya realized that the attitude toward her, an old woman, would be different there. Here she lived in her own house, everything for miles around was her own, came from her, and she was revered as mistress of it all. She didn't have to act it either—it was acknowledged automatically. There, Sonya would be mistress. She wasn't a spring chicken anymore, she knew that she wouldn't be in her prime much longer—it was time for her to come to the fore, no longer obeying but obeyed. Man can't live without that, bossing someone else, that's his sweetest job, and the longer he spends under someone the more he tries to make up for lost time.

The cutter pulled the ferry every day, and sometimes twice a day. They brought out the potatoes, and those who had cattle left brought them out, picking up whatever else might come in handy. There was no time left for putting things off: the very final deadline was here, mid-Setember. Many were helped out by a self-propelled barge that moored off the shore to buy potatoes—four rubles a sack. After thinking if over, and tired of bothering with the potatoes, Pavel sold the last twenty sacks. He had made three trips already, fifteen bags at a time, he had more than enough. He suggested that Katerina sell all of hers and he promised her whatever she might need for herself from his supplies, the potatoes were the same. But Katerina still kept three bags—you never know! And Sima was twenty rubles richer—she really had no place to put anything and nothing to count on, and the garden, which wasn't greedy, gave what was expected of it and then some. Later Sima sighed that she should have sold more, but she held back, and saved half the potatoes, which now lay on her porch in the sun and were turning green.

The old women couldn't decide what to do about Nastasya's garden. Nastasya hadn't come. In the summer, Darya kept an eye on it, watering and raking, chasing chickens away—would her labor and kindness go to waste? It was the last one in the village: the nurturing plots were bare. A few carrots, beets, and turnips stuck out here and there. Knowing that cabbage wouldn't have time to harden, most people didn't bother planting it. Seeing it was useless, the garden fencing fell down, the wind ruffled the dried, thin cucumber grass in the upper plots, and stirred the useless potato greens. Only Vera Nosaryova gathered it into a pile, as usual, but even she refused to haul it away and use it for feed: she had enough worries. She couldn't bother with the greens—at least she got her hay over there, and that was joy enough.

Nastasya hadn't come, and there was nothing for the old women to do but start in on her garden. What could they do? They closed the shutters in Nastasya's house and stored the potatoes in there on the floor, but why they dug them out and stored them—to let them burn with the house or to be put to good use—they didn't know. They also said that the arsonists bragged about the delicious roast red mushrooms that they picked when they burned down forests—and maybe this time they'd roast some potatoes. But it seemed sinful to leave it in the ground—how could they allow it to stay, that was unthinkable. Nastasya had to come, since she had promised—how were they going to live there without potatoes? Maybe something held her up, maybe she would surface from the Angara at the very last minute when it would be too late to dig, but sacking it would go fast, they would help her bag it.

And they dug it out . . . no Nastasya . . .

The cattle were moved out; Pavel was among the last to come for his cow. The cow, the sweet and docile Mayka, terrified by the disarray, fires, loneliness, and bustle, hadn't left the yard in several days. Darya chased her out to graze—Mayka mooed and huddled in her dirty, dark stall. It was only at night that she had the courage to come out, and even then not to wander freely but to go into the next garden, where she fed on greens and went back. She spent long hours standing still with her head bent, neck out, stretched toward the door, in constant tense anticipation, preparing herself for something. And when Pavel tossed a rope over her neck and led her away, Mayka went gladly—anywhere, to do anything, just as long as it was away from this terrible place. And she quietly went up the planks onto the ferry, and allowed herself to be tied with her back to Matyora, squinting at the distant opposite shore.

Darya, seeing her off, wept.

"Well, Mother," Pavel had said back at the house, "maybe we'll take you at the same time? There doesn't seem much left for you to do here."

"No," Darya refused firmly. "Don't touch me for now. I'm no cow to just leave Matyora like that. You have nothing to do here. But I do."

"They'll be burning it soon, Mother . . ."

"Let them."

And she couldn't resist, she asked with reproach and bitterness, knowing that it was too late and that nothing could be done.

"So we're leaving the graves then? Our family graves? To go underwater?"

Pavel's face sank; he was pitiful to see.

"You see, everything turned out differently," he began explaining. "We were planning to . . . if it hadn't been for that . . . incident . . . Now when could I do it? I owe my relief man three days. It probably won't work, Mother. We're not the only ones . . ."

"If we abandon them, no one will think twice about abandoning us," she prophesied. "Oh, we're inhuman, that's what we are. How will we manage without our family graves?"

When Pavel left, she went to the cemetery, still hot and upset

over their conversation. The day was coming to a close, the sun
was down more than halfway and warmed with a dry, quickly
cooling heat. The smell of burnt things was strong and stifling:
the fir barrens rose from the ground and flew up into the sky
behind the pasture, and the colorless, seemingly empty flame,
resembling a large playful sunspot, rose and fell. If it weren't for
the crackle and noise coming from there, you wouldn't be able to
tell that the barren was burning: you couldn't tell its smoke from
the smoke that came from somewhere else and settled over the
Angara. There was a feeble, high breeze from the upper end, and
Darya's throat burned, her head ached, and her feet stumbled as
they felt their way. From the right, beyond the turning promontory, came the putt-putt of the cutter on which Mayka left. And
now Mayka was off, sensing danger here and not sensing it there,
where the worry now was how to feed her until the frost so that
the meat wouldn't spoil.

The gate was open at the cemetery, and right beyond the gate
on the first meadow lay a large black spot of charred earth. Darya
looked up and didn't see crosses or headstones or beds on the
graves—what the old women had stopped at the beginning of the
summer, fighting off the strange men, had been done now under
cover of fire and smoke. But now she felt no outrage or hurt—
only the sense of ending. There was much that she had seen and
borne since then—her heart had turned to stone. She had lived to
see this, too—well, it was good, good that she had, it was meant
to be. She couldn't feel anger: she was joining her family and she
couldn't go there with an anxious, troubled soul, she would have
to turn back. The end, there was only one end . . .

She turned left and in the deep forest found the mound under
which lay her father and mother, the ones who gave her life. Soil
from the unearthed cross was scattered on the mound. On the left
lay her mother, she had been buried first, and her father on the
right. At the head of the mound, on the slope, grew a rowan tree
that Darya had planted long ago, and red berries, pecked by
birds, lay on the grass. There was a fir tree at the feet; in the days
when the graves were dug, there hadn't been a trace of it; it grew

on its own from a random seed. The mound had long seemed too short to Darya, and she had stopped herself more than once from stretching out and measuring herself against it to find out for sure whether the soul had run off from it over these long years or whether a person truly was so small. The branches of the rowan tree and the fir met on top. And it was terrible, and sinful, and satisfying to think that perhaps there was some measure of participation in their lives, as in hers, of the two who were lying deep in the ground where the roots were nourished. Everything here was familiar.

Darya bowed to the mound and lowered herself on the ground next to it. The breeze didn't get in here, it was quiet, only the prickly grass rustled drily. The smoke hadn't yet killed the special, tantalizing and sweet smell that exists only in cemeteries and which seems to be the smell of human departure.

She shut her eyes to keep from seeing the smoke and the ransacked graves, and swaying back and forth with lulling motions, as though flying from one state and heading toward another, gathering relief in unconsciousness, she quietly spoke.

"It's me, Papa. It's me, Mama." Her voice was unsteady, weak and she stopped and waited for the right voice and repeated it in another tone, good for distant penetration. "Here I am. I'm completely free now, they even took the cow away today. I can die now. And Papa, I'll have to die away from Matyora. I won't lie with you, it won't work. And I wanted to take you with me, so we could all lie together there, and that didn't work. Don't be mad at me, it's not my fault. I am guilty, I am, I'm guilty because it fell on me. And fool that I am, I didn't know what to do. You told me, Papa, to live a long life . . . I obeyed, I lived. And what did I live so long for, I should have gone to you, then we would all have been together. And now what? I can't die in peace knowing that I turned from you, that it was my generation and no other that cut off our family and swept it away. Oh, it'll be swept away . . . And I, accursed, will be separate, I'll start a new settlement. Who could forgive me that?! Papa! Mama! Is it my fault?" She buried her face in the grass of the grave's mound and her shoulders shook. And she complained bitterly into the grass and earth: "It's so smoky, so smoky here. You see that. But do you see me? Do you see what's become of me? I'm yours, I belong with you, I should be with you . . . I belong to your times. I should go to you . . . I'd see the house off and then join you. I don't care if there's fire or water . . ." She raised her head and fixed her kerchief. "Our house, Papa, will go . . . there . . . today or tomorrow. And I'll watch. I'll come as close as I can and I'll watch how it burns. And then I'll come and tell you. What can I do? Well?"

And suddenly it came to her—as though a barely perceptible whisper reached her from somewhere far, far away: "Did you prepare our house? You planned to see it off, but how? Will you just walk out and slam the door behind you? You have to clean the house. We all lived in it." With a shudder, Darya agreed hurriedly: "I'll clean it, I will. How could I have forgotten? I should have known that for myself. I will."

"And what else?" she asked, hoping for an answer. "What else should I do? What should I do?" And she strained, tensed, listening, gathering the sounds that floated past. But no, nothing else was said to her. The most important thing wasn't said. It was quiet, and the rustle of grass and leaves didn't form an answer. She asked once more, without hope this time—the graves were silent. And she decided that she hadn't been forgiven. Served her right. What did she think had earned her forgiveness? She couldn't forgive herelf, and she expected them to—wasn't she ashamed of herself?

Darya lifted her eyes—smoke hung in the tree tops, and a few merry clouds floated in the high sky. The sun was low and sent slanted rays through the cemetery woods, the long shadows seemed rounded and solid—and along one such shadow two birds with perky tails hopped as though along a log. But Darya didn't want to return to that world where the sun glowed as it set and birds hopped—it wasn't time for that. She imagined that when she left here to join her family many people would gather to judge her—her father and mother, grandparents and great-grandparents, everyone who had come before her. She imagined that she could see them standing in an endless formation, a spreading wedge—all with grim, stern, and demanding faces. And at the point of the multigenerational wedge, standing back a bit to be seen better, facing everyone, she stands alone. She hears voices and understands what they're talking about, even though the words aren't clear, but she has nothing to say in reply. Lost, confused, and scared, she looks to her mother and father, standing right in front of her, thinking that they will help, defend her before the others, but they maintain a guilty silence. And the voices get louder, more impatient, more violent. They ask about hope, they say that Darya has left them without hope or a future. She tries to step back but they won't let her: behind her a boy's voice demands that she stay where she is and answer, and she realizes that there behind her must be Senka, her son killed by a falling tree.

She felt spooky and dropped the vision with difficulty. The unfamiliar distant faces faded, but the voices, growing dim, still went on about hope. Coming to her senses, Darya had an unsteady thought: turns out that you need hope over there too. Everywhere. It must be so. But the faces of her father and mother and Senka, the people closest to her over there, still hovered above her, fading and disappearing behind a veil, then reappearing right next to her. Her parents looked at her silently and sadly, sorry and remembering that she was their daughter; Senka, an orphan there, kept demanding something.

She got up, reeling, steadied herself, bowed to the mound, and went in the direction of the shadows. Her head was spinning more now, but it wasn't far to Senka's grave, thirty paces, and when she reached it, she sank to the ground once more. "It's pulling me, the ground," she noted. "More than ever today." She was afraid to talk to her son: she really tricked him, she didn't show up, and the poor thing would wander without a connection to his kin. There was nothing she could do now. She sat, her unseeing eyes fixed in space, and thought and thought, heavily, unwillingly, not knowing the answers. All around her, amid the familiar birches and pines, rowan and cherry bushes, lay the exposed, outraged graves, their grass-covered mounds hunched over, and almost every other one belonged to kin: brothers, a sister, an uncle, aunts, grandparents, great-grandparents, and further back . . . She had just seen in her weak imagination how many there were and that wasn't all of them. No, the earth was pulling at her. Leaves in the trees quivered above them, and the tall grass, turning white, swayed. A upper breeze carried a light cloud over the sun and without covering it, flattened it—the sunlight grew dim, and the shadows were lifted from the ground. It was cooler.

And Darya still questioned herself, still tried to answer and couldn't answer. And who could? Man comes into the world, lives, and then when he's tired of life like Darya or when he's not, inevitably goes back. How many there were that came before her, and how many more there'll be after! She was at the turn in the road: one half exists and will be, the other was, but any second the road would dip and a new crossroads will arise at the turn. Where were there more of them—ahead or behind? And who knows the truth about man, why he lives? For the sake of life itself, the sake of children, so that his children leave children, and the children's children leave children, or for the sake of something else? Would this movement be eternal? And if it's for children, the movement, this eternal pull, then why come to these graves? Here they lie in full Matyora array . . . silent, hundreds of them who gave up their all for her, for Darya, and for those like her, and what came of it? What should a person feel for whom hundreds of generations have lived? He feels nothing. He understands nothing. And he behaves as though life began with him and will end with him forever. You, the dead, will tell: have you learned the truth there, beyond the line, or not? Why did you exist? Here we're afraid to find out, and there's no time anyway. What was it—what people call life—and who needs it? Is it needed for something or not? And our children, born of us, will get tired later and think and ask what they were born for. It's crowded here. And smoky. It smells of char.

"I'm tired," Darya thought. "Oh, so tired. I wish I didn't have to go anywhere now, and could just lie here, cover myself and find my long-awaited peace. And find out the whole truth once and for all. The earth is pulling me. And then I'll say from there: you're stupid. Why are you so stupid? Why ask questions? It's only you who don't understand, but here everything is clear to the last drop. We see every single one of you and we'll make demands on each of you. We will, we will. You're on display before us, and we look and see who's doing what, who remembers what."

And it was hard for Darya to believe that she was still alive; it seemed that she was saying the words just as she learned them over there, before they stopped her from saying them. Truth is in memory. The person without memory is without life.

But she understood: that wasn't the whole truth. She had to get up and go see and hear what happened to the end, and then she had to bring what she saw, heard, and experienced with her and receive the full truth in trade. She got up with difficulty and went.

On the right, where the fir barren was burning, the flames splashed brightly in the twilight; stars were showing in the sky; the tsar larch stood stark and alone in the pasture. And quietly, without a single light or sound, abandoned by absolutely every-one, miserable Matyora lay alone, keeping watch with its last few houses.

19

MATYORA, both the island and village, was impossible to imagine without that larch on the pasture. It rose and towered over everything else, like a shepherd above his flock spread over grazing lands. It did resemble a shepherd carrying on his ancient watch. But no one, no matter how literate, ever used the feminine about the larch; no, it was a he, the tsar larch—it stood so eternal, powerful, and mighty on the hill a half verst from the village, visible from almost every point and known by everyone. And apparently it had grown so high and so strong that it was decided in the heavens for the sake of propriety and measure to shorten it—that's when that famous storm raged, during which lightning cut off the top of the tsar larch and threw it down on the ground. Without its crown the larch squatted and seemed weaker, but it didn't lose its powerful, majestic appearance; it became, probably, even more awesome and imperious. It's not known when the superstition was born that it was the tsar larch that held the island firm to the river's bottom, to solid ground, and that as long as it stood so would Matyora. It wasn't so long ago that on the important warm holidays, Easter and Trinity, people brought it offerings of food, which they piled up at its roots and which the dogs, naturally, picked up later, but they felt that if they didn't leave the offerings the larch would be offended. These offerings gradually disappeared with the new life, but the respect and fear for the important, masterful tree remained among the old people. And there were good reasons for it.

The huge thick branches grew straight out of the trunk instead of on the usual diagonal—independent trees growing to the sides, it looked like. Years ago the lowest such branch had hung alone some four yards from the ground and had been called Pasha's bough for ages: once upon a time a young Matyora girl named Pasha, maddened by unrequited love, hanged herself from it. The Kolchak troops that took the island had never ever heard of Pasha but they recognized her bough and picked it and no other to dangle two of their own soldiers. No one on Matyora knew for sure what they had done. The hanged men swung in the breeze all day, frightening young and old alike, until the men came and asked them to remove them from their nooses for the sake of the children. The dead were then subjected to another execution— they were thrown from the ravine into the Angara.

And the last, completely innocent death occurred under the tsar larch after the war: a boy fell from the same Pasha's bough and strangled himself on a cord—it was Vera Nosaryova's son. And only after that, and it should have been done way sooner, the men cut off the bough and the children burned it.

That's how many different incidents revolved around the tsar larch.

Over its century it had dropped so many needles and cones that the earth around it had risen into a light, springy mound from which rose the mighty trunk, too large to be encircled by one pair of arms. Cows rubbed up against it, winds buffeted it, the village lads came by with slingshots and knocked off sulfur growths to give to the girls—and the bark gradually came off, the larch was denuded and could no longer spread out green needles in the spring. Weak and thin, the far-away twigs in the fifth or sixth joint broke off and fell. But what did remain seemed to become stronger and more dependable, good for centuries. The trunk bleached out and petrified, its powerful, spread-out base, showing twisted roots, bespoke only solidity without the slightest hint of rot or emptiness. From the side turned to the lower reaches of the river, from the back so to speak, the larch had an old, broad, slightly concave, clumsy indentation—and that was the only one; the rest of the tree appeared whole, poured in one piece.

And not far away, some twenty meters closer to the Angara, stood a birch which still turned green and had leaves but was old and dying. It was the only one that ever dared approach the tsar larch. And he let her, he didn't kill her off. Perhaps their roots united underground and lived in harmony, but here where they were visible it seemed that the larch put up with a birch that had mistakenly wandered near only through his great and capricious mercy.

And now the day came when the strangers walked up to the tsar larch. It was no longer day, it was evening, the sun had set, and twilight was descending on the island. The people were returning from their usual work, which they had been performing on Matyora for a good two weeks now. And no matter how well, how assiduously they performed their work, time went even faster, and it was running out. They had to rush. Their work had the peculiarity that if you got it started going well, it could continue on its own. That's why it was almost night when two men with faces so sooty they were tanned turned off the road and approached the tree.

The one who walked in front swung his ax handle against the trunk, to test the larch, and barely managed to hold on to the ax, rearing in fright—it had kicked back with such force.

"Oh-ho!" the man said in amazement. "What a beast! We'll

show you, you beast . . . Two times two is four with us. We've seen worse than you."

The second man, older, was carrying a canister and yawned as he looked at the tree. He was wearing tall swamp boots that shuffled unpleasantly, with a rubbery squeak, when he walked. Considering the work their master did, the boots seemed unreasonable, ruined for no good reason, and how his feet stood it in them was beyond understanding. They weren't any good for use in water anymore, either; both had holes.

The men walked around the trunk and stopped in front of the hollow indentation. The larch rose upward at a slight angle, leaning over the indentation, as though to protect it from strangers' eyes. The one with the ax tried to chip off some wood, but to his surprise the ax kept slipping and ringing, unable to dig in and grab hold of the wood, leaving small dents and nothing more. The man took a quick swipe across the wood with his sooty mitten, held the ax blade to the light, and shook his head.

"Like iron," he admitted and threw out another unintelligible mathematical threat. "Ah, you won't get away. With us, five times five makes twenty-five."

He tossed aside the useless ax, gathered branches and twigs that were scattered about, breaking them on his knees, and laid them down crosswise under the niche over the indentation. His pal, still yawning, poured kerosene from the canister over the trunk and sprinkled the remainder on the wood for the bonfire. He set the canister behind him and struck a match. The fire caught immediately, rose, and lashed at the trunk.

"There," the talkative man said, picking up his ax. "Light up for us, because it's dark now. We don't like the dark."

And they headed for the village; they went to eat and sleep, sure that while they slept the fire would do its work. When they left, it had surrounded the lower part of the mighty larch so brightly and was striving upward with such force and energy that it would have been silly to doubt it.

But in the morning when they were headed toward the lower

end of the island, where there was still some work left to do, the larch stood in its place as though nothing had happened.

"Looky there!" the man cried in amazement. "It's standing! Well, stand, stand on . . ." He was a jolly fellow and he sang in a deep voice. "You stand, stand there my beauty, let me look at you."

But he had no intention of looking at the tree for long. Soon after lunch the fire setters—for it was they—came back to the larch in full complement—five of them. They circled the tree again, touching it with their axes, trying to chop it and dropping their attempts: the axes, scraping off a thin layer of burned wood, pushed off from the trunk as if it were rubber.

"The beast!" the jolly man squinted at the tree in pleased amazement. "He's like our landlord,"—he meant Bogodul—"just as abnormal. It won't burn down like a good tree and not drive people crazy. No. You'll have to give in at the end. As far as we're concerned, six times six is thirty-six."

"The hell with it," yesterday's other friend suggested, the one in rubber boots, looking over at their brigade leader. "Why do we have to scrape the island clean to the last bit?"

The leader, the least imposing of them all, by the way, but with a mustache to look older, threw his head back.

"It's a big bastard! They won't accept it. We'll have to do something about it."

"We need a saw."

"You'll be sawing till doomsday. You need a hacksaw for this."

"I mean a chain saw."

"It won't do. This thing is——" and he used an unprintable expression. "Your chain saw will just tickle this thing."

One of the men who hadn't been near the larch the night before picked up a thin burned strip and sniffed it.

"Why waste time?" he said with a smirk. "What's the problem? This is pure resin. Look. Just make the fire hot enough and it'll go up just fine."

"We made a fire yesterday."

"It wasn't good enough then. You need more fuel."

"Let's try it again. It has to burn."

Rubber Boots was sent to the riverbank where the barrel of gas was; the rest started gathering piles from fallen garden fences, cutting them and putting a high cage, as tall as a man, around the tree, and not just one, but two. They stuffed the inside of the cages with small twigs and birch bark, stripping the birch to its naked skin. By that time the gas was there—they didn't skimp and poured it over the entire trunk and started the fire from below. The fire crackled, crumpling the birch bark, letting off a black, tarry smoke, and suddenly exploded, gasping on its deep inhalation for a second, and flew up with a tall, sweeping flame. The men, stepping back, covered their faces with their mitts.

"Just like two times two is four," the jolly one shouted victoriously.

But he rushed to victory once again. The fire danced, danced, and once it had licked off all the gas, began creeping down, separating away from the tree, as though the air around it was blazing, but the larch was unharmed behind a dependable fireproof shield. Ten minutes later the fire had crept down completely, and the dry fence poles burned, but they burned alone; their fire didn't stick to the tsar larch, it merely coated it with soot.

The poles burned down quickly. It was pointless to drag over new ones. The men swore. And the tree rose above them calmly and majestically, recognizing no power but its own.

"We should try the chain saw tomorrow," the brigade leader agreed, only minutes ago insisting that the chain saw wouldn't work on something that big and wide.

And then, louder now, more confidently, their retreating words rang out.

"The hell with it—and that's that! Let it stick out—who cares! It won't be in the way! Think how high the water will be! We have to clear the village, and we're wasting time on that thing."

"It's easy to say the hell with it!" The brigade leader was angry. "We're all masters at that, we don't need to learn how to do that.

But when the commission comes—what will you do with it? Hide it in your undershirt? You don't think we can bring down that tree?"

"If it were only a tree..."

On the third day, first thing in the morning, as their most important project, rather than a tangential task, they started in on the larch with a chain saw. The brigade leader decided to do it himself. He sidled up to the tree without any confidence, squinted at its power once more, and shook his head. But he turned on the saw, brought it over to the trunk, and pressed. It jumped almost out of his hands, but it did leave a slight cut. Following the cut, the brigade leader pressed harder—the saw burst into a high, straining whine, a light stream of colorless sawdust sprayed out from under it, but the leader could see that the saw wasn't taking. The heavy trunk didn't let him shake the saw, all he could do was encircle it with a shallow cut and no more. It was like using a sharp razor to cut through a block of wood—the result was the same. And the brigade leader turned off the saw.

"It won't fall," he said, giving up, and now knowing the larch's true worth, measured it with his eyes from top to bottom. "Let it go—who's going to bother with you, you bastard!"

He handed the saw to Rubber Boots, who happened to be nearby, and nodded angrily at the birch.

"Cut that down at least. So it doesn't stick up. They're all over, you know."

And the birch, whose only fault was that it stood next to the mighty and powerful tsar larch that refused to submit to man, fell, breaking its last branches, revealing fiber no longer white but aged and red in the cut and breaks. The tsar larch didn't even rustle in response. Leaning slightly, it seemed to be looking sternly and attentively at the lower end of the island, where the Matyora forests stood. They weren't there anymore. There were a few green lonely birches and sharp, charred stumps black against the burned-out areas. Low, dying smoke crawled over the island; the stubble in the fields with their burned-out interrows was turning yellow, like smoke; the meadows were cooling off; and huddling up to naked, disfigured Matyora was naked, disfigured Podmoga.

The sole survivor, the insubordinate tsar larch, continued to rule over everything around it. But everything around it was empty.

20

SHE HAD NO LIME, and nowhere to borrow it. Darya had to go to the spit by the upper promontory and pick up white rock and haul it back in a bucket straining her hands, because all the bags were in the settlement with the potatoes, and then, with the last of her strength, burn the rock as in the olden days. But miraculously—for when she began she didn't think she'd be able to finish—she managed: she burned it and got lime. She found a brush—Darya always had her own brushes made of tall, light white forest grasses cut just before the snow.

Whitewashing the house was considered a preholiday event: they whitewashed twice a year—after the autumn harvest before Intercession and after the winter heating for Easter. After getting the house ready, renovated, scraping the floors with a knife until they were milky yellow, they started cooking and baking and puttering by the whitewashed stove with its smoothed hearth, amid cleanliness and order, and the sense of anticipation of the church feast day felt so good and sweet that the Sunday feeling remained for a long, long time.

But she wouldn't be preparing the house for holiday now. After the time at the cemetery when Darya asked at her parents' grave what she should do and heard, she thought, an answer, she bowed to it completely. You don't put a person in his coffin without washing him and dressing him in his best—that was the custom. So how could she send off her own house, out of which her father and mother, grandfather and grandmother, were carried and in which she had spent her entire life, except for what was left, and deny it the same dressing up? No, the others could do what they want, but she understood things. She would see off the house properly. It stood and stood, poor thing, for some one hundred fifty years, and now it was over, now it would be off.

And one of the arsonists came by and hurried them.

"Well, old women"—they were all there: Darya, Katerina, and Sima—"We don't have orders to wait until you die. You have to move out. And we have to finish our work. Come on, don't drag it out."

And Darya hurried or, God forbid, they might burn it down without asking. All of Matyora's upper end, except for the Kolchak shack, was cleaned up, and on the lower end there remained six little houses huddled in a group, clutching one another, that would be best lit from two sides at once. It would be impossible to pull them out one at a time.

Seeing the prepared whitewash, Katerina said guiltily: "I didn't prepare mine."

"You didn't know what would happen," Darya said, trying to comfort her.

"I didn't" Katerina said, without relief.

Her head spun when she climbed up on the table, sparkling fiery lines ran before her eyes, and her knees buckled. Afraid of falling, Darya quickly sat down, holding her head in her hands, and then when her head and balance were under control she got up again, first on all fours—it was a good thing the table was low and steady—and then on her feet. She dipped her brush in the bucket of whitewash and holding on with one hand to a stool she had prepared, she moved the brush across the ceiling with the other hand, with clumsy short strokes that should have been broad and sweeping. Watching her struggle, Sima begged: "Let me. I'm younger, I don't get dizzy."

"Sit!" Darya answered, angry that her frailty was evident.

No, she would whitewash herself. She might be half dead, but she'd do it herself, she couldn't let anyone else. Her hands hadn't fallen off yet, and she needed her own hands for this, just as it is your own tears and not borrowed ones that bring relief at your mother's funeral. She didn't need to be told how to whitewash, she had done enough in her lifetime—and the lime covered smoothly, the powder giving off a soft blueness, and the drying ceiling breathed. Darya noted: It's drying fast. It knows what's coming, it's in a hurry. Oh, it knows, it knows, it must. And it seemed to her that the whitewash went on dull and sorrowing, and she believed that it had to be that way.

And standing on the table with the brush in her hand was how another arsonist found her—they must have been taking turns rushing them. His eyes opened wide in surprise.

"Are you crazy, old woman?! What, are you planning to live here? We're setting fire to it tomorrow and she's whitewashing. What's the matter with you?"

"Set fire to it tomorrow, arsonist," Darya stopped him from above with a stern, judgmental voice. "But not before evening. And now march out of here, you don't have authority in here. Don't bother me. And tomorrow, you hear me, and tomorrow when you come to set the fire, don't you step into the house. Do it from outside. I don't want you defiling my house. Understand?"

"I understand," the bewildered man nodded, understanding nothing. And still surprised, he left. And Darya hurried, hurried even more. Hah, they were in a hurry, they couldn't wait. They wouldn't wait, no, no, she had to rush. She had to get it done. That same day she whitewashed the walls and the Russian stove, and at twilight Sima helped her wash the painted partition and window-sills. Darya had some washed curtains. Her legs wouldn't go, her hands wouldn't move, and pain rolled in waves through her head, but Darya wouldn't let herself stop until late at night, knowing that once she stopped and sat down she wouldn't get up. She moved and couldn't get over the fact that she was moving and not falling—that meant that some other strength had been added to her own feeble powers just for this work. Could she have done this much for any other reason? No, she couldn't, she couldn't even think of it.

She fell asleep to the pleasant, cool smell of drying lime.

And she was back on her feet with the first light of morning. She lit the Russian stove and heated water for the floor and windows. There was still so much work, no time to lie in bed. Thinking of the windows, Darya suddenly realized that she hadn't whitewashed the shutters. She thought that she was finished, but she had forgotten the shutters. No, that wasn't how to do it. It's a good thing she didn't use up all the whitewash.

"Let me," Sima offered again.

And again Darya refused.

"No, I'll do it myself. You'll have enough hauling as it is. Today's the last day."

Sima and Katerina were moving Nastasya's potatoes in a cart to the Kolchak shack. Bogodul was helping. They gathered them together and saved them today, only for destruction tomorrow—that was probably how it would be. The Kolchak shack wouldn't stand much longer either. But while the saving was good, they had to save it. There was no hope left that Nastasya would come, but what was left was the old and reverent feeling for bread and potatoes, as for God.

Darya was finishing the shutters of the second street window when she heard voices and footsteps behind her—the arsonists in full force on their way to work. They stopped near her.

"The old woman's really nuts," one of them said in a jolly, surprised voice.

Another voice cut him off.

"Shut up."

A rather homely man with a machine on his shoulder approached Darya. This was the day that the arsonists were trying their hand at the tsar larch for the third time. The man coughed and spoke.

"Listen, old woman, you can spend tonight here too. We have enough work for today. But tomorrow . . . move out. Do you hear me?"

"I hear you," Darya replied without turning.

When they left, Darya sat on the earth mound in front in the yard and leaned against the house, feeling its worn, raspy, but warm and living wood with her back. She began weeping with the full force of her sorrow and injury—with dry, tortured tears: the last day, bestowed out of pity, was so bitter and so joyous. And it might happen that before her own death they would say: here, live until tomorrow—and what would she do that day, how would she spend it? Ah, how kind and good we all are when considered separately, and what senseless and great evil we create together—almost as if on purpose.

But these were her last tears. She cried and then ordered herself to cry no more, and they could burn her with the house, she would bear it all without a whimper. Crying means begging for pity and she didn't want to be pitied, no. She had done no wrong to the living—perhaps only in living so long. But someone had to, obviously, and it seemed to be she who had to be here, cleaning up the house and seeing off Matyora in a personal, family way.

At lunch they all gathered around the samovar—three old women, the boy, and Bogodul. They were the only ones left on Matyora, the rest were gone. They took away Grandpa Maxim: they held him up and walked him to the shore, he couldn't get there on his own. Tunguska's daughter came for her, a middle-aged woman, very much like her mother, and with a shiner under her eye; she brought along some wine and Tunguska drank and then shouted from the river, from the departing cutter, in her ancient, unintelligible language. The elder Koshkin took out the window frames from his house on the cutter's last run and set fire to the house with his own hand, taking the windows over to the new settlement. Vorontsov came over that week too, talked to the arsonists, and when he spied Bogodul, began nagging him to leave the island immediately.

"If you're childless and homeless, I can fill out the forms," he explained. "The regional executive committee will take care of you. Come on, let's get going."

"Kur-rva!" Bogodul replied without much ado and turned his back on him. Go figure if he understood or not.

But that had been it, was in the past; no one had shown up on Matyora in the last two days. And there was nothing for them to do here; they had taken away everything that they needed, and what they didn't need—well, they didn't need it. That's why it was a new life, so that you didn't intrude on it with the old.

At tea, Darya said that the arsonists had put off the fire until tomorrow, and asked: "But you spend the night where you planned. I'll stay here for the last. Is there any place to lie there?"

"Japanese gods!" Bogodul was incensed, waving his arms. "Plank beds."

"And tomorrow I'll join you," Darya promised.

After lunch, crawling on her hands and knees, she washed the floor and regretted that she couldn't scrape it properly, remove the thin top layer of wood and dirt, and then buff it with Angara sand so that it reflected the sun. She could have managed it one last time. But the floor was painted, Sonya had insisted when it became her duty to wash the floor, and Darya gave in. Of course, the paint rinsed more easily, but this wasn't an office, it wasn't so terrible to get down on your knees at home; soon people would paint their skins so as not to have to go to the baths.

How many feet had walked here—there were ruts in the floor, almost as if the floorboards had sunk. Her feet would be the last to walk on them.

She cleaned and felt herself wearing out, using up her strength —and the less work there was left, the less there was of her. It seemed that they would expire at the same time, and that was all that Darya wanted. It would be good to finish the work and then lie down on the doorstep and fall asleep. And then let come what may, that wasn't her concern. She would be found either by the living or the dead, and she would go anywhere, she wouldn't refuse either one.

She went into the calf shed, open, abandoned, the stalls fallen down, found an old, rusted, yellow-spotted scythe in the corner by the partition, and cut some grass. The grass was matted and tough, and also rather rusty, and it wasn't right for spreading for a ritual, but there wasn't any other to be had now. She gathered it up, went back into the house, and threw it down on the floor; it didn't smell so much of vegetation as of dryness and smoke—but it wouldn't be lying there for long, and it wouldn't be smelling for long either. It would do. No one could complain about it.

The hardest part was done, only details were left. Without taking a rest, Darya hung curtains on the windows and stove front, removed clutter from the benches and cots, and neatly arranged the kitchen utensils. But she felt that something was still missing, that she had forgotten something. It wouldn't be hard to forget: she had never seen anyone do this, and probably few had. She knew what was needed to see off a person with honor, it had been passed to her by several generations of the living, but here she had to rely on a vague sense, at first unclear, on instinct, prompted by someone all the time. That was all right, this would make it easier for others. Just let there be a beginning, the continuation wouldn't get lost, it would exist.

And she realized what was missing. She looked at the front corner and then the other one and realized that there should be fir branches there. And over the windows. Truly, how could she manage without it? But Darya didn't know if there was a fir tree left on Matyora, everything had been burned and uprooted. She would have to go look.

It was getting dark; the evening was warm and quiet with a light blueness in the sky and in the distant twilight-covered forests. It smelled, as usual, of smoke—the smell never left Matyora now—but there was also freshness in the air, of cool, deep earth, as after plowing. Where is it coming from? Darya looked around and couldn't tell. "Why from there, beneath the ground," she heard. "Where else?" And it was true—where else would damp earthen smells come from if not the earth? We've become so clever that we look at the sky.

Darya headed for the nearer upper channel, the destruction had been less there, and it was amazingly easy going for her, as though she hadn't been working without letup all day, as though something was carrying her along, barely letting her feet touch the path to take a step. And she breathed freely and easily. "That means I was right about the fir branches," she thought. And the blessed, peaceful feeling spread over her soul that she was doing everything right, including not letting Sima and Katerina spend the last night. Something had made her turn them away without thinking about it beforehand. And something had prompted the arsonist to wait until tomorrow—he hadn't thought about it, either, it just came out. No, this all wasn't just happening, there was meaning to it. And she began to regard the yellow-breasted bird that flew ahead and to the side, landing and then taking off again, as a messenger from far away to show her where to go.

She found the fir that had saved itself for her and revealed itself to her immediately, gathered an armful, and returned at dusk. And only when she was home did she notice that she was back, but she didn't remember how she had walked back or what she had thought about on the way. She still had the blessed feeling, coming from a secret place, that someone was watching her constantly, directing her. She felt no exhaustion now either, at bedtime; her hands and feet seemed to be moving silently and independently.

In the light of the lamp, in its dull red flickering, she hung the fir boughs in the corners and stuck them behind the window lintels from her stool. The fir released the sorrowful aroma of final farewell, reminding her of lit candles and sweet, sad singing. And the house took on a grieving and estranged, frozen air. "It can tell, oh, it can, what I'm dressing it up for," Darya thought, looking around in fear and humility. What else? What had she overlooked or forgotten? Everything seemed to be in place. She was irritated and disturbed by the crisp rustle of grass underfoot; she put out the lamp and climbed up on the stove.

An eerie and empty silence enveloped her—not a dog barked, not a pebble squeaked underfoot, not a random voice called, not a single breeze stirred in the heavy branches. Everything seemed dead. There were dogs left on the island, three hounds abandoned to fate by their owners raced up and down Matyora, going back and forth, but they too were quiet that night. Not a sound. Frightened, Darya got back down from the stove and began praying.

And she prayed all night, guiltily and humbly bidding farewell to the house, and it seemed to her that something picked up her words, and repeating them, carried them off into the distance.

In the morning she packed her plywood trunk, which held her burial outfit, made the sign of the cross over the front corner for the last time, stumbled at the door, struggling to keep from falling down and weeping on the floor, and went out, shutting the door. She had put the samovar out earlier. Sima and Katerina stood by Nastasya's house, guarding it. Darya told them to take the samovar and without a backward glance headed toward the Kolchak shack. She left her trunk by the first entry and went over to the other one, that led to where the fire starters were quartered.

"It's done," she told them. "Set your fire. But don't set one foot in the house . . ."

And she left the village. Where she spent the entire day, she didn't remember. She did remember that she walked and walked without resting—where did she get the strength?—and some small animal she had never seen before kept running alongside, trying to peer into her eyes.

The old women searched for her, calling out, but she didn't hear.

In the evening, Pavel, who had boated over, found her quite close, by the tsar larch. Darya was sitting on the ground and staring in the direction of the village, watching the last of the smoke being carried off the island.

"Get up, Mother." Pavel helped her up. "Auntie Nastasya is here."

21

Nastasya moaned, her face in her hands, sobbing and rocking back and forth.

"Egor, oh . . . oh, Egor! . . ."

The old women kept silent, confused and subdued, not knowing whether or not to believe in Grandpa Egor's death. Who could say, perhaps Nastasya was even more touched in the head now, and if she used to make up stories about the old man crying and bleeding when she was here, maybe she had moved on to death over there? And maybe Grandpa Egor was sitting and puffing on his pipe calm as can be right now? But it was terrible to think that she was so far gone that she could bury a living person. And it was terrible to think that Grandpa Egor was gone . . .

Bogodul's living quarters were as narrow as a corridor and

dilapidated and filthy. The things that the old women had brought over yesterday and today only added to the disorder. On the plank bed over the strewn hay were scattered undershirts, blankets, and bundles of small clothes; a mound of dishes teetered on the pathetic, creviced, bare table. Darya's samovar stood on the floor by the only window, without a lower glass. There in that crack the sun was setting, and beneath it the glass pane baked in greasy warmth, opaque from years of fly droppings. The floor was covered with red dust tracks from the bricks where once stood an iron stove. There was no stove at all now, and there wasn't the slightest smell of habitation in the whole chicken coop with a plank bed, like a perch, running along one wall and a long table, like a trough, along the other.

But they didn't have to look for something more proper: by then only the shack was standing, and there wasn't a stall or bathhouse left. On the lower end the ruins of the houses still smoked, and from time to time something burst in the hot ashes like gunpowder; the Russian stoves out in the fresh air cooled off, horrible and deathlike. It was over: Matyora took off and flew away—may it rest in peace! This shack didn't count, it was built by strangers' hands and was always a fifth wheel, out of place, even the arsonists didn't care to bother with it; that evening they packed up and left on the cutter they had called. Two of them dropped in to say good-bye on Bogodul's side, where trembling with fright and hiding from the sight of the burning houses were Sima and Katerina.

"Well, old women, what are we going to do with you?" one of them said. "Not very smart of you—you'll be chased off anyway. And we're not going to wait for you . . . oh no! We're going to go to a steambath and wash off your soot. Set fire to this fortress yourselves, if that's what you want."

"Do you hear, barge hauler?" the second yelled at Bogodul. "Don't leave it standing after you, it's against orders. Do you have matches?"

"Kur-rva!" Bogodul barked, and Sima, frightened and over-joyed, translated.

"Yes, we have matches, we do. We'll do it ourselves."

And after the men left, Pavel came bringing Nastasya and then brought his mother back from the pasture. He didn't know what to do with the old women: they wouldn't fit in one boat, and there was that crazy loon Bogodul, and they wouldn't leave right away anyway. He understood that as soon as he saw his mother, but still he asked.

"Maybe we could go today? I could come back tomorrow for the others . . ."

She didn't even reply.

"All right," he said after some thought. "Since Auntie Nastasya is here—all right. But I'll take the cutter in two days. Hear this, Mother: in two days. I'm working tomorrow night. So be ready the day after. And I'll bring along some bags—maybe we'll be able to take your potatoes too."

He wandered in front of the hot ruins and left. And so they were left all alone, but no longer five—Nastasya made six.

A little calmer, quenching the pain that flared up at seeing Matyora, Nastasya told them:

"As soon as we got there and settled in, he wouldn't put one foot out of the house, he just stayed in. I said: 'Why won't you go out, Egor? Why won't you go see people? They're all just like us, they're all drowned.' That's what the others, who aren't from the Angara, call us . . . In the evening we crawl down outside the door, where the people go up and down the street, we sit and mumble and mumble . . . People are from everywhere: there's an old woman from Cherepanovsk, and one from Vorobyov, and some from Shamask. We talk and talk about the old life, about this . . . And he just sits at home, all alone. He turns on the radio, we have one of our own there, and listens and listens. I say: 'Let's go, Egor, and hear what people have to say. What good can you hear in the air?' But no, he digs in, you can't get him out at all. And gets mad at me for nagging. He turned into a house spirit. And he cried and cried . . ."

"When you left, did he cry too? When you came here?" Darya

asked, holding her breath and ashamed of the words with which she wanted to trap Nastasya.

"What do you mean, leave?" Nastasya asked, not understanding. "Where did I go?"

"You came here, didn't you?"

Nastasya's face jerked and quieted.

"He would have cried . . . He would have cried, but he was already . . . how could he cry? He didn't cry after he was dead—what's the matter with you?! He lay there all light, so light Egor was . . . I wept over him, wept . . ." She rocked back and forth again. "And he just lay there, silent, so silent . . ."

"Did anyone help bury him?" Katerina asked and Nastasya, as though happy to hear the question, spoke with greater control and animation.

"They helped a lot. I can't complain: the people are good. They're our own people, we drank water from the same Angara. Aksiniya from Cherepanovsk came to wash the body . . . Ah, the whole building came. Everyone who goes through the same door to reach the stairs is considered in the same building. They got a coffin somewhere and brought it, covered with cloth—I had nothing to do with it. Then they brought a car and took him out. Aksiniya took care of everything, she's a pushy one . . . you'd never know that she was an old woman, that she lived in a village just like this. But she got used to it, she was comfortable there. Egor, he couldn't, he wouldn't get used to it, he just mooned and cried . . . the radio was his whole world. He listened and sighed, listened and sighed. I ask: 'What are they saying there, Egor, that you can't get enough?' 'They say they're sowing.' 'How can they be sowing? how!—it's almost autumn, look out the window. Have you lost your reason?' I say: 'What are you grinding, Egor? What are you milling? You'd be better off crying some more and not making up things!' And he—and you remember how contrary Egor was—he says to me: 'That's why I'm grinding and milling, I'm getting ready to sow.' He said the strangest things toward the end. And without outdoor air he became tansparent, white, and he lost weight. And it kept getting worse. He was fading before

my very eyes. I ask: 'What hurts, Egor? Where does it hurt?' I'm
not blind, I could see he was melting away. He wouldn't tell, he
refused to the last minute. 'There, you hear,' he says, 'they're
tossing bombs?'—'Those aren't bombs, Egor,' I say to him,
'they're raising the ground with explosives, so that they don't
have to dig.' The old women on the bench downstairs explained it
to me that they were exploding the earth, for the first time I
heard it I almost died on the spot. But he never went anywhere,
and I had to tell him what was what. 'The ringing in my ears,' he
says, 'the ringing is killing me.' And that was the only thing he
complained of, nothing else."

"Did he die peacefully, without suffering?"

"He died peacefully. As peaceful as could be, I pray God to let
me die that way. He said in the afternoon: 'Nastasya, go buy
some red wine, I'm all cold. Go get some and I'll warm up my
blood, it's all stuck somewhere.' I went. There's a store across the
street, but they didn't have any red wine, and I went over to the
next street. There are cars there, lots of cars from all over—and
they race back and forth. I'm afraid to cross, I stood around a
long time. I look this way and that, this way and that, waiting for
them to pass. I guess I was gone a long time. I came back and
Egor is looking at me so closely. 'I brought it,' I say, 'Egor, don't
be mad, I'm not good at walking around the city.' He didn't say
anything. He got up to go to the table, got up and lurched, and
was so embarrassed that he shook and cursed himself. We sat
down, it was evening already. We sat a while, but he only drank
two fingers in a glass. 'No,' he says, 'I can't drink it, it won't go
down.' And he got back into bed. We slept apart. He slept in our
bed, and I slept on the city one that folds up like an accordion.
He lay down and I see that he's looking at me. 'What,' I say, 'do
you want something, Egor?' "

Nastasya's voice tightened, she leaned forward, the way people
do when they can't wait for an answer. " 'Maybe you need something?' I asked. I could see that he wasn't just looking." She
leaned back. "But he didn't say anything. I know that he wanted
to say something, but he didn't say it. He was afraid to scare me.

He sensed death, he did." She stopped again and nodded. "He sensed it. I turned out the light, went to bed, and fell asleep, the fool. I fell asleep!" she shouted and immediately corrected her voice. "I woke up in the night—I heard rain. I thought: where did it come from, there wasn't a cloud in the sky in the evening. You can't see the sky very well there, but I look from habit. And the rain was soft and quiet. Oh, I think, something's wrong. I go to the window and it was just starting, the earth wasn't wet yet. And I remember that Egor had mentioned rain once: there hasn't been any in a long while, he said. I say softly: 'Egor, it's raining. Did you want it for something? What—,' I ask Egor, 'did you want it for?' He's silent. I go for the light, running my hand all over the wall. I turn it on, and my Egor, my Egor . . .'"

Nastasya wept.

The sun set, and it grew dark in the chicken coop quickly. The old women sat in heavy, oppressive silence; the boy tugged at Sima's sleeve in fright, and she pulled away weakly. Bogodul inhaled and exhaled with a wheeze. Unwilling to wait for the old women to get to the samovar, he took it outside silently and started filling it with water.

"Gran, Gran," Kolka spoke up.

Nastasya turned and saw him.

"Kolka's still with you?" she asked Sima.

"With me, yes," Sima answered quickly. "Who else would he be with? While I'm alive where would I send him?"

"Egor and I had children too," Nastasya said. "Darya and Katerina must remember. Do you?"

Darya and Katerina looked at each other, counting on each other, and said nothing.

"Well, am I lying, or what?" Nastasya cried out, insulted.

"Heaven forbid, Nastasya," said Darya, smoothing her back soothingly. "Heaven forbid, Nastasya. What's the matter? You're here—that's good that you're here, that's fine. We waited for you . . . We dug up your potatoes."

"What potatoes?"

"Yours. From your garden."

"Ah," Nastasya waved it off. "What would I do with them?"

"Whatever—you can't let the potatoes go to waste!"

They realized they should put on the light, but there wasn't any: Bogodul was like a cockroach, he had no light—not a lamp, not a candle, and Darya had left her lamp in the house; it had added to the flames. Katerina went into the other half, where the arsonists had lived, but she didn't find anything there. They had to sit in the dark. It was meant to be, it had come to that. It was better that way, probably: the pathetic rootlessness didn't stand before their eyes and frighten them with thoughts of tomorrow. Matyora was finished. The last people who had a life to live had left, the light was gone, and it seemed that it was over—no one would come again and the light wouldn't return, and they, stuck to Matyora, would be borne off in the darkness somewhere, carried away until the final hour tolled for them all at the same moment. And as though sensing it, the boy sobbed pitifully, and Sima soothed him.

Bogodul brought in the boiling samovar, set it on the floor, found the brewing pot by feel in the mound of dishes, and started the tea. And they drank it without getting down from the plank beds, holding the hot enamel mugs in both hands. No one asked for sugar or bread—it seemed that none of that would be proper anymore. They were lucky there was still some tea. Fresh air came in the hole in the window; Sima, keeping Kolka from the draft, bustled and tried to put him to sleep—Kolka continued whining. It grew lighter, they could make out the walls, and Bogodul announced:

"Gypsy sun, kur-rva!"

"You took away your samovar—did you use it there?" Darya asked Nastasya, remembering.

"Only two times," Nastasya said with a sigh. "Once when Egor was still alive and the other—after. Aksiniya from Cherepanovsk came over and said, let's have some tea. But you can't call that tea! The water tastes terrible, they poison it with something to keep it from tasting of the Angara. And there's no charcoal. Aksiniya gathered some pine cones, we filled the samovar and took it down those stairs outside. Where else could we burn it? Nowhere. We sat with it, watching it, and people walked by and laughed. Aksiniya, she's a fighter, she's not afraid of anything. We got so tired of waiting—there's no draft without a stovepipe, the cones were like rocks. But we waited and then we had to drag it back up. Our apartment is on the fourth floor, I barely make it up there emptyhanded with my breathing spells. I stop on every step. The stairs are so steep. Aksiniya is on the third floor—not a big difference, but it's lower. Four doors open on each level, and hers is the furthest left as you go up. So we didn't get up to my place, my heart was leaping out by then, we went to her house with my samovar. She lives with another old woman; she's very skinny and can't even walk on a level floor. Well, we sat down and emptied the whole samovar. We knew that we wouldn't be able to warm it up—so we just went on and on."

"Will you go back?"

"Oh, I don't know, Darya. I don't know anything right now. I'd be happy not to go back, but where else can I go?"

"You're not tied to that place."

"I'm not, but I squeal anyway. Where can I go? Who needs me? That's so. And Egor's grave is there—how can I leave it? But it looks as though we'll have to lie apart; they say you have to die at the same time to lie together. I made inquiries. The cemetery is new, they bury people in order, no guessing who'll be next to whom. Oh, but I won't last long—maybe I'll end up not too far from Egor after all. I don't know if I'll get through the winter . . . I thought: I'll go and see you, take a last look at Matyora. And then I'll start getting ready. Did our house, Egor's and mine, burn?"

"Didn't you see? It burned down today. When you came it was still burning. Our whole side held out until today; it burned at once. Didn't you see it?"

"I didn't see a thing. I didn't see how I got here, how I was on the boat. It was all a dream. And as soon as it came into my head to see Matyora for the last time . . . that's all I could think about. I didn't want anything, I couldn't swallow a piece of bread. No, I think, I'll go, or I'll have no peace. I'll get my cat Nunya. Oh!'" she suddenly realized. "Is my Nunya alive? I didn't even ask. Darya, I left Nunya with you? . . ."

"Why don't you ask if I'm alive? You and your Nunya . . ."

"Where is she then? I asked you to look after her."

"Last night she was still alive. I don't know where she is now. I remember that I chased her out of the house last night so that she wouldn't burn. Maybe she squeezed back in, maybe she's wandering around outside somewhere."

"I have to look for her tomorrow. How will I live without her? Oh, how will I live now? How will I be all alone?" In the darkness Nastasya blew her nose and rocked.

Darya suggested: "Take Sima and the boy with you. They don't know how to live either, which way to go. Or Bogodul. And you go on about Nunya . . ."

"Y-ick!" Bogodul refused. "The ci-ty!" And he snorted in disgust.

"That would be wonderful, of course, if Sima would come." Nastasya was happy. "We would live together. Otherwise, Aksiniya says, they'll give me someone to share with anyway. Why have a stranger when we Matyora women could live behind one door. It couldn't be better."

"I don't know," Sima said in confusion. "You must need some permission. They might not give it. But it would be good . . ."

"I don't know anything about that. Aksiniya helps me now and then, without her I'd be completely lost. Life isn't easy there. The city is the city. You have to buy bread, buy potatoes, buy onions. Bread isn't expensive . . . that's all right. Aksiniya took me to a bazaar once. We rode and rode on wheels—my head began spinning. Well, we got there. And what did we find? A pot of potatoes costs three rubles, a head of garlic, a ruble. What is this, I thought, where are you supposed to get all these rubles? It was pure robbery! I went back without anything. But I saw plenty. Those suburban types are raking in the money all right. What are they doing with it all, what do they need it for?! Oh, why talk about it? While our money for the calf lasted, we lived. But now,

I don't know. They're trying to give me a pension for Egor. I don't know. Pay money for the apartment, for gas. Maybe I'll manage, I don't eat much anymore. I don't need it. I don't need anything at all anymore. I'll forget to put a single crumb in my mouth, and it won't ask for some. I'm turning into a saint. Just something to hold the soul."

Bogodul made noise as he settled down to sleep by the door, and Nastasya stopped talking. Katerina sighed a series of fast sighs, one after the other; neither Sima nor the boy made a sound. A distant, cold light coming from the depths circled the chicken coop, falling on the walls and faces in a murky pattern, shading the door opposite the window. Under the spell of that light the old women, lost and silent, slipped away.

22

PAVEL reached the settlement at dusk. The duty car, which had zipped back and forth from the bank to the settlement, was no longer working, and Pavel, after he put away his boat and spoke with the guard, old man Vorotila from Podvoloshensk, nicknamed in his youth for his great strength and now much frailer and weaker, started the ten-verst uphill climb, but he had an unexpected stroke of luck: somewhere on his second verst he was overtaken by a motorcyclist wearing a helmet over his sharp, severe, and wrinkled face, who stopped on his own and gave him a ride. There was need to ask where he was headed: from the turn the road led only to the settlement, and no one needed it to go any further or any closer. And so the lucky fellow-traveler got Pavel home in ten minutes. By the garage at the entrance to the settlement the man braked, nodded silently in answer to his thanks, and turned left down the street; Pavel went straight, his street was on top, right by the forest.

The sun had set, and in the remaining gathering light that clearly outlined every object, the settlement most resembled an apiary. Identical houses with identical low, solid fences stood in even, measured rows, falling off at right angles in two directions —to the left and toward the Angara. Actually, the settlement was off to the left, for the road that Pavel was following was the limit, its right side was made up of industrial concerns—the garage, shops, welding unit, boiler shop, and also the steambaths. It was called Rabochaya Street. Always noisy, clattering with machinery, stinking of gasoline, coal, and iron, the street was amazingly quiet and empty this time; Pavel was the only one walking on it, staying on the residential side, where there were fewer potholes. Life went on beyond the fences—there dogs talked and muttered, rattled their chains, and barked as Pavel walked by (Vorontsov had ordered all dogs chained up, and they were—after the local cop, Vanya Suslov, a young friendly fellow who used to be with the border patrol, shot half of them), and it was there, beyond the fences, that people ran their own lives, perhaps even planting cherries and birches. But here on the street, as in every street without exception, it was spacious and bare—not a single front lawn, not a single tree. Either people hadn't gotten around to it or they thought: why bother, we're surrounded by woods.

Down in the lower street came the steady whine of motorcycles —the kids were racing around, practicing. There were so many of those motorcycles now—in every yard—and people traveled to Bratsk, even to Irkutsk, to get them; they were buying them with abnormal haste, racing one another, as though these would be the last ever made, or as though they were showing off before their neighbors: there, you see, we can afford one too. Not understanding the haste, Pavel nevertheless was considering the fact that he'd have to get a motorcycle himself by spring. He didn't need one on Matyora, everything was close at hand there, but here he'd have to walk more than an hour to get to work, and in the

summer the water, if he wanted to fish, or the fields with mushrooms, or the berries—wherever he might want to go—couldn't
be reached on foot . . . It wasn't Matyora.

What was true, was true—this wasn't Matyora. Matyora was
no more, may it rest in peace, as his mother would say, crossing
herself. Matyora village was gone and soon the island would be
too. He'd be able to go down there by boat and circle, trying to
guess whether it had stood here or there . . . And amazingly,
Pavel pictured it simply and clearly, like something that he had
done more than once—the boat on the huge raised water, and
himself in the boat, trying to determine the spot that was Matyora from the distant river banks, staring into the dark still mass
of water—perhaps there would be a sign from the sleepy depths,
perhaps a flickering light. No, no sign, no light. Crossing the
water, if you head from one bank to the other, you could say: it
was here—because somewhere at some point you would cross
it—but lengthwise, no, lengthwise you couldn't even estimate
where it was, on what line it had stood, where it was buried. All
you could do was remember the name. But amazingly he also
couldn't understand why he felt nothing now except a pain that
brought relief: it had festered and festered and finally burst. It had
to happen anyway and it happened, and the anticipation of the
inevitable tired them and exhausted them more than the actual loss.
It was enough . . . he didn't have the strength for any more. Now
he wouldn't have to torture himself with Matyora, comparing one
against the other, going back and forth, suffering, straining his
soul to its limits—now, seeking a new like here, he would have to
settle permanently, letting down his surviving roots.

Pavel turned left and cutting across one street—it was closer to
his house that way—went back uphill again. There was a whiff of
sweet smoke from one of the yards, and Pavel who had just come
from a place where the smoke had hovered for over a month,
interfering with your breathing, involuntarily stopped and inhaled the pleasant smell, which was related to this past, which
should have faded and hadn't. For it was true they didn't heat
stoves or bathhouses here, and there were no smokehouses either,

but no one had forbidden just having smoke on your plot; Pavel tried to remember whether he had started a fire for any reason in his yard this summer, and it turned out that he hadn't. The garbage, gathered into a heap, was rotting in the corner, grass peeping through it; he had planned to burn it in the spring but imagined that they'd come running—what's burning? is it a fire? why doesn't anyone else burn their garbage and you do?—and he gave up the idea even though no one would have come or said anything. He wasn't used to it there yet: he did everything looking over his shoulder, the way you do at some uncle's house, waiting for instructions. His thoughts returning to Matyora, to today's trip; Pavel remembered with shame how he stood by the remains of his house and pulled and pulled at himself, trying to find a strong, powerful emotion—it wasn't a stick, but his house that was burning—and how he couldn't pull out or find anything except bitter and uncomfortable surprise that he had lived there. That's how hardened his soul had become! As though excusing himself Pavel thought that he often had to recall that he was alive and nudge himself toward life: since the war, lo these many years, he still wasn't himself, and there weren't many who had fought in it who were, he thought. Pavel knew that he often suffered blackouts during which he lost himself and was released into a kind of freedom, sometimes for a long time; and he didn't remember where he'd been, where he flew off to, or what he had done. After such a spell he would hold his memory closer, step more cautiously, do everything to get a tighter grip on himself—and a week or two would go by, sometimes more, and then another fall, once more he would be pulled into a skewed and estranged state, like a lunatic, when a person goes through the motions, but by rote, not by will power.

Children's voices spilled out in a mighty roar and Pavel realized that it came from the school; classes were over. Its roof with the drainpipe handsomely painted in aluminum paint was visible from there, attracting the eye, and Pavel looked at it with a sigh and felt sorry that his sons were grown and weren't going to school here. It was a good school, even by present standards—

cheerful, three stories above everything else, full of windows—
and if the settlement did resemble an apiary with neat rows of
hives it was only the noninhabited structures—the school, store,
kindergarten, cafeteria, and even the bathhouse—that brightened
it, saving it from its beautiful and boring monotone. How good it
would be if someone, not his sons but, say, a grandson, went to
this school and he'd be called in for meetings over bad grades and
mischief. But no, it wouldn't be. That's why depression grabbed
him by the throat when he looked at the school and heard the
children's voices, like now. Life was over, then—it wasn't time,
but it was. And thinking about it, he remembered his mother and
that he would have to move her somehow and once more he
refused to believe that she would ever set one foot in this settlement. Something wouldn't let him believe it—do what you
want!—no matter how he tried to picture it, a veil descended
over his eyes.

Here, from the top of the hill, it looked lighter now, and the
tall, shingled roofs of the houses rippled from street to street in
calm heavy waves. The motorcycles were still buzzing, raising
dust; the straining whine of a tractor came from the fields on the
left; the schoolchildren, spreading out over the streets, were still
making noise; and a cow in some yard mooed over and over,
locked away, with a bitter and suffering sound. Far far away,
beyond the Angara, the opposite shore showed blue, and the
clean, still sky rose above it sharply with a single airy, tinted
cloud, stuck like a feather into the horizon. Here, above his head,
the sky had cooled and was turning to dusk, leaning down toward
the Angara. It was—not like on Matyora where it was cool as
soon as the sun went down—it was warm and dry, and the
warmth came from the earth and buildings heated during the
day; they still gave off the smell of paint and gasoline.

Pavel reached his street, built up only on one side opposite the
forest, reached his gate, and stopped, looking to see if Mayka was
among the cows wandering through the brush, stepping on twigs.
She wasn't there—Pavel looked through a crack in the fence and
saw her in the yard. What a smart cow!—even here, where the

cattle had run wild without pastures or attention, wandering through the forest like wild animals, she came home every day on her own. And they would have to kill such a sweet and docile animal soon. Pavel thought how he would have to call someone in to do it, because he wouldn't take it on himself—even if you killed him—and would even run off from the house and wander around until they cleaned up. He couldn't watch a pig being stuck or a rooster decapitated, and Sonya, who was a determined woman about these things, could only wave her hand at him in exasperation as he tried to run off. He had been through the war, he had seen more death than he needed; he still fought the war and bid farewell to the dead in his sleep, but he couldn't do anything about his feelings, he was just born that way.

He didn't feel like going home. He just didn't feel like it and that was that. The evening flowed quietly and languidly, gentle caressing his face, and the darkness hadn't settled in yet. All the sounds and noises of the large settlement seemed to be moving away—as though they were carefully borne away by the same flow as imperious time. A red leaf fell from the aspen across the way and stopped in midair, choosing a direction, but the movement lifted it and carried it out onto the road and dragged it along the ground. Pavel nodded without thought or memory; that's the way it must be. But what must be that way, what the far-away anxiety was about, he didn't know. He probably should have insisted and brought his mother over today. He had left Matyora without any anxiety, certain that he would get the cutter day after tomorrow and take them all off the island at once rather than separate them during the move, but suddenly he felt uncomfortable. And it was not only "suddenly"—something had been nagging at him and slashing constantly from the moment he left them—but he had thought that it was something else. But how could he have insisted? If his mother didn't feel like talking she wouldn't, and she wouldn't have left the others. And even without the others, if she had been all alone, she probably wouldn't have left right after the house burned down anyway, without a chance to calm down a bit on her native soil near the cooling ashes.

And once again he felt that she would never walk through that gate . . .

He stood there a bit longer, worrying without finding comfort, and went in the house—it was time to go to bed, he had to be at work early in the morning. Sonya, waiting for him downstairs, sat in the kitchen knitting, red, green, and black yarn stretching from a large pot on the floor. She picked up knitting here in the settlement when the store got a shipment of rare yarn, either from Riga or Paris, and the office workers without exception, to keep up with one another, bought it up in large amounts. Sonya had never knit a single piece of yarn from their own sheep on Matyora; his mother had made mittens and socks a finger thick and those socks and mittens never wore out. You could pour water in them and it wouldn't leak out—not like Sonya's work, which was full of fashionable holes.

Getting up to feed Pavel, Sonya said: "One of our native villagers was here twice this evening, asking for you."

"Who was that?"

"Petrukha. 'Where,' he says, 'is my mother?' "

"Now he remembers her."

"That's what I said: 'Aren't you thinking of your mother too soon, sonny? Why don't you wait until she's been drowned, and then go look for her.' I can't tell if he's drunk or sober. He gabs on the same way."

Pavel didn't ask what Petrukha had "gabbed," he didn't care. But he had to see Petrukha: let him help bring over the old women day after tomorrow. And let him take his mother, whom he suddenly remembered, with him—but where, to what kingdom would he take her? But that wasn't Pavel's concern. He felt and foresaw that he would have the responsibility of finding a home for Sima and the boy and Bogodul and bringing Nastasya back. Who else would help, who else cared about them? He'd have enough problems, he would . . . But that wasn't so terrible, he could manage that, what scared him the most, what he didn't even dare think about or try to guess, was what would happen to his mother. Another day's delay wouldn't do anything; before he knew it, it would be the day after tomorrow and he'd have to go for her, bring her here . . .

He had just finished dinner and hadn't gone upstairs when there were steps on the veranda, and the loud, determined, and warning footsteps announced that it was Petrukha. Speak of the devil. But Petrukha didn't show up alone, he was with—and Pavel couldn't understand that at all—Vorontsov. He came in and even before saying "hello" began searching the corners with his round bulging eyes in his round and ruddy face.

"Pavel Mironovich," Vorontsov asked quickly and demandingly, "where is your old woman?"

"In Matyora," Pavel replied, beginning to understand what it was all about.

"What do you mean in Matyora?! You went over there today! Why is she in Matyora?"

"I went all right, but she didn't come."

"Are we going to tell jokes, or what?" Vorontsov cried, completely lost. "What do you mean, she didn't come? What does that mean?!" He still looked around, still not believing him, and even ran over to the stairs and looked up.

"She's not there." Pavel stopped him, or he would have climbed upstairs. "Why would I lie? She's not here. She's over there. Says she hadn't spent enough time there. She stayed to live there a little more."

"And my mother?" Petrukha shouted—you'd think his heart was bleeding for his mother just then. "Is she there too?"

"Well, if you didn't take her away, she's there too."

"When ?" he howled. "When am I supposed to take her away? I only got back today, I was on assignment. Boris Andreyevich will tell you." He used Vorontsov as a reference, shaking his dirty hand, bandaged with a black rag, right under Pavel's nose. And that wild shaking, and burning eyes, and piercing screech told Pavel that Petrukha was drunk.

Vorontsov grimaced.

"Ass-ssignment!" he boiled over. "Ass-ssignment! Why is your mother located in the wrong place, you miserable drunkard? Your assignment is have her here. She can be anywhere you want, but not there. And what do you do? There's an order out, it affects everyone! Are we going to understand, or what?"

As for understanding, Pavel understood that it was being said and yelled not so much at Petrukha as for his sake.

Petrukha decided to take umbrage.

"I may be a drunkard," he looked at all of them from beneath his bushy brows, inviting them all to feel the responsibility of that confession, "but as for being miserable—excuse me for living, Comrade Vorontsov, Boris Andreyevich—I will not be called that. I don't have the right! Yes!" He threw back his head like a spoiled child and held the pose, enjoying the strength of his words. "As for drunkard . . . so I'm a drunkard," Petrukha went on. "What would you do without drunkards?"

"Where are they living over there?" Vorontsov asked quickly and nervously, not listening to Petrukha.

"In the shack."

"In the shack? The shack is standing?! The shack is up?!"

"Yes."

"What is this? This is . . ." Vorontsov shook and ran to the window—what he wanted to see there wasn't clear. "And you"— he attacked Pavel, running away from the window—"you, Pavel Mironovich, what were you thinking of? How could you let them? You're a Communist, not like that one"—he nodded in disgust at Petrukha—"and you can't keep your mother, a hundred-year-old woman, in line! The shack is still standing!" he moaned. "And the state commission is coming tomorrow. In the morning. What am I supposed to do—show them the shack? People who took the law in their own hands? The state commission—do you understand, Pavel Mironovich?! What am I supposed to tell them? My man went over and came back. And is now sitting around drinking tea. No problems! And who'll be held responsible tomorrow?" His own question: Who'll be held responsible? scared Vorontsov and he ordered decisively: "Get ready. Enough playing games. You must understand the situation. By morning there will be no people and no shack. Don't you even think about taking off," he warned Petrukha. "You're going. On assignment. With me. You, Pavel Mironovich, you get ready too. I've had enough. This is government business. Devil knows what's going on!"

Pavel didn't want to go, he was tired, it was late, and he had to be at work early in the morning; that meant he wouldn't get any sleep at all, but more than that he didn't want to disturb the old women, chase them out of their nest, and burn down the last remaining object on Matyora before their eyes—the shack that gave them their final shelter. But there was nothing he could do—they had to go. He pictured Vorontsov screaming at the old women in the dark, rushing them and herding them down to the cutter, yelling at them without choosing his words, cursing them along with everything else in the world. He pictured his mother and how she would talk back to the authority and how she would look at him, at Pavel, with expectation and pain. He pictured Nastasya, lost and trembling in fear, nodding constantly in fear . . . the crying boy . . . the ruffled and angry Bogodul, whom he would have to watch so that—what else?—he didn't attack Vorontsov . . . He pictured all this and suggested to Vorontsov: "Maybe you shouldn't go? We'll manage somehow."

"Oh no," he yelled. "No, Pavel Mironovich, I can't count on you anymore. Enough. I no longer trust you. I have to give an accounting tomorrow, and I have to be sure that the territory is cleared, and if I depend on you—you'll let me down again. You must understand the problem. I'm the one who answers."

He told Petrukha to go wake up the cutter pilot, gave them a half hour to get ready and down to the garage where they were meeting to save time, and ran out.

"And why not?" Sonya said. "He's right. Why put the man in a difficult position? He has to answer."

"Let him answer," Petrukha got angry. "Let him answer, nobody's stopping him. But let him respect a man. I'm not a step for him to sit on and call me names. Excuse me for living. I have my pride. Some yeller! I've seen the likes of him before."

But while they got ready, while Petrukha found the pilot, a grim middle-aged man called Galkin, one of the motor pool, and woke him up and then ran off on an errand of his own, while they did this and that, a whole hour went by. They left in darkness—the stars were out—in a van that took workers to distant areas in the morning. Pavel drove. The road was good, and they went downhill fast; the forest rushed toward them and just as quickly parted; small, winged nocturnal bugs flitted in their lights, managing to swoop into them; the gravel underneath rustled steadily with a muffled sound. No one talked behind Pavel. Petrukha tried to start up a conversation, teasing Vorontsov with remarks about after-hours work, but Vorontsov didn't even deign to stop him, and Petrukha shut up, suffering and grimacing (Pavel could see in the mirror). Old Galkin napped. Vorontsov sat in front of them so straight that he didn't seem to lurch when they hit bumps, staring intently and angrily out the side window.

They were halfway there when Pavel felt dampness splash into the window on a turn. And the forest came at them more slowly, lazily, and the rubber tires rustled more softly. And when they reached open ground a kilometer and a half from the river, gray damp tufts moved on the car, a few at first, and then thickening quickly, growing, also seeming to fly into the headlights. Pavel didn't realize right away that it was fog. Old Galkin sat up behind Pavel and asked uncertainly and anxiously: "Fog?"

"Fog," Petrukha confirmed. "Maybe it's—" He didn't dare express his desire and only jerked his head back. "Why run around in the fog?"

Vorontsov didn't consider an answer necessary this time either.

Without turning around, Pavel parked facing the river and got out first. The cutter, docked to the right of a string of boats, wasn't visible; the fog was still hanging in the air, but you could make out a strip of water below it quite well considering the dark. There was a deep, solid silence: the water didn't splash, the usual sound of the shallows on the upper Angara didn't reach them, the whistle of the current, loud and even and at other times audible to the keen ear, didn't break through, and the earth was silent—everything seemed stuffed with dead, impenetrable mass. They got up on the cutter, not hearing their own footsteps. Galkin started the motor, but it didn't fire as usual, with a broad, wide-ranging roar that deadened the area and hurt the ears, but putted, as if catching its breath, quietly and cautiously, and its putt-putt couldn't have penetrated more than thirty feet. Petrukha was the last on the cutter, and he bragged to Pavel with a happy smile: "I locked in Vorotila. He didn't even stir, he's fast asleep."

"Still fooling around?" Pavel frowned.

"So what? If you're the watchman, then watch and don't sleep. When he wakes up he won't be able to get out. He'll have to climb out the window. And when he does get out, he'll see the cutter's gone. Boy, Vorotila will be mad."

Petrukha laughed and seeing that Pavel didn't care for his joke, went into the pilothouse, which the peasants called the booth.

They backed out and turned around on water. The bank was gone, and the fog came in closer, and it began drizzling, beading up not with moisture but with fine, dustlike, sticky gray sweat. Pavel felt his face and clothes grow heavy, swelling with the repulsive dampness, but he didn't want to get up and go into the booth; he settled down behind it on a block of wood turned into a seat and lit a cigarette, the cold and his anxiety making him inhale with particular pleasure and greed, but the anxiety didn't dissipate. In fact it got worse. They would be there soon—and then what? He couldn't think or imagine what would happen, everything inside him froze and went numb from the question, and he wanted to get off the boat so much he was ready to jump off. He was sorriest about agreeing to this night raid; he had already forgotten that he had no alternative. How, how could he have agreed? And how could he have refused since his mother was there, since he couldn't relegate her move to someone else: his mother would never forgive him.

Matyora lay at an angle some two versts from the bank where they started. Galkin headed straight out onto the Angara and was now steering blind, by touch: five minutes after they set off they got into such thick pea-soup fog that it was impossible to make out anything two yards away. Pavel thought in hindsight that they should have gone down a bit with the current and then turned across the river; that way they would hit Matyora for sure, follow its shore, and come up where they wanted to be. But it was too late to bring it up now, he should have thought of it earlier. It would be all right, Galkin had been boating here all summer, he knew the way, he could get there by memory, by instinct. He steered cautiously, at low speed; Pavel could hear Vorontsov demanding that he speed up and Galkin refuse, and their speed remained steady: at full speed they could run aground and then they'd be in trouble. The pilot was responsible for the cutter. The motor putted ever so softly deep inside, he imagined that it was underwater. He could hear clearly the hiss of the tearing fog and tearing water, and Pavel, anxious and quiet, lost himself in reverie to the sound of that soft and monotonous hissing.

He started when the cutter tilted and lurched on a turn, shuddered, and got up to look at the shore for which Galkin was headed, but he didn't see land no matter how hard he looked. The fog was a solid wall, and the cutter seemed to be running in place, unable to fight its way out of the fog, beyond the heavy wall, slipping off time and time again; Pavel couldn't remember ever being in fog that thick, so thick and solid that the vague shimmer of the water barely broke through, as though coming from a deep and dark well. His eyes pushed against the thick gray soup and shut involuntarily, avoiding its nearness. According to the time, they should have gotten there by now, but it didn't look like they were landing; Pavel went into the pilothouse and guessed from the way Galkin peered into the dark, intent and anxious, sticking out his neck, hoping to see something, that they were lost. Well, they should have expected it. Wise people didn't set out in this kind of weather, especially on water. And he was just like a child; he went where they led him, he didn't even try to argue. Well, now they had to circle until they hit one bank or the other. They must have missed Matyora higher up and then turned without noticing and followed the current. Probably that's what happened. And if that's what it was, then they had to head right and try to meet

Matyora from the other side, from Our Angara. Pavel gently nodded to the right, merely suggesting it, and Galkin, overjoyed at sharing the responsibility for steering, turned without a second thought.

"It's taking a long time," Vorontsov said, standing on Galkin's left, sensing that something was wrong. "Where are we? Why is it taking so long? Did we lose the island, is that it? Hah?"

"We'll find it," Galkin said without confidence.

Petrukha, napping in the corner, was wakened by the voices, shivered from the cold (he was still wearing a loose shirt), and peeked out the door.

"Oh-ho, some fog that is!" he said in amazement, shut the door, and stood up, rubbing his chest with his hands to keep warm. "You can cut it with a knife. We're turned around, hah? We're lost, we are . . . I told you . . ." Petrukha hadn't said anything worthwhile, hadn't warned them about anything, but he certainly wasn't going to pass up an opportunity to mention that he was right, even if he hadn't known it—and he didn't pass it up. "In fog like this a fish could get turned around. Really!"

They traveled another fifteen minutes—twice as long as necessary to bump into Matyora or Podmoga from Our Angara—and found nothing: no shore, no sign, no light, just endless fog that had grown even thicker, like pudding. Galkin turned to Pavel, asking where to turn, what to do, and Pavel shrugged: I don't know.

"Cut the engine," he said.

Galkin got up and turned it off. Pavel went out on deck, listening to the rustle of fog and water stop—he couldn't see the water anymore. He picked up the block he had sat on and threw it down—there was a deep viscous splash; that meant there was still water down there. Then he lay flat and leaned over the side, looking for the wood he had thrown—it rocked in the fog, as though suspended in it, nearby, but look as he might, guess as he might, Pavel couldn't tell the current from it: the block fell and stuck where it had fallen next to the cutter. Now they couldn't tell which way they had been traveling, where they had come from—everything had blended into a single indistinguishable circle. Vorontsov couldn't stand it.

"Are we going to fool around much longer? What is it—do you understand, or what? It's almost morning, we have work to do."

"Don't shout," Galkin said curtly. "This isn't a meeting, you know."

And Vorontsov, strangely enough, held his tongue, realizing that orders wouldn't help here at all. But the "don't shout," which hurt his feelings because he wasn't used to being treated that way, prompted him to make another decision, and he told Petrukha: "Shout."

"Shout what?" He didn't understand.

"Whatever you want. Scream for help if you want. There are living people around here somewhere. Maybe they'll hear you. Or is this a conspiracy? Well?"

Petrukha waited a bit to show that he thought it over and agreed with Vorontsov and went up front, and they could hear him shout.

"Mo-other! Auntie Darya! Where are you? Hey!"

Not a sound in response. And it was silly to hope that someone would reply: the fog immediately absorbed and drowned his voice, nothing could escape from its nets.

They started the engine again and went on, headed they thought toward the right shore, not finding it, turning the other way, and then a third—and they didn't reach any of them. Everything was lost in the fog's pitch black. It was morning, but the fog had no intention of lifting; it lay with such heavy power that there was no hope left that it could ever lift. Pavel resigned himself: what would be, would be—and he didn't tell Galkin to bear right or left, and Galkin headed in some direction, toward some emptiness on his own. Vorontsov resigned himself to it too; he sat with downcast head, staring ahead senselessly with swollen red eyes, but he still woke up Petrukha, who was sleeping next to him. Petrukha would wake up, go up on deck, and shout, barely hearing himself, yelling the same thing: "Mo-o-ther! Auntie Darya-a-a-a! Hey, Matyora—a!"

Then he would come back in, leaning familiarly on Vorontsov, and go back to sleep.

Finally, despairing of ever reaching anything, Galkin cut the engine. It grew absolutely quiet. Only water and fog around them. Nothing but water and fog.

23

THE BOY CRIED as he woke up, anxiously and inconsolably, and the old women woke up, stirring, stretching, and sighing—they hadn't gone to bed, they had napped sitting up where they had been in the evening and had remained after their conversation. Sima, muttering to herself, started to console the boy, and he gradually quieted down, giving an occasional weak and held-back sob. It wasn't dark in Bogodul's chicken house, but blind: there was a hazy damp light in the window, like under water, in which something moved listlessly and shapelessly—it seemed like a thick weak trickle passing by.

"What's this—night again?" Katerina asked looking around.

"Well, it's not daytime," Darya replied.

"There won't be any more days for us."

"Where are we, though? Are we alive?"

"Must be we're not."

"Lord! ..."

"That's all right. We're together—so it's all right. What else could we need?"

"We should push the boy out of here. The boy should live."

Sima's frightened and determined voice: "No, I won't give up Kolyana. We're together, Kolka and I."

"Together, fine. What would he do without us, anyway?"

"Where are you, Darya? That is you talking, isn't it?"

"I'm sitting next to you. Don't you see? That's me sitting here."

"It's you, is it?"

"It's me."

"I flew off somewhere, I wasn't here. It feels like I just sat down. I don't remember anything."

"Where you flew to—are there people there?"

"I didn't see, I don't know. I flew in darkness, I didn't look at the light."

"And this? Who's this at my side?"

"Me? I'm Nastasya."

"From Matyora?"

"From Matyora. Are you Darya?"

"Darya."

"Who lived next door to me?"

"Yes."

"I recognized you, girl."

"I recognized you first."

"What's the matter with you two? What are you going on about? Are you crazy?"

They answered in unison.

"We're crazy."

And they stopped talking, either put down by the scolding, or embarrassed by their own disloyal, strange words. The anxious, oppressive silence was cut by the hoarse, scratchy breathing of sleeping Bogodul. In rhythm to his snores, calming themselves, the old women rocked back and forth as one.

"What can you see out the window? Take a look. Someone go look."

"No, I'm afraid. Go look yourself. I'm afraid."

They stared out the window and saw in the dull washed-out light large shaggy shapes, looking like clouds, rush by as though under a strong upper wind. Bogodul, finally awake, crept down from the bed and looked out the window. They hurried him.

"What's out there? Where are we? Talk—why are you quiet?!"

"Can't see, kur-rva!" Bogodul replied.

The old women crossed themselves, whispering, touching each other. And then once more, but even more faint and lost:

"Is that you, Darya?"

"Yes, it's me. And where's Nastasya? Nastasya!"

"I'm here, I'm here."

Bogodul stomped over to the door and opened it. Into the open door, as though from the gaping void, rushed the fog and the sound of a nearby lonely howl—that was the Master's final voice. It was washed away immediately and the window seemed brighter, the wind whistled louder, and the faint, barely audible hum of a motor came from somewhere, from below, sounding like a hopeless wail. Its putt became clearer and then moved away again, and then once more, sharper and closer, rose the voice of the Master.